SINFUL
crown

A FORBIDDEN AGE GAP ROMANCE

ELEANOR ALDRICK

SINFUL
crown

A FORBIDDEN AGE GAP ROMANCE

ELEANOR ALDRICK

ISBN: 9798810962939

FIRST EDITION

10 9 8 7 6 5 4 3 2 1

For the broken girl in every woman.
Don't worry, baby. Daddy's got you.

"Sometimes the people with the worst past, create the best future."

- Umar ibn Al-Khattab

Playlist
ON REPEAT

Hands to Myself - Selena Gomez

Tutu-Remix- **Camilo, Shakira, Pedro Capo**

Deserve It - Shenseea

Emiliana - **CKay**

Freak - Doja Cat

ТАЙМАУТ - **Nikitata**

Feel It - Jacquees

Prologue
JACE

*J*essa, Jessa, Jessa. What's my favorite girl doing today?

Pulling out my cell phone, I let myself sink into the buttery leather of my chair, my fingers deftly scrolling to the app in question. At this moment, I've never been more appreciative of the airport's VIP lounge and the privacy it offers.

It's been a hellish month and I could sure use a fix of caramel skin and luscious tits to keep me sane. I've been holed up in Colorado for the past couple of weeks, without so much as one available female in sight. To say that my dick is at risk of shriveling up and leaving me would be an understatement.

Yes, it was a sacrifice I'd willingly take on all over again because family is everything and my brothers needed me. But holy hell, am I ever glad to be going back home.

Miami is the exact opposite of Loveland, Colorado, and I plan on taking full advantage of that as soon as the plane's wheels hit the ground. But first, I need a hit of my girl.

I scoff. *My girl.* There's no such thing. Like I told my brothers, I'll never settle down. Love isn't for me, and the closest thing I'll ever come to it is this camgirl on *OnlyFriends.*

Well, she's not really a camgirl. *Bingo.* My eyes land on her profile, her haunting eyes the first thing that drew me to her. They're somewhere between an aqua green and pale silver, but they shine so brightly against the dark caramel of her skin. It's the most stunning pair of eyes I've ever seen.

I found her on one of the many restless nights up at the ranch. She was on a suggested account on my social media. I tapped the profile, unable to resist her photo and instantly, I was hypnotized by the many pics she'd posted, all covering the important bits but showing enough skin to let the imagination wander. And man, did my imagination wander.

It was then I noticed the link in her bio, and equal parts of jealousy and lust clouded my vision as I pushed through to the site she'd connected—an *OnlyFriends* account.

To my utter horror yet relief, she wasn't sharing videos of herself with another man, but she was doing something that I wasn't sure was much better. This little tease was getting herself off in the most innocent ways, all with no penetration.

Why, one might ask. And that's the part that had the horror

setting in. My girl wasn't showing anyone or anything sliding into that tight cunt of hers because she was auctioning that privilege off.

Two months. Two months left of her teasing men. Driving them to bid higher and higher for the pleasure of taking that ripe cherry. Something I'll never allow myself to do.

I might want to taste her, savoring her essence like the finest of liqueurs, but I would never be her first. Women form a bond with that person, whether or not they like to admit it, and I have no intention of tying myself to *any* woman any time soon. Regardless of how arresting their eyes are.

Still, it doesn't stop me from fantasizing, and that's just what I plan on doing until my jet arrives. Well, it was until I caught sight of the approaching woman.

She has the same naturally bronzed skin as Jessa's, though not as supple. This woman seems to be in her forties, but she's stunning nonetheless. And to my luck, her eyes are this pale jade color. Not as bright as Jessa's, but definitely noteworthy.

Shit. Here I was about to play out a fantasy in my head when there's a more than willing woman sitting next to me, her come fuck me eyes in full effect, letting me know she's ready to warm my bed.

"Hey, handsome. Looking for some company?" She trails a hand up my arm, her bright red nails not something Jessa would ever wear, but beggars can't be choosers. She's as close to the girl I've been obsessing over for the past month and I'm not about to look this gift horse in the mouth.

Licking my lips, I give her a once over and come to terms

3

with my decision. I'm taking this lady good and hard, and I'll be thinking of my girl during every minute of it. "Sure, sweetheart. Why don't you come here and sit on Daddy's lap."

She doesn't need to be told twice, having succeeded at her objective. Knowing that she's getting hers only serves to dim my guilt just a bit, and as she settles her fine ass onto my lap, I pray for absolution.

To whom and for what, I have no fucking clue.

Jessa isn't my girl. She doesn't even know who I am. I shouldn't feel ashamed.

Hell, this lady gets to come at least twice, and I get to play out my fantasy of fucking Jessa. Win-win, right? But if it were that simple, then why do I feel the way I do? Like there's a cement block attached to my legs, and if I'm not careful, that fucker will drown me.

SINFUL CROWN

My finger hovers over the bid button for the millionth time, battling whether I should go through with it and lay claim to something I have no business owning.

It's been over a month since my encounter with the Jessa stand-in and it's only made my obsession worse. I've grown possessive now, and the thought of anyone else touching her for the first time sends homicidal thoughts running through me.

Fuck it. Someone's taking her innocence, so it might as well be me.

I'm about to hit the bright red button when the screen turns black and the number to the guard tower comes through.

I live on Millionaire row, and though living on the water

does have its perks, nosy tourists aren't one of them. Armando, the head of security, does an amazing job at keeping nosy Nellie's out of my hair, but *right now*? I'm not his biggest fan.

"Mando. Everything okay?" The sooner I get him off the line, the sooner I can hit that bid button and secure my girl.

"Sorry to bother you, sir, but you have a visitor and she says she has some rather *sensitive* information for you."

My stomach knots at his words. I just went through hell and back with my family and the last thing I need right now is more bad news. Tilting my head back, I pinch the bridge of my nose and answer. "That's fine. Send her through."

"Yes, sir." Armando cuts the line and I shove the phone into my pocket, getting up from my comfortable down feather sofa and regretting answering that call already.

There's a soft knock just as I reach the door, but as I go to turn the knob, I get this impending sense of doom. Maybe I'm just jaded, and maybe this is all just in my head, but as soon as my eyes land on the woman standing in front of me, I have a sinking feeling my intuition was dead on.

"Jason." The Jessa stand-in is blinking up at me and I feel like an ass for not remembering her name. Thankfully, she supplies that and more on her next breath. "It's Catherine. From the airport lounge?"

More like the bathroom at the airport lounge.

"Yes, yes. Of course. Please come in." I'm ushering her through the door, wondering how in the hell she found me when we barely exchanged a few words. "Can I ask you what brings you into town? If I remember correctly, you said you were a local in Colorado."

She's blushing now as I direct her to the sofa I'd just vacated minutes ago. With a hand on her stomach, she gracefully lowers herself into a seated position. She's talking. I can hear sounds coming from her general direction, but my eyes are trained on the hand she's kept on her abdomen this entire time.

Oh, hell no. This shit cannot be happening right now.

"Jason?" The woman's brows are furrowed and she's looking at me with concern. Rightfully so, I feel like I'm about to pass the fuck out.

"Yes. I'm sorry. What were you saying?" I beeline it to my bar and pour myself a healthy serving of my brother's private label, Tortured Crown whiskey. It's the good stuff and it'll definitely provide the dulling of emotions I'm no doubt about to need. "Catherine, would you like some?"

Her brows shoot up and I suspect it's because of what she's told me, but I've yet to really hear. "Um, no thank you. In my condition, I don't think that would be wise."

Yup. I'm fucked. Needing to plant myself in a chair before I topple over, I walk over to the opposite sofa from what I can safely assume is my baby momma. As my ass sinks into the plush seating, a conversation with my brothers comes flashing back in vivid color.

"To be honest, I'm surprised you haven't knocked someone up or called us to bail you out." Mathew *sighs as he puts down his tumbler.*

"I'm not stupid, Matt. I wrap it up. No glove, no love," I state matter-of-factly while Jack, our eldest brother, chokes on his drink.

"You do know that those things aren't one-hundred percent foolproof, right?"

God, oh, god. How I wish I could take that all back. But hey, Karma sure has a way of keeping you humble, doesn't it?

"It's still early, but I'm positive it's yours." Catherine has picked back up where she left off, as if the information she just dropped on me was whether or not we'll be having pizza for dinner.

Yeah. No, Catherine. This is so much bigger than pizza.

Her brows push together and her nose scrunches up. "Pizza? I'm sorry, did you want me to order some?"

Shit. I must've said that out loud. I've clearly lost my mind. "No. It's me who needs to apologize. I was just thinking. Pay that no mind." I rub a palm over my face and let out a slow breath before continuing. "I sort of blacked out for a moment there. Could you please repeat why you're here?"

Catherine turns a bright shade of pink and I feel like a dick all over again. This can't be easy for her either. "Um. Well, as you know, about a month ago we were intimate. The condom must've failed because here I am, a week late and three positive tests deep."

"And these are pregnancy tests we're talking about, right?" *Fuck.* I'm not trying to be dense, but I need her to spell this shit out for me.

At this, she smiles. "Yes, we're talking about pregnancy tests."

I'm nodding. Letting her words sink in. "Okay, at the risk of sounding like a major douche. How sure are you that *I'm* the father?"

Her smile drops, and even though her feelings are clearly hurt, this is something that needs to be asked. I double glove for a reason. With my assets and family name, there have been many who have tried to land themselves a Crown through less honorable means, and I can't put it past anyone—not even my Jessa stand-in.

"Well, I can assure you that you're the only man I've been with in the last couple of months."

My eyes narrow, remembering how forward she was with me when we met. I have a hard time believing a woman who's so aggressive in her flirting is someone who goes celibate for long. But implying otherwise is a line of assholery *I* won't even cross.

"Okay." I take a big sip of whiskey and let it all sink in, trying to come up with a game plan of how things are going to change moving forward. "I'm not sure how long you'll be in town, but I'll give you the number to my financial planner. He'll set you up with an account that should cover all of your medical expenses through the pregnancy, and as soon as the baby is born, we can confirm paternity."

I'm speaking the words that have yet to sink in. *I'm going to be a father.* I'm still lost in my head when I notice Catherine hasn't said a word since I last spoke. "Is everything okay?"

Her eyes are glistening with tears, and I'm not liking the direction this is going. I'm the light and fun brother. Always joking, never taking things too seriously. But as this woman sits in front of me, her hand still clutching her abdomen, I fear those days are long gone.

"I just… I thought this would go so differently. I've been

terrified that you'd ask me to abort the baby, and even though this is a late-in-life pregnancy carrying its own set of dangers, I still could never part with this child."

Straight up bile crawls up my throat. I may be an asshole, but I would never in a million years ask a woman to do that. "Catherine, only dickless men fail to show up for their responsibilities, and as you've clearly experienced, mine is still very much attached."

She lets out a strangled laugh as she wipes away her tears. "Yes. I'm very much aware of your *member.*"

Hearing her talk about my cock makes me want to vomit. Fifteen minutes ago I was about to bid on Jessa's virtue, and it makes the memory of what I did with her doppelgänger not sit right with me.

Needing to change the topic quickly, I ask about the baby. "Have you had your first appointment yet?"

Catherine shakes her head. "No, you're really the first person I've told. It's been a bit of a surprise, to be honest. I wasn't exactly sure how everything was going to play out."

I nod, wanting to take her at her word. "Right. Well, my niece and brother's fiancé are both pregnant. They're in Colorado, too. I can call them and see who they're using as their doctor if you don't have one."

As life would have it, the Crown men have been inundated with pregnant women, and all I can say is at least I won't be alone when all the baby questions start to come in. I've never changed a diaper in my life, and there's no doubt I'd probably fuck it up without the help.

Jesus. This is really happening, isn't it?

"Um, I was actually finishing up with a contract in Colorado and thought maybe I could find work here in South Beach. That way, you'd be close to the baby." She's pressing her lips together, her eyes going wide. "I mean, I wasn't trying to be presumptuous that we'd be together, but since I'm just an interior designer and you're... well, you. It just made sense for me to move instead of the other way around."

I'm nodding, probably looking like a damn bobble head at this point. What she's saying makes sense, but it all seems *too* convenient. The cynical side of me rears its ugly head and I start to wonder if she'd planned all of this from the beginning.

"Catherine, can you answer something for me?"

"Yes. Of course. You can ask me anything."

"How did you know who I was and where to find me?" The smile she'd been wearing falls for the second time, but I just can't find two fucks to give.

"Um, I thought you'd probably wonder." She opens her small pocketbook, retrieving one of my business cards and handing it to me. "This fell out of your pants after we... well, you know."

My cheek twitches. She's acting all shy, the complete opposite of how she was at the airport lounge, but I'm in no position to make baseless accusations. Not if there's a chance she's really carrying my child.

"Okay. Thank you for telling me. Please take no offense, but one can never be too sure these days." I get up, walking toward the bar for a refill. "So, where will you be staying then? I can have my realtor find you a nice little apartment close to my office. She deals in commercial real estate, but I know she'll make an exception for me."

Silence descends and it has me turning back toward Catherine. She's blushing again, her fingers now picking at the hem of her dress. "Yes. I wasn't really sure how this would go, so I'd held off on deciding that. I came here straight from the airport."

I'm blinking, jaw clenching tightly. Surely this woman didn't think we'd become an instant family, did she? I mean, yes, I'd probably ask her to marry me, eventually. I've seen what growing up in broken homes does to people and I wouldn't want that for my child if I could avoid it. But to assume that she'd be moving in from day one seems a bit presumptuous, doesn't it?

Clearing my throat, I ask the obvious. "Where are your things?"

"They're at the guard station. I didn't want to impose. Just thought I'd leave the option there in case you were as excited as I was about the baby. But I can see that isn't what's happened." She gets up in a rush, her words punching me in the gut where I probably deserve.

I'm about to apologize for my callousness when Catherine goes pale, her body crumpling to the floor before me. *Shit.*

I rush toward her, hitting the ground as soon as I've reached her, my arms scooping her up like an injured child. "Catherine. Catherine. Talk to me. Wake up, sweetheart."

I'm about to pull out my cell phone and call 9-1-1 when her lashes flutter open, those captivating jade eyes looking up at me.

"Jason," she whispers. "I'm okay. Really." She goes to remove herself from my hold, but I only grab on tighter.

14

At that moment, I know I can't ask her to leave. Not if her passing out is going to be a regular occurrence. I might not love this woman, but there's an inexplicable bond to that child already growing inside her. "Does this happen often? Your losing consciousness?"

"Just for the past week. That was my first clue that something wasn't normal. I've been extremely tired and if I get up too quickly, I end up on the ground."

I roll in my lips, coming to a decision as I help her up onto her feet. "I'm calling Armando and telling him to bring your things. You'll be staying in the room next to mine and first thing tomorrow morning we'll get you set up with the best doctor Miami has to offer."

She's beaming up at me now, flashing me her pearly whites. "Thank you so much, Jason. This has all been so overwhelming and it makes me feel better knowing that we're in this together."

I just nod, unable to form words. Overwhelming is putting it lightly. It's more like I've been hit by a Mack truck, blindsided and left on the road for dead.

Taking out my phone, I dial the guard house and make the call that will forever change my future, kissing any hope of having Jessa goodbye.

Chapter Two
MILA

wo weeks later...

TTen o'clock hits and I couldn't get out of this seedy bar fast enough. I've been waiting tables for the past year thanks to my fake I.D. and tons of make-up—the only useful skill I've learned from my mother, but I can't wait until the day that I can finally give my notice. *Just two more weeks.*

"Need me to walk you out?" One of the bouncers calls out to me as I'm heading out the door.

Whipping around, I give him my brightest smile. "I'm good, Johnny. But keep an eye on Melissa. I think she may have an obsessive fan."

I snicker, knowing full-well Mel will be pissed. She's had

a crush on the brooding mountain man who's become a regular, and sending in Johnny to cock block will definitely get me an earful later. *Oh well.* My roommate should've thought harder before eating that last sleeve of Oreos.

Leaving Johnny to it, I turn on a wistful sigh and walk toward my beat up civic, fantasizing about the day that I get to leave this town once-and-for-all. Sure, bar money isn't a lot, but I've got a plan that'll get me where I need to go. And best of all, it'll just be a one-time thing, meaning I can shove it in my rear-view mirror as soon as I'm done with it.

I've just shut the door to my car when my purse vibrates. *Oh, God. What now?* There are only two people who have this number and one of them is inside dancing.

Clicking the line through, I pray it's nothing serious.

"Mila, darling. Are you there?"

"Yes, Catherine. I'm here. Is everything okay?"

"Is that any way to talk to your mom?" she admonishes, and it takes everything in me not to laugh in her face.

She isn't my mom. Not in the truest sense of the word. She may have carried me in her womb, but there isn't a maternal bone in that woman's body.

"Spare me the hurt feelings and get to the point. I've had a long day and I just want to get home so I can crawl into bed."

"Mila Kournikova, you watch your tone or I won't let you be around your little brother or sister."

Her words have my breath halting and my heart picking up.

"What did you just say?" The words come out so low I wonder if she heard me.

"Surprise! You're going to be a big sister! I wanted to tell you in person but figured you wouldn't fly out without my telling you why."

I'm gulping in air, wondering how this is even real life. She doesn't even like kids, and she wasn't with anyone the last time I'd seen her.

"What? When? How?" So many questions slam into me at once that I'm surprised I'm able to get any out.

"I admit it was a surprise, but a pleasant one. The only problem is that because of my age, I'm having a bit of medical issues this time around."

I'm nodding, though I know she can't see me. "Right, you're forty-six, not the typical age for a pregnancy, but science has come a long way. I'm sure everything's going to be fine, right?"

Despite the animosity between us, I still want my mother and the baby to be okay. *I'm not a monster.*

"Yes. I've been able to see the best doctors for the little peanut and me. But that doesn't change the fact that I'm having horrible morning sickness. It's even worse than when I was pregnant with you." She laughs as if we're the bestest of friends. "Anyway, that's why I was calling you. I remember you saying you'd taken a couple of design courses in high school and I'm sort of in need of your help. Don't worry, I'm not expecting you to do my job, but it'll get you by with the menial tasks I'll need your help with. The mornings are so hard for me, and I need another hand with the business. There are deadlines from the project in Colorado that are coming up and I want you to help with the little things. Put that administration course you took in prep school to good use. And don't worry, it'll only be until the baby is here."

I'm shocked at her words. Never in my life has she asked for my help, always swatting me away and telling me I'd just mess up her precious boards and files.

A part of me preens, but the one more connected with reality wonders what's really in it for her. Yes, I'd be helping her with her work, but aside from the obvious, why now?

"I thought you'd finished the project in Loveland. At least that's what you told me the last time we spoke."

"I did, but the couple wanted to put in an addition at the last moment and I just couldn't say no. You know how it is."

Yes. I do. Mom can't turn down money. It's her driving source, and never enough. Everything always plays second fiddle to it. Including her daughter.

Sighing into the phone, I finally give her my answer. "Fine. But I can't promise that I'll be there for long. I'm planning on attending college in the fall."

Two more weeks and I'll have the funds to make that dream a reality. Yes, I could've asked mom for the money. After all, she's been getting child support from my father for the past eighteen years, and thanks to his position in life, it's been a pretty penny—not that I've seen a dime.

Catherine likes money, and whatever she received from my father went to feeding her love of everything designer and luxe.

Right then, the memory of my thirteenth birthday hits me strong and fierce.

Covering my mouth, I tried to hide the crooked imperfection that got me teased more often than not. "Please, momma. I just want to fix my teeth."

Catherine scoffed. "Who do I look like? The money tree? We don't have enough for frivolous things, Mila. Just wait until you're older. You can buy yourself braces then."

"But dad gives you more than enough. He always says so." I didn't have a relationship with my biological father, but we talked once a month, and one thing he'd always mention was how much money he'd been giving my mother.

"Stupid girl. That money goes to important things, not superficial ones like your teeth. You'll understand when you're a grownup. Life isn't cheap, and everything costs money."

I cried myself to sleep that night, taking her words to heart. But the next morning, when she walked into the kitchen with her hands full of designer goods and I saw that one bag was worth well over what a set of braces would cost, I knew what she really was. *Selfish.* And I vowed right then and there to never be like the callous bitch my mother was.

"Mila. Are you still there?" She'd been talking this whole time I'd been lost in my head, and I can't say that I'm sorry. I needed that strong reminder of who I'm really dealing with.

"Yes, I'm here."

"Okay, good. Does that mean you'll be coming to South Beach? For the baby?" She tacks on that last part, knowing it's probably the only reason I'd agree.

And she isn't wrong. I already feel a sort of camaraderie with the little one. Poor thing will need a friend against the Wicked Witch of the West when navigating this world.

"Yes, I'll come. I'll need to let my shift manager know, but girls bounce all the time. I'm sure it won't be a problem."

Mom hisses. "Ugh, Mila. Please tell me you're not still working at that strip club."

"Save it, *mom*. It's the highest paying bar in our town, and it's not like I'm asking you for money, right?"

She quiets at that, knowing that the only reason I'm at that place is because I refuse to ask her for a dime. I haven't asked this woman for a single red cent since I turned thirteen and I sure as hell don't plan on starting any time soon, which is why I'll be buying my own ticket out there. "Just tell me where I need to go and I'll give you my flight number."

"Oh, perfect! I can have Armando pick you up from the airport."

"Armando? Is that the baby's daddy?"

"Oh god no. That's the head of security. But you'll meet Jason Crown soon enough. He's going to be your new daddy, after all."

Her words have my stomach lurching. *What the fuck?* "Um, I'm all good on that front, but thanks."

Jesus. What do you say to that? I've never had a dad, and definitely not a daddy. "Head of security? Is Jason some sort of celebrity or something?"

Shocker that mom would get pregnant by some other

affluent schmuck.

"No, he's not a celebrity, but he does have a large profile. You'll see when you get here. There's always security milling about the house. Anyway, I'm so excited to see you, baby."

Her words have my brows hitting my hairline. *Am I in the twilight zone?*

Needing to get off the line before she starts singing Kumbaya and telling me she loves me, I give her some bullshit excuse. "Hey, mom. I see my boss walking out. I'm going to talk to him about leaving."

"Okay, sweetheart. Don't forget to text me the flight later."

"I won't. Bye mom."

"Bye, baby. I lo—."

I end the call before she could get the words out. I don't want to hear them. Not now. Not ever.

They aren't true, and if there's anything I hate worse than avarice, it's deceit.

Jason

"I have the best news, Jason!" Catherine walks into my office without knocking and it takes everything in me not to yell at her.

"For the millionth time, it's Jace." I don't know why I bother, because no matter how many times I've told her my friends and family call me that, she insists on calling me by my birth name, saying it fits me better.

"Anyway, don't you want to hear the news?" She waves away my words as if they're of no importance. How I'm going to spend the rest of my life with this woman is a mystery to me. I'll probably end up in a straitjacket at some point. *Maybe that's her plan.*

"Sure. What's the news?"

"My daughter Mila is coming to town. Since I've been having problems in the mornings, I thought maybe she could help me finish out my contracts. I'd hate to flake on my clients and the baby is just taking all the energy out of me." Catherine sits on the edge of my desk, her skirt riding up her thigh and exposing her tanned skin, but the vision does nothing for my cock. "I hope it isn't a problem that I told her she could stay with us."

I've been trying to make a go of things since she's moved in. And if I were being honest with myself, I know that decision was made when my eyes landed on the ultrasound monitor, the little peanut visible to me for the first time.

My childhood was full of so much happiness, and the memory of my parents being very much in love was a big part of that. I've always known that, if possible, I'd want to give my kids the same. A happy and stable home. Too bad for me. It seems if I want any chance of having that, it'll have to be with Catherine.

Resigning myself to my fate, I rub at the back of my neck and sigh. "Yes, that's fine. When will she be getting in?"

"That's the second thing I'd been wanting to talk to you about." She's fidgeting with a strand of her hair, and I have half a mind to tell her that coy doesn't look good on her. "I know we briefly discussed it when I moved in, but I hoped that Mila staying with us could mean that we could move our relationship to the next level."

My stomach knots at her words, realizing just how much I hate the sound of that. Needing to nip this in the bud, I respond as quickly as humanly possible.

"Now, Catherine. We'd agreed. Until the baby arrives, there's no need for us to be together in that way." I run a hand through my hair, tugging at the ends, intentionally inflicting pain—anything to distract myself from this sense of impending doom. "We're both adults, and we both know that this," I wave a hand between us, "is all a result of a one-night stand. There's no need to complicate it any further by playing house and forcing a relationship where there isn't one. Maybe with time we'll get there, and things will look different when there's a child in the mix, but as of now, I still think we should wait."

Catherine outright pouts. But thankfully, the phone she'd been holding vibrates, cutting off any argument she'd been ready to offer.

Like a magnet, my eyes are drawn to the screen and the caller's photo flashing across it.

What the—?

All at once, my heart stops, my world tilts, and there isn't enough air to be had. *Fucking hell. This has to be some sick joke. This can't be real, can it?*

As Catherine speaks, I know I must've been an evil fuck in a past life. There's no other explanation. No other reason life would be so cruel.

"Mila, darling. That's great news. I'll let Jason know and we'll have someone pick you up." There's a pause and I assume *Mila* is talking. "Uh-huh. Okay, sounds good. We'll see you soon, sweetie. Love you."

She ends the call with a huge smile on her face as I try to figure out how to word my pressing question.

"Catherine, that photo that flashed when Mila called. Whose picture was that?" I'm praying that by some miracle she's just as obsessed with the same camgirl as I am, but I highly doubt it.

"That's Mila, silly." Her brows are furrowed, but the smile still hasn't left her face. That's because she's oblivious. Oblivious to the fact that I fucked her to the thought of her own daughter. That the only reason she's pregnant with my child is because I hadn't been able to stop fantasizing about her little girl.

Bile inches up my throat and I need to excuse myself before I hurl all over my desk. To say that this is one fucking twist I didn't see coming is the understatement of the century.

"I'll need a minute. See you at dinner." I wave toward Catherine as I head for the attached bath, needing a splash of water to the face or the toilet for hurling. Either will do.

And as I shut the door behind me, I have only one question playing on repeat in my head. *How in the fuck am I going to survive this?*

Chapter Three
MILA

I've just stepped out of the terminal and into the open air, but I'm second guessing everything already. Two seconds in and I'm assaulted with so much humidity. It's a miracle my long brown hair doesn't curl on the spot.

I've never been to Florida before—hell, I've never left my little town in Colorado—so this is all a shock to my system. It's beautiful, I'll give it that, though I could do without the dampness in the air. It hasn't even been five minutes of being outside and I already feel like I could use a second shower.

"Miss Kournikova?" A tall man with broad shoulders approaches me and I flinch, realizing I hadn't been paying attention to my surroundings. A big *no-no*.

Focusing on my caller, I let my eyes skim the tailored

uniform he's in before falling to the whiteboard in his hands. "Armando?"

Mom said she'd have security pick me up, and he definitely looks the part. Those broad shoulders are housing impressive muscle if the fabric going taut is any indication.

"Yes. I see Catherine told you I was coming." He smiles before waving a hand toward a large SUV with tinted windows. "This way, Miss."

"Armando?"

He whirls around so fast I almost slam into his chest. "Yes?"

"You wouldn't mind showing me some I.D., would you? I don't typically make it a habit of getting into cars with strangers, and this being a new city and all, I'd feel safer knowing you are who you say you are."

His smile goes from ear to ear as he pulls his wallet out of his back pocket, his bicep flexing and threatening to split his shirt with the movement. "Not at all, Miss."

"Please, call me Mila." Looking down at the open wallet, I see his driver's license. *Armando Cartagena.*

"Very well, Mila. Shall we?" He tilts his head toward the Escalade again and I nod.

"Thanks for indulging me and my paranoia. I've seen one too many true crime stories to not ask."

Armando chuckles as he opens the back door for me, taking my luggage in the process. "Oh, you definitely don't have to explain to me. I have a little sister and I wouldn't let her go anywhere without doing the same."

I get into the back seat and sink into the rich leather, so different from the scratchy fabric of my old civic. Mom did always have a thing for luxury, and it seems her new man is very much the same.

I roll my eyes as Armando gets into the driver's seat, his eyes meeting mine in the rearview mirror. "Everything okay, Mila?"

"Yes." I blow out a breath, wondering if my new friend will spill the beans on his boss. "Is my mother's new boyfriend nice?"

Nice and wealthy rarely go hand in hand in my limited experience. The ballers at my work? Mean. My mother? Mean. My biological father? Well, he's more indifferent than mean, but still.

"Can't complain. He's the best boss I've ever had."

We'll see about that.

Armando pulls away from the terminal and all I can see is palm trees for days. *Wow, it really is beautiful here.* My face is glued to the window, mesmerized by the scenery when we drive onto a bridge and I get my first glimpse of water, the sight alone making my jaw drop. I've never seen the ocean, and this is one hell of an introduction.

Rows and rows of massive beach front homes line the street we're on, and in between each I get a glimpse of the sand and water beyond.

"Do you think we can drive by the beach before we get to our final destination?" I'm practically kissing the window when Armando's words cut into my fog.

"We're already here, Miss." The SUV pulls up to a set of large white gates, the massive slabs of steel parting and exposing a circular drive. "But if you want to see the beach, then you just need to walk past the backyard. The residence holds a private entry past the swimming pool and garden."

My mouth hangs open. *I can't help it.* Just how much money does my mom's new boyfriend have? The house I'm staring at has to be in the millions, and to be right on the water like this? Yeah, the guy is loaded.

I try to compose myself as Armando rounds the SUV and opens my door, but my mouth goes dry and all thoughts leave my body as my eyes fall on the man standing at the door.

Lord have mercy. I've seen Adonis himself. He must be six-three, all muscle and hard edges—topped with the thickest head of hair, he could make the CEO of Monat salivate with envy.

His massive frame fills the doorway, and even though he's dressed in all linen, the casual nature of his clothes does nothing to hide the power and steel beneath them. It radiates from him, reaching me from over twenty feet away.

I'm still standing there, staring, when Mom's voice slams into my bubble of lust. "Mila! You're here, baby!"

Her term of endearment is enough to shake any remaining fog I was under. I see her now, speed walking around the adonis and heading straight for me with arms outstretched. *What the fuck?*

I'm so shocked at what I'm seeing I don't have time to brace myself for the hug.

"Mother?"

Catherine squeezes me harder, a sharp squeal emanating from her throat. "I'm so glad you're here, sweetie!"

She finally lets me go, but moves to grab my hand, and because I'm still in a daze, I let her. She's dragging me up the stairs and toward the man I saw earlier, and the closer we get, the finer he seems. *How is he even real?* I swear, not even actors with all the Photoshop in the world have anything on this man. Is he her boyfriend's brother? Son?

"Jason, meet Mila. Mila, meet Jason." Catherine's hand falls to her stomach and I instantly want to vomit. "He's the baby's father."

Yup. I want to vomit. I was just drooling over the man who gets it on with my *mom*. Nausea hits me and it takes everything in me not to gag.

"Mila. It's nice to meet you." Jason's deep voice reaches me and any ailment I had leaves my body, his deep baritone enough to keep it all at bay. That is, until his hand reaches for mine and our skin makes contact.

Fire. Nothing but liquid heat burns between us. It's so intense I quickly pull my hand away, unable to let myself feel this with him. For him.

It's wrong.

"Jason." I nod, trying to school my features but failing miserably if Catherine's furrowed brows are any indication.

"Do you two know each other?" She's looking between us, her eyes landing on mine for an answer, knowing that I can't lie to save my life.

"Nope. Never met him before." I roll in my lips, not

trusting myself to add anything more.

And Jason saves me from having to do that, but to my horror, he does it by placing his hand on my lower back and ushering me inside. "Armando, I'll take Mila's luggage."

As if in a trance, I let his free hand take the handle of my suitcase. All the while the other remains pressed to my back, never once dropping from its perch as he walks us inside.

I never let a man put his hands on me, *but Jason*? It's as if I've never heard of the word *no*.

"You don't have to do that, Jason. I can show her to her room." Mom's shrill voice sounds off behind us and I can't bear to turn and look. The shame of how much I'm enjoying her man's touch is too much for me to face.

"We can both take her. It's not like I'd let you pick up her luggage in your condition." He never once turns toward Catherine while he speaks. In fact, he bristled beside me with every syllable. *Interesting.* Does he resent her for her weakened state? Well, that's a jerk thing to feel.

I quickly add it to an invisible tally, anything that'll make me dislike Jason. Not because I want to hate him, but because I need to absolve myself of the sinful thoughts I've already had.

I may not like my mother very much, but there are lines that not even I will cross. And fantasizing about a man who's going to be my stepfather is one of them. Catherine might not have a ring on her finger yet, but knowing her, it's only a matter of time—and how awkward would that be? Yeah, no thanks.

We reach the top of the stairs and my steps halt. There's a massive picturesque window right across the landing and the view is nothing short of breathtaking.

"It's so beautiful." I've only seen the ocean through video or photos, but none of it does it justice. The sky is shining down onto the crystal-clear water of the surf, but the waves do nothing to hide the azure of the shoreline.

"If you like that, then you'll love your room." Jason finally drops his hand and I instantly feel the loss.

How could his touch affect me so much when I've just met him? I'm not left any time to ponder because my mother is quickly inserting herself between us.

"Jason, I didn't know you were putting her in the Ivy."

Mom's boyfriend rolls his eyes as he walks into the room Catherine so aptly named after the vine. The walls are all in a deep green, contrasted with the dark blue jewel tones of the furniture and velvet bedding. It would be over the top in any other situation, but the way it's balanced with the minimalism of the room makes it chic and elegant instead of gaudy and pretentious.

"Did you decorate this room, Mom?"

Catherine blushes as she wraps an arm around Jason's waist, the contact making him visibly bristle. "Oh, no. Jason had his designer put this together. He's been so protective, not wanting me to lift a finger if I don't have to. Isn't he the best?"

My brows reach toward my hairline. I highly doubt she wants my opinion of her beau. Something tells me she'll have a problem with my lusting after his Greek physique and protective ways.

I've never had that before—*someone looking out for me*—

and the thought of this man taking charge is making me ache in all the naughty places.

Jason clears his throat, and it's then I realize I've been staring at him, not giving my mom an answer. "Right. Well, I bet you're tired from your trip." He walks over to the bed and lays my luggage on top of the plush comforter. "But before we let you rest, why don't you push this?"

He pulls a remote from the bedside table and hands it to me, our fingers brushing and sending another violent tingle through me. *God, what is it with this man?*

Needing the distraction, I push the button and a soft whirring sound has me turning. The deep green curtains part, seemingly gliding on a mechanical tract and exposing the room to the beauty just outside the window. Floor to ceiling windows open onto a balcony overlooking a strip of beach.

"Oh my god. Does this open up?" *Holy hell.* It's stunning.

I'm walking up to the panel of glass when Jason comes up beside me and pushes another button on the remote I'm still holding, making the entire window slide to the left and converting the room into an instant outdoor space.

"Does that answer your question?" Jason is smirking down at me while I'm just standing there with my mouth hanging open.

"Yes. It definitely does." I'm blinking up at him, still in a daze, when Catherine steps out onto the balcony and points toward the right.

"Best part is we're all connected! That's Jason's room, and then mine is next to his." She points to the wall of windows next to mine. *That's weird.* They don't share a room? "We have an adjoining door and eventually my room will turn into the nursery."

Her eyes widen at that last bit as if she can't contain her excitement, making me wonder if my mom did in fact become baby crazy since I last saw her.

Just then, Jason coughs before turning back toward my room. "My number is on your bedside table, Mila. Call me or Armando if you need to leave the property. If you ladies will excuse me, I have some work to get to."

I'm staring at his back when Catherine waves him off, blocking my view. "Don't worry about us, Jason. We've got some catching up to do!"

It takes everything in me not to cackle at my mother's words. She's really playing up the mothering role, isn't she? The door clicks and the charade doesn't end there. She's apparently committed to becoming my new BFF, plopping herself on the bed as I start to unpack.

"So, tell me all about this college you're planning on attending."

I raise a brow, my hands stopping mid air with a swimsuit I'd bought just for this trip. "You really want to know?"

"Of course I do, Mila." She's looking at me like I'm crazy, and maybe I am. Maybe I'm being a little too jaded and she really wants to mend our relationship.

"Okay. It's for the best design school in the nation. It's a miracle I'm able to swing—"

I'm about to open up and let her in on how I'm planning on

paying for it when her cell phone goes off and she holds up a finger.

"One minute, baby. This is work." She gets up and walks over to the blue chase, answering her phone and getting lost in her conversation before I can even put my heart back in my chest.

I should've known better. Work always comes first with her. Why did I think this would be any different? I'm here to help her with that after all.

With a deep sigh, I resign myself to playing her pawn. *She wants to parade me in front of Jason?* Fine. I don't care as long as I get to be there for the peanut she's bringing into this world. With a mother like her, they'll need all the love they can get, and I definitely plan on showering them with it.

SINFUL CROWN

Chapter Four
JACE

My finger hovers over the bid button one last time. Now that I've seen her in the flesh, there's no way I can let any other man have her.

I may not follow through with the claim, but I'll be damned if I let her sell herself like some prized show pony.

There's a little over a week left until the timer on her *sale* runs out, and she has to be out of her damned mind if she thinks I'll let her go through with it.

That girl is innocent and there will be no cherry popping while she's under my roof. I may not be her parental figure, but as soon as she stepped through my door, an unexplainable need to protect her came over me.

No, I'm not her father, but I'll definitely be her daddy.

Clearly, she needs guidance if she's out here willing to sell such a valuable treasure.

Before I can talk myself out of it, I press the button, agreeing to transfer over two million dollars at her behest. That should be enough to outbid any motherfucker out there who thinks he's worthy. If not, I can always send more.

A sense of peace settles over me as the confirmation screen appears, but it's quickly washed away by my brother's flashing face. *God. I hope it's nothing but good news.*

Sliding the call through, I pray that it is. "Talk to me, Austin."

"I need you to come back to the ranch."

My stomach knots at his words. "Is everything okay?"

"Yes. But I can't get married without one of my best men here."

I let out a whoosh of air, both elated and relieved at the news. "You finally settled on a date?"

My brother had asked Anaya to marry him last month, but they had some loose ends to tie up before that was made possible.

"Yes. Got the divorce papers being mailed to me as we speak. That shit couldn't happen fast enough. But now that it's done, we're ready to move forward and become a real family."

I smile so wide my cheeks hurt. "That's good to hear, brother. Just let me know when and I'll be there. Though I'll be bringing company." My chest tightens with the bombshell I've still to drop on my brothers. "There's something I need to tell all of you once I'm there. Just know that I'm bringing two guests with me."

My thoughts drift to Mila. Now that I've had her in my home, there's no way I'm letting her out of my sight. Especially now, with the sale of her virginity hanging in the air.

"Oh? Is it anyone special you're bringing home? Has the eternal bachelor finally settled down?" Austin teases, but if he only knew.

"Something like that. Just save me a cabin with three rooms."

"Three separate rooms?" His curiosity is evident but I'm not budging on telling him. Not until all the brothers are together.

"Yes. Now, when's the date?"

Austin lets out a sigh. "I would've liked to have had the info from Cardenas' men, but it looks like we'll be having to move forward without it. Raul isn't budging, no matter what *tactics* are thrown his way."

He pauses and I know he can't say more. This isn't a secured line and who knows if the Feds are listening. My family got mixed up with rival cartels long ago, and the fallout of everything is still with us 'til this day.

And to be honest, I'm glad he hasn't been able to get his hands on the information he's after. If he only knew what it really was, then he'd be sorry.

Unfortunately for me, that tidbit is something I've had to carry for most of my adult life, and I'll be taking it to the grave if I have to. Dad trusted me with it, and there's no way I'd betray him.

"Jace? You there, brother?"

"Yes. Yes. I'm here. Sorry, a work email came through. What were you saying?"

"It's next month. The wedding."

"God, I'm so happy for you and Anaya. I bet the kids are excited as hell."

"They sure are. They love my woman more than they loved their own momma." He hisses, probably remembering how Blanca treated her own children.

It was clear she loved them, but she never really engaged with them. Not like their nanny, and now soon to be stepmom.

"Well, count on me being there. Just email the details. I wouldn't miss it for the world."

"Looking forward to meeting your mystery guests. Make sure to come a couple of days early. I want Anaya to meet them without having to worry about the wedding planning."

"Sounds good, brother. See you soon."

Austin cuts the line and I'm left wondering how in the hell I'm going to break all of my crazy ass news to them.

I'm going to be a father. And I've fallen for my baby momma's daughter.

Mila

My phone vibrates on the bedspread and I jump for it. Anything to take away from the sting of my mother's rejection.

You'd think I'd know better by now.

Rolling my eyes, I unlock my phone, the sight i making my heart freeze in my chest. *Holyfuckingshit.* Two million dollars. Two. Million. Dollars.

This can't be real.

My eyes flit to the bidder's name and I practically swallow my tongue.

First Name: Your

Last Name: Daddy

What the fuck? Is this a joke? It has to be. Double checking the figures, I see they haven't changed. Two Million dollars. That would be more than enough to cover any tuition and living expenses. Waitressing at a seedy strip club? Yeah, that would be a thing of the past.

But what kind of sick fuck signs off as *Your Daddy*? I'm about to email the bidder when I see he's left behind my email instead of his own. Was that intentional? Now I have no way of tracing him.

Technically, I can wait out the bids—knowing none will come close to his—and then accept his transfer. The system cleared all of his banking information. It would slip into my account, no problem. All the while knowing there's no way for him to collect on his prize.

I squeeze my eyes shut. That'd be shady though. This entire process is already a bunch of gray lines as it is. But if I renege on my side of the bargain, that takes it to a whole other level of fuckery I'm not even willing to contemplate.

No. I can't accept the money. Not if there's no way of

contacting the bidder.

"You know, if you keep frowning like that, no amount of Botox will help."

Mom's words have me tripping out of my dilemma and into the here and now. "What?"

"You may have youth on your side right now, but trust me, that fades all too quickly. And then where will you be?"

I roll my eyes. "I'll be a nationwide sensation, known for my design skills, making my beauty or lack thereof moot."

Catherine scoffs. "You think beauty won't matter? News flash, it always matters."

I'm about to retort with something spiteful, but a knock at the door saves me from saying something I'll never be able to take back.

"Am I interrupting?" Jason's impressive frame stands just outside the hallway, but even from here, I can feel the heat in his gaze. Did he hear what Mom said?

"Not at all, darling. I was just catching up with Mila's school of choice. Where was it? Missouri?"

I sigh, wondering why I even bother. "Montana. They have the best—"

"Design school," Jason interjects, and I'm left speechless. How does he know?

"Yes. That's why I'm going there."

"It's pricey. Do you have enough to cover the tuition?" His eyes narrow, focusing on my own which shift to the phone still in my hand.

"Not now, but I will." Even if I don't accept the two million from the mystery donor, I'll still get enough for tuition. The bidder before him hit sixty thousand. With that and a part-time job, I'll manage.

"Hmm. Well, you can always ask me if you need anything." His tone has me looking up and I wish I hadn't. His gaze hasn't left me, his steely eyes boring into me. It's almost as if they see right through me, skating past all of my defenses and tearing them all to shreds, leaving me nothing but an exposed pile of nerves.

"I—I don't think that'll be necessary." Hyper-aware of his eyes on me, I don't have time to process what Catherine says next.

"Don't be shy about it, Mila. Jason is practically your daddy now. He's just being protective of you like he is of this little peanut." Her hand flutters to her abdomen as a smile plays on her lips. "And despite how hard I work, you know as well as I do that all of my money went to fixing your snaggle tooth and the fancy private school you went to. Nothing but the best for my little girl."

My mouth falls open, but I quickly snap it shut when she raises a brow. *What alternate universe have I walked into?* How can this woman say those things with a straight face? My father payed for the private school *she* insisted I go to, and *I* paid to fix my fucking snaggle tooth.

I have half a mind to call her out on her bullshit, but then she'd lock me out of that baby's life, and that's not something I'm willing to risk. It'll be a cold day in hell before I let that child grow up the way I did.

Thankfully, Jason saves me once again, his hand rapping on the door frame only once. "Alright then, it's settled. Mila, if you need anything, just ask. Like Catherine mentioned, I'm practically your daddy now." A shiver wracks me, all while those eyes threaten to steal my soul. "I mean it. Whatever is mine is yours." Something flashes behind those orbs before a jovial facade falls into place, and I can't help but wonder how often he has to do that—hide himself. "Speaking of which, my yacht. I was wondering if you ladies were up for a sunset cruise along the coast."

"I'm sorry, what?" His change of subject shocks my system. Did he say yacht?

"Oh, I'd been wondering if you'd invite me out!" Mom practically squeals as she saunters over to him, her hands wrapping around one of Jason's massive biceps. "We'd love to go. Right, Mila?"

I swallow hard. Not sure if being in close quarters with a man who sets my girly bits a flutter is such a smart idea.

"It'll be short," he prompts, as if reading my mind.

"Okay. Sounds good." I nod, unsure if it's a good idea at all, but deciding I should try. He's going to be family, after all. I should desensitize myself to his presence. Maybe after repeated exposure, I'll be numb to this effect he has on me.

"Great. The boat is at a marina not far from here, so let's meet out by the cars in ten." His eyes flit between Mom and me as if unsure, but then he turns and leaves.

"Did you bring a bathing suit, Mila?"

Are you kidding me? I was literally holding it in my hands

48

not twenty minutes ago, but instead of giving her sass, I simply bite my tongue and answer. "Yes, I brought a bathing suit. We're in Miami. I thought I'd hit up South Beach at some point."

Mom's eyes widen. "Well, if you go, you're taking Armando with you. And don't do anything that will embarrass me." She rushes over to me before grabbing my biceps and squeezing. "And for the love of God, whatever you do, *do not* tell Jason where you work."

I rear my head back as if slapped. "I'm not going to hide it, *Mother.* If he asks me, then I'll tell him."

Catherine's face is turning beet red, and it takes everything in me not to laugh. If I wanted to pay her back for all the things she put me through, this would be a fantastic idea. *Embarrassing* her in front of her beau.

Ugh. I can't. I'm not that petty, and I just know karma will bite me in the ass.

But it's fun to imagine.

"*Mila.*" Mom is pleading with her eyes, her fingers still digging into my flesh.

"Fine. I won't say anything unless he directly asks me. But I won't lie. That's a line I won't cross."

Mom scoffs. "Look at you. The pinnacle of morality, working at a strip club."

"There's nothing wrong with what I do, Mother. I wait tables and serve people their drinks—but even if I were to get up and dance on the stage, there's no shame in that."

Catherine rolls her eyes. "Let's agree to disagree." She finally releases me before sauntering over to the door. "I'm going to get ready. Meet you downstairs in a bit."

"Looking forward to it," I murmur under my breath.

It hasn't even been twenty-four hours and I'm already wanting to pull out my hair, the whole situation turning me into an unstable head case.

What will I be after enduring *months* with her? I don't even want to think about it.

SINFUL CROWN

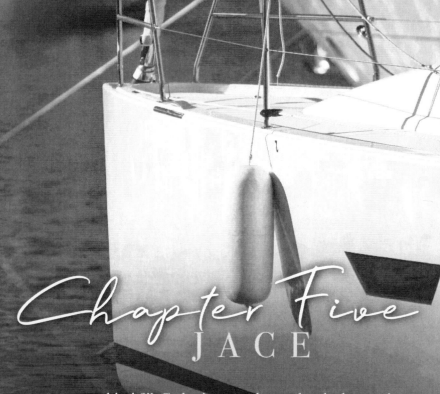

Chapter Five

JACE

"Is this it?" Catherine stands on the dock, peering over her large sunglasses at my sailboat as if it had the bubonic plague.

"Yes. This is her. My baby." I look between both women and see that they couldn't be more different.

Catherine is decked out with wedge heels, makeup done to the nines, a massive hat that almost blocks all of that makeup, and a leopard print cover up that looks like it could double as a dress for the Met.

Meanwhile, Mila is wearing cutoff shorts, a white tank, and Converse with not a lick of makeup—not that she needs it. She's naturally gorgeous, and God help me, but I can't stop staring.

"Jason." Catherine's shrill voice cuts into my admiration

and a shudder wracks my broad frame. "I don't think boating is such a good idea in my condition. When you said sunset cruise, I pictured a yacht. Not a small sailboat."

I choke on my saliva. *Small?* Acts of Grace is a seventy-two-footer, with dual helms and three staterooms. I'm blinking, unsure of how to respond.

"What I mean is, I thought you meant you had one of those." Catherine points to a large motored yacht. "I'd seen a picture of you in one of those recently, so naturally, I assumed. But I guess I assumed wrong."

I bite down on my lower lip, debating on whether to tell her that the yacht she pointed at is also mine, but her next words have me swallowing my tongue.

"I see you're upset. You were probably looking forward to this sunset cruise." Her eyes shift over to her daughter who's been silent this entire time. "Why don't you just take Mila out instead? It'll give you both some time to get to know each other." She hitches her thumb down the dock. "I saw a gorgeous little bistro that opens up onto the water. I'll just wait for you there."

My brows furrow as they fall on Mila. She appears to be mortified on her mother's behalf, and I don't blame her.

Catherine was all but jumping for joy when I first mentioned coming out here, but one look at my love and she's ready to bail. Yes, she's smaller than the other yacht. But she's special to me and doesn't need an entire crew to be taken out.

"Is there a reason you don't like sailboats?" I turn back toward the mother of my unborn child.

54

She bites on her bottom lip nervously before answering. "They pitch to one side. I'm afraid it'll make my nausea go crazy, and the last thing we all need is me going green and getting sick."

"Yes, of course. I'm sorry I didn't think of that." My eyes fall back on the motored yacht, the offer to take it out instead right on the tip of my tongue, but then Mila turns, and those cutoff shorts do nothing to hide how tight her little ass is.

My cock lurches, deciding for the both of us. God help me, but I'm taking the sailboat.

"*Mom*, are you sure you wouldn't rather us go home instead?"

"Nonsense. I have my phone with me. I can just do a little work until you come back." Her eyes narrow at Mila, as if sending a message.

"Well, if you insist. But I'll just message Armando and have him pick you up. I won't have you unguarded. We'll wait until he arrives, and then Mila can have some bonding time with her daddy."

I bite the corner of my lip, trying to suppress a full-on grin. It's obvious that the term has an effect on Mila if her reddened cheeks are anything to go by. But hey, it was Catherine who started it with her comment earlier. So, am I *really* to blame?

"That sounds good." Catherine grabs Mila by the arm, her red fingernails digging into her caramel skin and leaving half-moons behind—the action making my blood boil. I'm about to say something when Catherine's next words cut me off. "Why don't we all head to that little bistro and wait on Armando. We can all have a cocktail in the meantime."

My brows raise. "I'm not drinking before sailing and you're pregnant. That only leaves Mila."

"Actually…" The object of my obsession looks at the ground, her feet shuffling in place. "I just turned eighteen."

My vision blurs and I'm robbed of all breath. *What the fuck did she just say?* My mind goes to the bid on her virtue, and it hits me like a ton of bricks. She'd been waiting until she was legal enough to give that cherry away.

"I thought I told you, Jason. Mila celebrated her birthday a couple of days ago." Catherine is blinking up at me. "And I meant mocktails, silly. I've gotten very creative since finding out about this little peanut." Her hand drops its death grip on Mila and moves to her abdomen, that one motion sobering enough to help me get my shit together.

I can't be lusting after Catherine's daughter. I'm going to be a father and that child deserves the best of everything. Including family.

If I'm going to do right by his mother and make her my wife, then I need to pull my head out of my ass and smother the last of my desires for Mila. For fucks sake, she's barely legal. But *she is* legal.

No. I can't think like that. Especially when temptation is a hairbreadth away.

As we cross over the threshold to the Singing Fish, I vow to kill any and all thoughts of my soon to be stepdaughter. They're wrong and will only lead us down a path to destruction.

SINFUL CROWN

Chapter Six

MILA

"Oh, wow. This is absolutely stunning." My eyes are trailing the entirety of the boat as my heart and mind try furiously to ignore the way Jason's hand feels in mine.

He's walking me aboard *Acts of Grace*, and thank god it's breathtaking, helping to diminish the flutter I feel in my tummy just a little.

"Thank you. She's a lot of fun." There's a twinkle of mischief in his eyes, and I'm dying to know what's behind that.

Like a Mack truck to the face, my thoughts drift to orgies on the boat, the vision making my stomach sour.

He's handsome, there's no denying that. Who's to stop him from partying hard?

I'm still lost in my head when Jason stops short, and I almost run into him—all six-foot-plus and hard as steel.

I'm about to ask him what happened, but my tongue gets tied up when our eyes meet. He's frowning, and the intensity with which he's staring at me leaves me breathless. "Why are you upset, Mila?"

His words have me blinking back to reality. "What? What do you mean?"

"Your face. It's doing that thing." His eyes narrow and my brows raise.

"What thing?"

He quickly looks away, avoiding my gaze. "I meant you pursed your lips to the side. Most girls do that when they're pondering something or if they're upset."

I shake my head, clearing it of the fog he has me under. "Oh. I was just thinking of all the women and parties you must've had on board. So... pondering, I guess you could say."

Flashing him a megawatt smile, I hope my explanation is enough to hide that my stomach still sours at that thought. Why? I have no clue. He isn't mine to be jealous over. He belongs to my *mother.*

"Mila. Look at me." Jason steps closer and places the pads of his fingers under my chin, lifting until my gaze is on his. "You are the first woman that's been on this boat who isn't family."

His words soothe my heart that has no business feeling the flutters it does. Taking a step back, I put some much-needed distance between us. *Not that I want it.*

"You don't owe me any explanations." I gnaw on my bottom lip and watch as Jason's frown returns. "I mean, it's not like I'm Catherine."

At my mother's name, he clears his throat. "Right. Well, you seemed upset." Jason drags a masculine hand across his face while letting out a sigh. "Anyway, we should get going. Have you ever been on a sailboat before?"

I quickly shake my head no. "This is my first time."

Almost immediately, Jason's pupils blow out and his nostrils flare. "It's alright, sweetheart. I promise I'll take it easy." *Holy shit.* Is that....? Is he...? No. That can't be.

"All you need to know is that's the bow" He points to the front of the boat. "That's the stern." He points to the rear. "And this is the helm." He grabs on to one of the massive wheels, all stainless steel and shiny.

Following his mannerisms, I repeat what I just learned. "Bow, stern, and helm."

"Good girl."

Jesus. His praise goes straight to my clit, and it takes everything in me to stay upright. I want this man like I've never wanted anything in my life.

This is bad. Very bad. Not only do I hardly know him, but he's the ultimate definition of off-limits, making the sensual images running through my mind so very wrong.

I should probably get off this boat while I still can. I'm about to jump out and start swimming when Jason takes control of the conversation once more, putting a stop to any plans of escape.

"As soon as we're out on open water, I'll teach you how to steer. After all, you'll be helping moor this baby."

My jaw drops. "You can't be serious. I don't know what that means, but it sounds important. What if I wreck her?"

His eyes narrow on mine as he guides me to a bench seat, the new vantage point allowing me to openly stare while he steers us out of here. "As long as you're not hurt, then nothing else matters."

My throat gets caught on a swallow. Why does everything he say sound so *intense*? Like it's all or nothing, all the time. Is he like this with Catherine too? It must be what drew her to him. His presence exudes alpha energy. You can't help but feel safe when you're near him.

How amazing would it be to be loved like that? I'm just his girlfriend's daughter and he's already so protective of me. I can only imagine how he'd be as a lover.

"Isn't it beautiful? I could never tire of the evening sky." Jason's deep voice pulls me back to the present, and looking past his frame, I see the sky has turned a gorgeous shade of orange.

I'd been so lost in my head that I hadn't noticed we'd already slipped out of the dock and headed towards the sea.

"I can see why. If I had a boat at my disposal, I'd be out here every night."

Jason chuckles. "You don't get it yet, do you? You already have a boat at your disposal. Whenever you want it. Just let me know."

There he goes again, being all intense. He hasn't taken his

eyes off the horizon, but I feel the veracity in his words from where I sit.

"Well, thank you. I'm not used to all this, so you probably won't get many requests from me. I'll just enjoy the view. We definitely don't have *this* back home."

Jason chuckles. "Yes. Open waters are pretty hard to beat, but mountains and fresh air have a draw all their own." He turns back toward me, his brows dropping slightly as he assesses my face. "What do you miss most about being back in Colorado?"

"Mel, my roommate. Hands down." I throw my head back and laugh, remembering her crazy antics. "She's the life of the party wherever we are, and that includes our tiny home."

Silence. Dead silence has me lowering my head and searching out Jason's eyes. *Shit.* I wonder if I fucked up. Did Catherine tell him a different truth?

"Your *roommate*?"

I roll my lips in and nod but don't dare speak another word, knowing this little slip up will have pissed off Catherine enough. I'm not a fan of her tall tales, but I also don't want her baby daddy so upset that he leaves her and the baby.

Growing up without a father figure takes a toll on a child, and that's something I'll fight tooth and nail to avoid for my little brother or sister.

Unfortunately for me, it doesn't look like Jason is dropping it. "So, you don't live with Catherine?"

I shake my head no, but verbalize nothing, hoping that he'll move on.

"You just turned eighteen, Mila." He turns his head, eyes

locked on the horizon. "Since when have you lived on your own?"

I don't answer. Hell, I'm barely breathing.

If I tell him the truth, there's no doubt he'll judge Catherine, me, or both.

"Answer me, Mila." Jason turns from the helm and walks toward me until he's standing between my thighs, his deep gaze locked on mine. "Don't lie."

That makes my eyes narrow and nose scrunch. "I don't lie. Ever."

His hand cups my cheek so reverently it makes my heart stutter. "Then answer me."

I dart my eyes to the side, all the while he keeps his palm pressed to my cheek. I don't dare break contact, even though it soothes me far more than it should. "Fifteen."

Jason sucks in a sharp breath before asking, "Why?"

The one word comes out so harsh and full of anguish, it has my eyes pulling back toward his. They're bouncing back and forth between mine, trying to find a truth I'm not sure I'm willing to share.

"I met Melissa in school. She was going through some stuff with her family and she'd asked me if I wanted to move out with her. She was my best friend, so I said yes." I gnaw on my bottom lip, deciding how much of my truth I should let him have. "I didn't really have anything keeping me at home and she couldn't afford the rent all on her own, but between the both of us, we could make enough to rent out this adorable little tiny house."

My eyes light up as I think of the small cabin we've called home for the past couple of years. Yes, it's miniscule, and yes, we've found jobs that pay more and can get us another pad, but that would sort of feel like a betrayal to the place where we set our dreams free and gave them wings.

I've been so caught up in memories that I failed to see the deep scowl that's now formed on Jason's face.

"And Catherine was okay with this? Did she help with your part of the rent at least?"

I'm holding stock still, harboring this irrational hope that if I stay quiet long enough, he'll drop it. But of course, that's stupid. He's not moving on.

"Mila, so help me god... if you don't answer me, you're earning yourself a spanking." He's growling down at me and *oh my god* why did that make my lady bits clench?

I clear my throat, hoping it'll rid me of my wayward thoughts. "Melissa and I bussed tables at a diner, since it was the only place that would allow us to work that young. That or sacking groceries, but the diner let us make a little more."

Jason's face is turning a deep shade of red, making me panic and blurt out whatever I can to make his discomfort go away.

Holding both palms up, I try to downplay my childhood. "But hey, it's okay. We make more money now, and even bought our own car. Don't even have to wait on the bus to take us into town."

My eyes go wide, realizing what I've done once more. *Jesus.* I really need to keep my mouth shut.

Jason's eyes have shut and his breathing is coming in through shallow bursts. I'm about to say something when his hand drops to the back of my neck and squeezes, the one action rendering me speechless.

Why do his hands on me feel so good?

"And where was your father through all of this?" His eyes are still closed, but his hand has never left me, his fingers digging into the column of my neck.

"Um. He's never really been in the picture, aside from the obligatory monthly call."

This makes Jason's eyes flash open, his piercing hazels drawing me in and sinking me deeper into this fog of lust and adoration I'm in.

"Now you listen to me and listen to me good. *I'm* your daddy now. Anything you want and need, you come to me." One dark brow raises as his eyes sear into mine. "Do you hear me, baby girl? You're not alone anymore."

Oh, fucking hell. I think I might've died and gone to some twisted part of heaven. One where I get to call this man Daddy and have him make all my filthy dreams come true.

Snap. Out. Of. It.

He doesn't belong to me. He belongs to my mother.

"I appreciate that. I really do. But it's not your job to be there for me like that." I roll my lips in and bite, stopping myself from taking my words back like I really want.

"It *is* my job, Mila. From the moment you stepped through my door, you became my responsibility, and I'm not taking that lightly." He steps away and I instantly miss his touch. *This is bad. So bad.* "Now, get your ass up here. You're about to help me moor this boat."

My brows shoot up. "I'm what?"

"You're helping me moor. You'll steer us toward a buoy, and I'll tether our boat to it."

I suck in a deep breath and stand, walking toward his outstretched hand. "Steer. That's like driving. I can do that. It's not like we'll be going fast, right?"

Jason smiles, the action making his dimples pop and melting me further. "No, baby. We'll be taking it real slow."

He takes my hand and places it on the wheel, all while the butterflies and tingles never cease, despite the repetitiveness of our touch. *So much for my theory of becoming desensitized.*

Jason points toward a round bobbing object in the water up ahead. "Just steer us toward there. You think you can do that?"

He's standing behind me, both arms caged on either side of me as his front presses into my back. Right now, feeling his heat against my own, I think I could do or promise just about anything.

Unable to form words, I just hum and nod. "Mhm."

Jason takes in a deep breath, and I might be losing my mind, but I swear I felt him scent me.

"Good girl," he whispers into the shell of my ear before he drops his hands from the big metal wheel. "Just keep her steady and if anything goes wrong, turn the engine off by pushing this button here."

I'm nodding, lost in all these new sensations when I see he's leaving for the front of the boat. He's bending down to pick up a long pole, and *Jesus* does his ass look edible in those shorts.

I'm still staring at his rear when he shouts something from the bow. "Okay, steady. Steady. Hold."

Hold. Yes. I'd like to *hold* those hard cheeks in my hands…

"Mila, kill the engine!"

Dammit, I wasn't paying attention. "What!?"

"We overshot the buoy. Kill the engine."

"Shit. I'm so sorry."

"It's okay, baby. We'll catch the next one. Just kill the…"

There's a sputtering sound and the engine cuts out right along with my heart. Oh god. I messed up his boat. I don't know how I did it, but now it's dead.

Jason is rolling in his lips, his chest heaving as if trying not to cry or laugh. Shit, I hope it's the latter.

"Oh, god. I'm so damn sorry!" I'm trying to figure out what the hell to do as our boat turns backward and I panic. "We're drifting! We're drifting out to sea!"

Meanwhile, Jason quickly navigates back toward the helm, taking me in his arms and pressing his lips to the top of my head. "Shhhh, it's okay, sweetheart. But I need you to calm down in case we need to radio for help."

Squeezing my eyes shut, I press my face into his hard chest and breathe him in, letting his masculine scent center me. "God, I'm so sorry."

"Baby, look at me." He's holding onto my arms but gives us enough distance so I can look up into his eyes, so full of warmth and… *love?* "I meant it when I said as long as you're okay, nothing else matters. Not even this boat."

"But—"

"No buts. As long as you're okay, nothing else matters." He quickly looks away, and I'm left wondering if he's hiding something. "And as for the boat. Don't worry. It's just a fouled prop. It happens plenty."

"Has it happened to you?" I tilt my head to the side, waiting for his answer.

"No, but it did happen to Hunter, my brother." His chest starts to rumble and his eyes dance with mirth. "Damn, that was hilarious."

I blow a raspberry. "Yeah, yeah. Laugh it up at the expense of us poor land lubbers. I bet he was just as clueless as I was, wasn't he?"

Even as I say that, I doubt he'd been distracted by the same thing I was. Biting my lip, I quickly avert my gaze and hope my cheeks aren't giving my thoughts away.

"Fair enough. I'm probably not the best teacher if I'm down two-for-two." Jason drops his hold on my small frame and sighs. "We better get her untangled, and if we're lucky, the prop is still in working order."

With my teeth still sunk deep into my bottom lip, I nod. *Lucky*. I don't think I know the meaning of the word.

Yup. Lucky is not something associated with my name, and Jason's next words prove it.

"I'm so sorry, Mila, but I forgot to reload my scuba gear. The position of the prop makes it so I have to be submerged to cut the line free, and I can't do that without my gear."

All color drains from my face. *We're stranded. I'm stranded.* Stranded with the sexiest man alive, and he's completely off-limits.

"So, um. What are we going to do? How will we get back?"

He sits on the bench next to me, his hand finding mine and squeezing. "I've got some good news and bad news. What do you want to hear first?"

I throw my head back and groan. "Just lay it all on me."

Jason chuckles as his hand squeezes mine once more. "Everything is going to be okay. I've radioed for help and they'll be sending someone out."

My head flies back toward his. "That's wonderful news!"

"Mhm. But it won't be until morning. They run on island time around here and everyone who's capable has already gone home for the day."

My lips form a silent 'Oh.'

"Don't worry, though. The line is good and caught. We're not pulling free from it tonight. And as far as sleeping arrangements," Jason shifts in his seat as the black in his eyes spreads, swallowing up all color as the inky dots extend toward the outer rim. "You can take the master."

So much information to process that it's not really sinking in. I'm blinking, staring at him in a daze and letting the facts settle in my brain.

I'm spending the night. With Jason. Alone.

Holymotherforkingshirtballs.

Licking my suddenly dry lips, I finally answer. "That's unnecessary. I'll sleep on this bench if I have to, but I'm not taking your room and putting you out."

Jason scoffs. "You're not sleeping on this bench, baby girl. And there are three staterooms. You'll hardly be putting me out. It's just that the master is the most comfortable, and I want your memories of being out here to be fond ones."

My eyes flutter up toward him. "But they already are."

With those words, an intensity settles between us—a silent

acknowledgement that we're playing with fire, and if we're not careful, *we'll get burned.*

Seconds pass in a dangerous game of chicken, but I'm the first to look away. It's too risky. Whatever this is between us, it's clear we both sense it, and it's clear that it's wrong.

"How about I fix us something to eat? I usually keep the essentials stocked. Nothing fancy, but it'll hold us over for the night. You game?"

Turning back toward him, I give him my most convincing smile. "Of course. You're looking at a girl who survived on ramen for a whole month. I can handle just about anything."

I'm laughing, but I see Jason isn't fond of my humor. No, his eyes are narrowed and his lips have formed a thin line.

"I have an idea." His deep voice comes out low and measured.

"Oh, and what is that?"

He's walking us down into the boat and I can see there's a beautiful kitchen with windows that capture the perfect pink and oranges from the setting sun.

"Have a seat." Jason ushers me toward a u-shaped seating area and I oblige, taking in every detail of this beautiful vessel.

"Jason, she really is beautiful. I'm sorry Mom missed out on all of this." Bringing Catherine back up is a strategy I hope works toward taming whatever this is I'm feeling toward my soon to be stepfather. And I pray it works, because as Jason bends over to retrieve two waters from a fridge, I just about pant.

"Speaking of, I forgot to tell you I had the marina update

her on our situation. I didn't want her worrying about you being out here without her."

I snort, unable to stop myself in time.

"Right. I forgot. You've been without her for some time now."

I don't know what to say, so I simply nod. It's not a lie. It's a glaring truth I won't deny.

Jason walks back toward me, placing two water bottles and some chips between us. "Look at me, Mila."

I'm staring at the chips as if they're the most fascinating thing in the world, refusing to look away.

"Mila." Jason cups my face, forcing me to look up. "You're not alone anymore. Those days are over. You have me. You have my brothers. And when we visit them, you'll have Pen and Anaya too. They're your family now."

A lump forms in my throat, making it impossible to swallow. *They're my family now.* My family because of my mother and this beautiful man being coupled.

Why the fuck is life so cruel? I've never in my life reacted to a man the way I do Jason. Yet by some cruel twist of fate, he belongs to my mother.

"Hey, pretty girl." A thick finger swipes at my cheek, and it's only then I realize that I'm crying. "Dry those eyes. I can't bear to see you upset."

"Ugh. I'm not typically a crier. That's usually Mel's department." Sniffling, I press the pads of my fingers to my eyes. "Anyway. Was this your idea? Coming down here, eating and making me get all emotional?"

I chuckle half-heartedly, trying to make light of the situation but clearly failing.

"No. But I do think my idea will lift your spirits."

My brows raise at this. "So, are you going to tell me or keep me guessing?"

"Feisty little thing, aren't you?"

I laugh. "You have no idea."

At this, he raises a brow. "Truth or dare."

"What?" I feel my eyes bug out.

"Truth or dare. That was my idea." He lifts my legs from the seat and sits on the edge, as if it's the most natural thing to have my feet on his lap. "We're stuck here until morning, so I figured we'd get to know each other. What better way to do that than a little game of truth or dare?"

I'm pretty sure my jaw is touching the floor now. It has to be. "You can't be serious."

"Serious as a heart attack." Jason picks up his water bottle and takes a sip. "So, you want to go first?"

He wants to play this game? Fine. I have a million questions at the ready. "Truth or dare?"

"Truth." He brings the bottle back to his full lips, and it takes everything in me not to sigh.

Inwardly groaning, I ask my first question. "Why did you fall for my mother?"

Jason coughs, sending water spraying all over the table. "*Holy shit.* You don't hold back, do you?"

"Can't live a life worth living if you're holding back, right?" I bite the corner of my lip and fight a smile. I'm so full of it right now. Truth is, this is the boldest I've been with any man.

Yes, I don't take shit from people, but I'm never this forward with what I want to know—and god do I want to know what he sees in Catherine.

"Right. God, how right you are." He's blowing out a long breath as he scrubs a palm over his face. "Look, I don't know if there's a good way to answer this, but... there was no falling involved. It's more of a 'fate gave us a child after a one-time situation, so here we are,' sort of thing."

My brows raise and I'm left gaping. "You didn't date?"

Jason clears his throat and it's obvious he's uncomfortable with my questioning. I purse my lips, feeling no pity. If he didn't want to answer uncomfortable truths, then he probably shouldn't have picked *truth or dare*.

As if reading my mind, Jason narrows his eyes before arching a brow. "There was no dating involved. But these are questions better left for your mother, and this is your second question, so now you owe me two rounds. Pick, truth or dare?"

"Truth."

Jason's masculine jaw clenches as he pins me with his stare. "Earlier you'd said that you had little keeping you home. What did you mean by that?"

My stomach knots and I feel any bravado I had deflate. *Fuck.* If I'm going to throw hard punches, then I better be ready to take them.

"Gosh, we really know where to dig, don't we?" I shake my head and chuckle.

Jason winks at me and smiles. "Just call me Dick Tracy."

"Dick who?" I scrunch my nose, but my question only serves to make Jason groan—his head falling back and exposing the delectable column of his neck as he sighs.

"Thanks for the reminder, baby girl. I'm so much older than you." He lowers his head, our eyes meeting once more. "Dick Tracy was a detective in a comic book. But that's beside the point. You still haven't answered the question."

I squeeze my eyes shut before peeking out through one. "Okay. But promise not to judge me."

Jason rears his head back as his mouth goes slack. "Mila, look at me." He grabs my shoulders and squeezes until I'm looking at him dead on. "I will *never* judge you. Know that in my eyes you could do no wrong."

I snort. The idea of this adonis putting *me* on a pedestal seems absolutely ridiculous, it can't be real. He has to be joking.

But when I've stopped laughing and my eyes have refocused, I see that he's dead serious, the realization making my brows drop and eyes blink. "But why?"

"The *why* doesn't matter. All that matters is that it's true. That and you still haven't answered my question."

"Fine." I pout, something I never do, but this man has me acting all out of sorts. "I was home alone more often than not. And when I wasn't…" *How do I say this without putting my mother in a bad light?*

"I won't judge, Mila," Jason cajoles.

On a sigh, I answer the best I can. "Mom was busy with work whenever she was home, so I didn't really see her."

Pressing my lips together, I hope that wasn't too bad of an admission, but Jason's ticking cheekbone is telling me different. Needing to change the subject ASAP, I try for a diversion.

"Anyway, I owe you another round. Dare. I pick *dare* this time."

Jason's eyes are still narrowed on me, his hazel orbs assessing, as if they could somehow find all of my childhood scars and unearth them. *Good luck.* I've buried those suckers deep, and I doubt even his Dick Tracy will be able to find them.

"Good. I dare you to ask me for help."

My heartbeat thuds in my ears. "*What?*" I'm blinking at him in disbelief. "Out of all the things you could dare me to do, you choose *that*?"

He's grinning like the Cheshire cat. "Yes."

"But why?"

"Honestly? Because you don't strike me as the type of person who ever does. From where I sit, you seem to shoulder everything. Things like helping your best friend with moving in, or even now, coming to help your mother when you should be getting ready for college in the fall."

My cheeks heat and face flushes. He's spot on. I'd rather die than ask for help. Help others? No problem. But me asking for help? Yeah, no.

Melissa says it's my achilles heel. That it'll be my downfall. And as I stare into this man's eyes, I can't help but think she was right.

"What's it going to be, baby girl? What can I do for you?"

Teleport me back to Colorado. To a point in time where I

didn't know you were real. *But of course, I don't say this.* Not only because it isn't possible, but because it's not what I really want. To not know that he exists, that this sort of connection is possible, would be nothing short of a travesty.

"I don't know, Jason. I'm not sure that I need help with anything." And that's the truth. I'm so used to doing everything on my own, I'm drawing straight blanks when I try to think of one solitary thing.

Calloused fingers graze my cheek. "It'll get easier with time. You'll see."

Goosebumps rise across my skin and I shiver. "What will get easier?"

"Relying on me." Something like possession flashes in his eyes but he quickly tempers it. "For now, just think of a task you've been meaning to do but haven't had time to get around to."

"That's easy. I've been meaning to research cars. I'll be trekking to Montana in a couple of months and I don't think my little Civic will make it." I sigh. "It'll need to be something that can drive in a harsh climate, is decent on gas, and is around thirty grand."

"I can definitely help with that." He's smiling as if I've just given *him* a gift, instead of the other way around. "And now it's my turn again. I choose *dare.*"

I snicker, knowing that what I'm about to ask is nearly impossible. "I dare you to come up with a three-course meal, using only ingredients found on this boat."

Jason's eyes go wide. "Oh, you're good. Real good."

"I know," I preen, my cheeks hurting from how hard I'm smiling. That is until Jason answers, his words making my mouth go slack.

"Too bad, I'm better." And with a wink, he's off. Gone to conjure a small miracle.

SINFUL CROWN

Chapter Eight
JACE

God must hate me because looking at Mila eat is the cruelest form of torture.

Each little moan of appreciation signals an early grave for my dick. It's as hard as stone, and just one more mewl will have it breaking off.

"How in the hell did you manage to come up with all of this?" She's sucking on her fingers now and it takes everything in me not to reach over and make her straddle my cock.

She's been the object of my desire for the past couple of months, and to have her here in front of me, making obscene sounds that belong in an adult film instead of her innocent mouth is just too much for me to bear.

She's *not* yours. Hell, she's barely even legal.

That knowledge alone should make my cock wilt, but instead it makes it twitch. Knowing that nothings been inside that tight little hole, and nothing ever will be if I have my way.

Now that she's in my care, I'm not letting another man near her. *Ever.* She'll be a virgin until the day she dies.

"Jason. How?" She's staring at me as if I've grown a second head. And I have. It's right between my legs, the fucker lurching with every lick of her lips.

Focus. "It's not hard to be creative when you're surrounded by such beauty."

I'm staring right at her, trying to convey she's the beauty I'm referring to. If she only knew. None of God's creations could compare to her, because she's the best thing he's ever made. Bar none.

The color in her cheeks tells me she gets what I'm putting down and I'm not the least bit ashamed.

"Seriously, though. Using the chips to make tartare nachos—*so* good. It's making me turn a blind eye to your using the fishing rod to catch us a large part of tonight's dinner."

"Hey. It was on the boat, so it technically counts." I smirk, knowing full well that she's enjoying the labor of my love.

Love. Shit. There's a word I never thought I'd use.

Sure, I feel love for my family, but never have I expressed it for someone outside of it. Didn't think it could be possible, and the ease with which it did has my stomach knotting.

"You okay? You look sort of green." She puts down the chip and presses her fingers to her lips. "Oh, god. You don't think the fish is bad, do you?"

At this I smile. "No, baby. It's as fresh as it gets." I reach across the table and grab her hand. "I was just lost in my head. But I'm glad you're enjoying the dinner."

Mila blushes once more, and I swear that shade of rose is my new favorite color. "It really is delicious. Using the lime from the bar is absolute genius."

"And you haven't had dessert yet."

Her bright blue-green eyes light up, making me want to capture this moment forever. "Dessert?"

I bite the corner of my lip and nod. "But you have to have it on the deck with me."

"I'm ready now." Like an excited little girl, Mila pushes her plate away and bounces in her seat—the sight serving as a reminder of how young she really is and how wrong my thoughts have been.

She'll be my stepdaughter soon, and everything I've ever thought of her will have to be shoved deep into a closet, never to resurface again.

"Mila, I'm second guessing our dessert for the night."

She pouts, the action making my cock throb as I imagine sucking that plump bottom lip between my teeth.

"That's not fair. You can't just tease me with something sweet and then take it away."

Jesus. That's what she's done to me every second since I first laid eyes on her. "I know, baby. But I was going to offer you cognac on the bow of the boat. And now, I'm not sure that's such a good idea with you being so young and all."

She snorts. "God. Don't let that stop you. I handle drinks

for a living, and it's no secret I've enjoyed my fair share."

My eyes narrow and her face heats up once more.

"*Mila.*" Her name comes out as a warning. I know she said she doesn't bus tables at a diner anymore, so where is she coming into contact with drinks? Thoughts of her drunk and vulnerable assault me, making my vision go red. I'm about to pry for answers when she abruptly cuts into my rage.

"Anyway." She shakes off my stare, equal parts horror and fury, and continues as if what she's disclosed is no big deal. "Look. All I was saying is that I'm not as innocent as you might think. A little drink won't kill me… or you."

She gets up, sauntering over to the bar where I'd pulled the limes from earlier, and makes herself at home. As if it's the most natural thing in the world, she pulls out the bottle of Marancheville and pours us two healthy tumblers.

"So, are you coming or what?" She peers over her shoulder as she waits by the stairs that lead us out.

I'm shaking my head as I get out of my seat, already knowing this'll lead us nowhere good. I shouldn't be enabling her. Yes, she's done it before, but it's never been under my care.

With two large strides, I'm by her side, reaching for the glasses and placing them back on the bar. "No, little girl. You might've been able to do whatever you wanted before, but not on my watch." I pull two fresh waters out of the fridge and hand her one. "I know you're not used to having an authority figure. That much is clear. But now you do. I'm your daddy, and part of that is watching out for you, making decisions that might not seem like the most fun, but are the best for you in the long run."

Her brows raise, and her nose does that adorable scrunching thing. "Are you worried I'd tell? Because I wouldn't. It could be our little secret."

Fuck. Why does that have my head filling with visions of railing her hard against the deck, and keeping it *our little secret?*

I close my eyes and take a centering breath, needing to shove those filthy thoughts out of my head. "No, baby. As much as I want to make you happy, I just don't want us doing something that could get you into trouble."

And if I'm being honest, myself too. Not legally. I couldn't give two fucks about that, for her or myself. I know I'd get her out of any bind if needed.

No. It's the thought of being around her while intoxicated and having lowered my inhibitions with alcohol. It's a disaster waiting to happen. There's something between us, and it's clear she feels it too.

It's up to me to protect us from it because I'm already hanging on by a thread. Add alcohol into the mix and I'd be sure to pounce on that virgin pussy and make it mine.

Like a petulant child, Mila's eyes narrow before finally snatching the water out of my hand. "Fine. But you owe me dessert. And I get an extra round of truth or dare."

As she turns and walks up the stairs and onto the deck, I can't help but stare, those juicy cheeks of hers peeking out from under her shorts drawing me in like two round bullseyes begging to be bit.

Blowing out a deep sigh, I make my way behind her, willing my cock to stand down.

Whatever her questions are, I hope they're not about the constant bulge in my pants—something that's become the norm around her.

As soon as we're topside, I guide us toward the bow and gesture her to sit.

"Wow. The sky. You can count every star." Mila is looking toward the heavens, enjoying the very reason I brought her out here.

"Yes. It's one of my favorite things of being on the water and away from the city lights. There's a sense of—"

"Peace." She finishes my sentence and my heart hitches.

"Yes, peace. There's a bar on that island right there. But it doesn't operate during the week, so it's pretty much just us and the owners who live on the other side."

Mila's eyes go wide as she focuses back on me, the only light illuminating us being that of the moon and the stars above.

"It's unbelievable how detached from the world you can feel when Miami is such a short boat ride away."

I nod, smiling down at her. "Yes. That's why this is one of my favorite escapes. Few people know of the older couple who own this little piece of land. Makes for a great getaway when life is too hectic."

"Is it hectic? Your life?" She's looking at me with so much concern it fills me with warmth. How could this perfect creature worry about me when she just met me?

"More than I care to share, baby girl." I suck in a breath and look away for fear of spilling everything right on this deck.

"You can always share with me. No judgment. Ever."

That has me looking back toward Mila. This girl keeps surprising me at every turn. What started as nothing but sheer carnal lust is quickly turning into an appreciation of so much more, and I'm not sure that's a good thing. Not when I owe her mother and my unborn child what I do.

"I appreciate it, I really do, but the last thing I want to do is weigh you down with all of my thoughts. For now, let's keep it light and fun. Yeah?"

Mila narrows her eyes, but the wind blows strands of dark brown hair across her face and takes her indecision with it. "Fine, where were we?"

"It's my turn. Truth or dare?"

She nibbles on her bottom lip as her eyes dance with life. "Dare."

I grin so wide my cheeks hurt. I'm a fucking bastard for what I'm about to demand, but I need to know what had her turning several shades of red in a matter of seconds. "You got a text message on our way to the marina."

She'd been looking up at the stars, but the mention of her phone has her eyes trained back on mine, something akin to panic racing behind the jewel like orbs. "Yes? But that's not a dare, that's a statement."

"I *dare you* to read it to me."

All color drains from her face and I now more than ever need to know what's on that phone. *Did someone outbid me?* Fuck if I'll let them.

"Um."

"What is it, baby girl? Backing out of our dare?" I flick the tip of my tongue to the edge of my mouth and watch her pupils dilate. *Lord help us.* I think she might be as attracted to me as I am to her.

"No." She clears her throat as she rises. "I just have to get my phone. It's in my bag."

"Hmm." I give her a soft smile as I try hard—*okay, maybe not that hard*—to avoid staring at her ass. "Okay. I'll be right here—"

I'm still looking at her behind when suddenly she's dropping like a sack of potatoes, her head hitting the metal railing.

"Shit, baby!" I'm off my feet and at her side in two seconds, but it's two seconds too slow. I should've helped her up. Should've helped her in. It's clear this is her first time on a boat. She's probably not used to the rocking and bobbing on the water. "Talk to me, Mila. Tell me you're okay."

I'm patting her down, assessing her body for injury when she groans. "I'm okay. Probably going to have a nasty knot, though."

She's rubbing at the side of her head and I'm wondering if I need to get on the dinghy and get us out of here. To where? I have no fucking clue.

My mind is a blur when Mila brings her hands to my face, instantly calming the storm inside. "I'm okay, Jason. Seriously. There's no reason to freak out."

I scoff at that. "Freak out? I never freak out." It's true. At least it was. I've been the laid-back brother, but I'm quickly finding out that she's changed that. "I just want to make sure your mother doesn't kill me for maiming her little girl."

"Ha—ow!" She started to laugh, but then quickly grabbed her head.

"That's it. I'm getting us out of here." I pick Mila up and throw her over my shoulder, but she kicks her legs.

"Oh my god, stop!" She's laughing. Laughing at the fact that I'm worried out of my mind for her. "Stop! I promise I'm okay. Besides, where are you going to take me?"

"I'll take you to the island. I'm sure they have a boat we can take out and get back to the mainland with."

I'm about to lower her when she struggles against me, the action making her slide down along my front and letting me feel every inch of her delectable body. *Yes. She was sent to torture me for my transgressions.*

"There's no need for that, Jason. I promise. We can wait until morning if you still feel the need to get me checked out, but I swear it's just a little bump. Nothing more."

I'm staring into her eyes, trying to assess if she's telling the truth or just putting on a brave face.

'I don't lie. Ever.' Her words from earlier come to mind and I know I can believe her. It's like a strong pull in my gut letting me know that she would never lie to me. Not when it really matters.

"Fine. But I don't like it, and you're taking it easy for the rest of the night."

"Yes, Daddy. Whatever you say." She's smiling, clueless to the effect those words are having on my body.

"You're laughing now, but you won't be when I'm waking

you every few hours just to make sure you don't go comatose on me."

Mila giggles. "You're overreacting. It's just a bump, not a full-on concussion."

I'm shaking my head and directing her inside the cabin. "How would you know? You wouldn't let me get you checked out by a professional."

"I know because I know my body. Every twinge, tingle, and flutter. I know it well and what it all means."

Her eyes flit to mine and my chest tightens as I will those tingles and flutters to be mine. God, what I'd give to own every single one.

And as she ducks inside, I know right then and there that there is no hope of killing whatever this is I feel for this girl.

She's embedded herself into my being, and no amount of distance or restraint will ever douse the flames that only light for her—my baby girl.

SINFUL CROWN

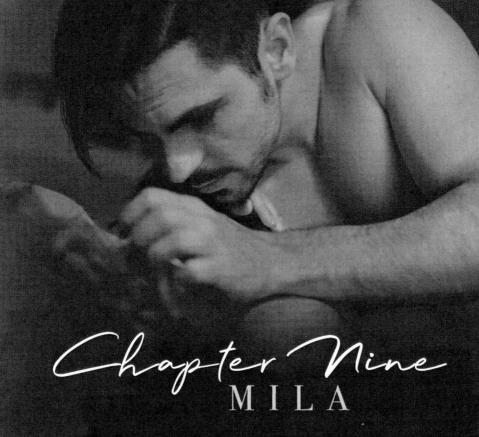

Chapter Nine

MILA

S *hit. Shit. Shit.* What did I get myself into?

This has got to be the longest night of my existence. True to his word, Jason has checked on me every couple of hours, but for the last four he's been asleep in the bed beside me, his hard toned body wrapped around mine, spooning my back to his front. And what was meant as a distraction from having to get my phone has now turned into an all-out shit show.

I was certain he would've taken me to the island and hot-wired a boat if I'd let him. And I probably would have if he hadn't dropped the text message.

Inwardly groaning, I remember the messaging between Mel and me.

MELISSA: Just how hot is this new daddy of yours?

MILA: Drop it, Mel. I only told you so you could help me feel better about unknowingly lusting after my mom's baby daddy. It was an accident. I didn't know who he was.

MELISSA: I call bullshit. You can't just stop attraction. Especially you, who never feels it toward anything other than a pint of rocky road ice cream. He really must be something if he had you all tongue tied and tingly. SHOW. ME. For real, though. If you don't send me a pic, I'm hopping on the first flight to Miami.

MILA: You wouldn't!

MELISSA: Oh, I would. Just one little pic. ::pouty lip and puppy eyes::

MILA: Fine.

MELISSA: Holyshitballs, Mila! I'd let him spank my ass and call him Daddy!

Yeah… That was the last message I got, and there was no way in hell I was going to read it out loud. Jason would know it was about him, and there's no coming back from that. Can't put that cat back in the bag, no matter how hard I'd try.

So, what did I do? I faked a slip and fall that turned into a real slip and fall, and now I'm in the most delicious, yet inappropriate, position with a man that will soon be my stepfather.

A shudder wracks me as I think of him lying next to my mother—day in, day out—for the rest of their lives, and I want to vomit.

I'm sure it's my sudden movement that disturbs Jason's sleep because he's inhaling deeply, his big broad hand finding the flat of my stomach and sliding underneath my top.

I stop breathing, my heart hitches, and my entire body is one vibrating rod of energy. Every little slide of his fingers lighting me up like the fourth of July.

Yup. I'm in deep shit.

As his thumb gently strokes the sensitive flesh, I know I've made a mistake, and it happened around the fourth time he'd come into the room…

"Stay, Jason. I feel so bad that you have to keep waking up just to check on me." I pull the covers tight over my chest. "I'll stay under the sheets and you can stay on top. That way you can just roll over, make sure

I'm breathing, and then go back to sleep."

His eyes narrow and jaw tightens. "I don't know, Mila. It's really not that big of a deal."

"Yeah, that's why you yawned as you said that and why your eyes look like you just smoked a bowl."

Jason's eyes narrow further as he crawls onto the bed. "I'm too tired to ask what you know about smoking and bowls. But don't think I'm forgetting that nugget of info, young lady."

And of course, I have to poke the bear, because why not? "Yes, Daddy. Whatever you say."

"You keep that bratty mouth of yours on that side of the bed." Jason groans, patting a line down the comforter between us. "And try to get some rest. Help will be here in five hours."

Giggling, I secure the flat sheet to my shoulders, keeping my hands to myself. My emotions might be doing all sorts of gymnastics over this man, but that's a line I won't let my body cross. Not if I have any intention of keeping my soul out of Hell.

God, how blind had I been? I mean, what did I think would happen?

As I feel his chest rise and fall against my back, I wonder how much of me knew this was a possibility, how much of me wanted this to happen.

After all, we shift in our sleep, and most levels of consciousness fly out the window. *Yeah.* Some part of me knew this could happen.

With a shaky breath, I try to ease myself from under his hold—a seemingly impossible feat.

Just when I think I've done it, his thick fingers dig into my hip, dragging my front to his side. And making matters worse, his arm secures my waist, the action pressing my pelvis to his outer thigh.

I bite my lip and whimper as my eyes land on his boxers. *When did that happen?* At some point in the night he must've lost his shorts and all this time he'd been pressed up against me with nothing more than the thin material of his underpants keeping him from my body.

He's clearly erect, and if he isn't, lord help the woman he slides that thing inside of. Just then, it twitches, making Jason shift and a shudder wrack through me with the new vision.

I'm staring at the bulbous part of his manhood pushing out of his waistband. And it is glorious.

Poking out at me, the pink mushroom tip is making all the wrong parts of me tingle. And my treacherous nipples—not being ones to be left behind—start to ache, the tiny buds tightening to a point against the side of his chest.

Oh, this is bad. So bad.

Visions of me bending down and licking the pink flesh has me clenching, the sudden need to be filled so very new to me. Never have I wanted—*scratch that*—Needed. Never have I needed a man so badly.

I need to get out of this bed, ASAP, because if I don't, god knows what I'll let myself do.

Bending my knee, I try to roll onto my back, but Jason's

hands go to my waist and the next thing I know, I'm straddling my soon to be stepdaddy—and lord help me, but it feels so fucking good.

The way he's hugging me to his front, it's aligned my core right over his hard length, the barest of pressure from my weight on him making me grow wetter by the second. *Shit*. Biting my lip as my head lies on his chest, I wonder how bad it would be if I pressed down a little harder, shifting on him just the tiniest bit.

This is so wrong, but thoughts of growing up with my mother, or more like her absence, is helping ease the guilt I feel inside.

I haven't asked that woman for a damned thing since my thirteenth birthday. And the thought of taking her man, if only for a moment, seems more right than wrong.

I'm justified in taking some sort of compensation for her neglect, right?

Ugh. Who am I kidding? It isn't right. Jason isn't a bargaining chip. He isn't mine, and no matter what I try to tell myself, it's wrong.

No matter how big of a bitch my mother was or is.

I'm about to roll off Jason when one of his hands goes to my lower back, the tip of his fingers slightly sliding under the elastic of my waistband as his hard length jumps up against my slit.

Christ, that felt so good. It felt good, and I did nothing wrong.

I mean, I'm still wearing shorts... and most of him is

covered. So it's not bad, right? It's not like he's awake. If it happened again. Over and over, it wouldn't be bad. It'd just be my little secret.

Just.

One.

Little.

Roll.

Ohhhhhhhhhhh. Fuck. That felt so good, my eyes rolled back in my head. *Jesus.* If one little grind, fully clothed, felt like heaven, what would it feel like if I was bare? My slick flesh rubbing up and down against his hard cock.

Another whimper falls from my lips as my hips do an involuntary pivot. *Shit. Shit. Shit.* I just want to keep moving. I know I can make myself come like this, rubbing my aching core on his hard-as-fuck rod. That thing smokes past any and all of my toys.

It's huge. Pair that with this insane attraction I have toward this man, and the battle that's been waging in my head comes to a tail end—the victor, my pussy claiming her release.

I lift my head, looking up toward Jason, trying to gauge whether or not he's close to waking up. Should I do this? I mean, it's so wrong. So very wrong.

But as I stare up at this gorgeous man, with his chiseled jaw and dark stubble, I know there's no real question. I'm already thrusting into him, clamping my thighs against his waist and praying he doesn't wake up, because I'd have no excuse.

It's obvious I'm using him, my breath coming in harder and faster as I slide my pussy against his length, riding his cock up and down—wishing against all logic I was naked and ready to take him into my body.

That thought alone has me rubbing harder and harder as images of his thick flesh sliding into me assault me over and over again. *Oh god.* Is he getting harder? I swear it feels like he's growing beneath me, the tip of his cock catching on my clit and making me bite back a moan.

I have to look up again, making sure that he isn't awake, because his fingers dig into my ass just then, his nostrils flaring as he helps me rub him raw, pushing me faster and harder into him.

His mouth parts and his breathing is coming in rough and ragged, just like mine. Should I stop? Is he awake? I can't tell. His eyes are still closed. He could be dreaming, right?

A wave of guilt hits me in the gut, and it has my movements stuttering. *Is he dreaming of her?*

"Mmmmph." As if reading my mind, Jason mumbles in his sleep, "Keep going, baby. Ride Daddy's cock."

Oh shit. I'm full-on panting now, and one word keeps flashing brightly in my head. *Daddy. Daddy. Oh fuck, Daddy.*

Jason makes a pained sound, but I don't stop. I can't. *But shit. Did I say that out loud?*

Jason's jaw is clenching and his chest is rapidly rising and falling, making me wonder if he's about to wake up because of my slip-up. *Fuck it.* There's no stopping this runaway train now.

The world has blurred and there's nothing but this beast of a man beneath me. That and the building pressure that's taken up residence in every cell of my body. It's on a countdown, unable to stop until the pleasure he's bringing me has detonated my soul right onto another plane of existence. One where the only thing I know is the pleasure his body brings.

I've rolled in my lips, biting down hard. All in an effort to drown out my moans as I continue to fuck this man with my clothes on. *Jesus.*

I'm.

Almost.

There.

One more roll of my clit and I'll shatter.

Just then, Jason makes a strangled sound as a rush of warmth hits my stomach. Oh shit. I just made him cum in his sleep.

His sticky release is coating my shirt, making the thin material cling to my heated flesh and bringing me the heady knowledge that I gave this man pleasure. It's what takes me over the edge, spiraling me down a supernova of release that has an audible moan breaking past my lips.

God. It was worth it. And I'll gladly go to Hell with the memory of this moment in the recesses of my mind.

Lifting my upper body, I'm able to see the mess that we've made, and I know I've never seen anything more scandalous yet beautiful.

As I remove myself from his now laxed body, I know I'll be taking this glorious secret to my grave.

I had him, Jason Crown, if only for this stolen moment. And I don't regret a damned second of it.

Chapter Ten

JACE

A loud knocking sound has me waking up from the most amazing dream of my life. Mila's tight little body grinding on me, making me—*what the fuck?*

I'd been reaching for my dick, about to give it a stroke to the memory of my obsession when I was met with a sticky wetness. *Wow.* I came in my sleep.

I'm laying there, not really shocked, but more so concerned. I haven't had a wet dream since I was a teenager, and the fact that I had one with Mila sleeping not one foot away could have been disastrous.

What would I've said?

'Um, yeah. Sorry about that. I was dreaming of you riding

me raw. Couldn't be helped.' *And it couldn't.* Not with Mila moaning, '*Oh fuck, Daddy.*'

Yes. That was definitely the moment that did me in.

Even now, my cock twitches at the memory.

I'm getting lost back in the dream when I hear steps in the galley coming closer with every second that passes. *Shit.* Hopefully Mila didn't see me like this.

Making quick work, I remove my shirt and swipe the soft fabric across my abdomen, erasing any trace of my lust for the woman who's rocked my world like no other.

I'm shoving my shirt under the covers just in the nick of time, only to realize that I'm in my damn boxers. *When did that happen?* Damn. I know I'm a heavy sleeper, and I usually sleep in the nude, but I thought I had enough of a grip on myself last night.

Apparently, I was wrong.

"Jason? You up?" Her voice tinkles in and I'm glad as hell she didn't just barge in. But honestly, she probably already saw me in this state. Probably the reason she hightailed it out of the room before me.

"Yes, I'm up. I'll be out in a second."

"Okay. The boat guy is here. He's been working on cutting the prop free."

In two seconds flat, I have my shorts on and the door open. There's no way I'm leaving Mila alone with another man. I don't care if I called him myself.

I'm about to have her take me to him when I see she's wearing nothing but two thin white triangles over what are the most delectable pair of tits I've ever seen. And god, how I remember every single curve and pucker of those nipples that have starred one too many times in my dreams.

No, I've never seen them in the flesh, but her little teasers on her *OnlyFriends* account have my spank bank stocked for life.

"Your shirt. Where is it?" My question comes out more like a demand, but I can't help it. The thought of her being alone with another man while she wears close to nothing has absolved me of all manners and rational thought.

She cocks her head but smiles. "Well, good morning to you too." She turns to walk away as she answers my question, and her response leaves a pit in my stomach. "I got something on it, so I washed it. It's drying up top."

It's on the tip of my tongue, asking her *what* she got on it, but I pull back at the last minute. What if I got myself on her?

Instantly, my cock fills. Every inch of it preening like a fucking peacock at the idea of marking her with its seed.

I'm staring at her ass as we exit onto the helm when a clearing of someone's throat has me looking to my right. There on the aft is the man who's presumably come to pry us free, an all too knowing look dancing in his eyes as he smirks at me.

I just shrug. Can the man blame me? He has eyes. He can see how irresistible Mila is.

Too bad for him. He can't have her. No one can. Not even myself. I won't allow it.

"Mr. Crown. My work is done. I've released you from the mooring line and dropped your anchor until you're ready for departure. As for costs, your account with us has covered everything." Out of respect, he avoids looking toward Mila, no doubt sensing my territorial nature. Hell, I have an arm draped over her, positioning her body slightly away from his in a clearly possessive posture.

Who the fuck am I, and what caveman snatched my soul?

If you would've told me three months ago that I'd be ass over tit for a girl, I'd have told you that you'd lost your mind. And the kicker? I could never act out on it. Not if I had any sense of decency.

"Thank you—" I extend my hand, dropping a tip into his and wait for him to share his name.

"Ramon, but my friends call me Moncho." He tips his head as he backs up to the dinghy he'd arrived on. "I'm always a call away if you need anything."

Looking down at Mila, I nod. "Thank you, Moncho. I have a feeling we'll be seeing you soon. I'm teaching my girl here how to sail, so we'll be getting a lot of open water time." Finally looking back at him, I smile. "Next time we're out this way, we'll take you to Carolina's. Our treat."

"Sounds good, Mr. Crown."

"Please. My friends call me Jace."

At that, he smiles. "Jace and Miss Mila, it was my pleasure."

I'm watching him get onto his boat when Mila speaks, pulling my attention back to her. "So first, were you ever going to tell me you go by Jace? And second, you must be out of your damned mind if you think I'm learning how to sail. I just about killed Acts of Grace. You should be terrified of ever having me behind the wheel. I know I am."

She's so fucking adorable. Shaking her head back and forth, the mere thought of her steering sending her into panic mode.

As if on autopilot, my hands go to her hips and I position her so that she's directly in front of me. "To answer your first question, I hadn't corrected you because I like the way my birth name sounds coming out of your mouth." *And that's the absolute truth.* I hate it when Catherine does it, but somehow, it coming out of Mila's mouth sounds perfect. "And as to your second question, haven't you heard of the term getting back on the saddle? You can't let one little mishap scare you off from what is arguably one of the most amazing pastimes ever."

Her eyes are sparkling with the promise of tears—happy or sad, I'm not sure—and her bottom lip quivers. My eyes hone on the supple flesh, and I know I'd love nothing more than to take it into my mouth and suck.

Blinking, I recognize how wrong that thought was. And the way I'm holding her? With my bare abdomen brushing against her exposed softness…Yeah. It's definitely inappropriate for a stepfather and daughter.

I take a quick step back and drop my hands. "I think it's time we head back. What do you think? You ready?"

Mila sucks in a sharp breath through her nose and nods. "Mhm."

My brows drop at her sudden change in demeanor. It's like she shut down right before my eyes, her arms wrapping around herself and her gaze locked on the ground.

Placing the tips of my fingers under her chin, I lift her gaze back to mine. "Hey, baby girl. If you're not ready to leave, we don't have to go. You just let me know what you want."

Her eyes are searing right into mine, making my heartbeat overtime, the amount of emotion behind them arresting me on the spot.

"We should go. It's for the best." Mila answers with a clenched jaw, and I can't help but feel there's something else she's not saying. "I'll go check on my top and then we can be on our way."

I nod, watching for anything that will give her secrets away. But as she pulls her shirt from the mast where it'd been drying, I know she's right. Leaving this behind *is* for the best.

If only forgetting our shared time together was as easy as heaving anchor and sailing away. *No.* The memory of her sleeping by me, the smell of her coconut shampoo, and even the way she softly snores. They're all things that have been engraved into my memory. All of which I'll pine for until the day I die.

Mila

"When are you coming home?" Mel's voice is like a blanket of warmth, enveloping me when I'm nothing but a bundle of frayed nerves.

I almost broke down on the way back to the house. Knowing what I'd done, and that Jason would go back to *her*, it took everything in me to keep it together for as long as I did. So of course, the first person I called was my bestie.

"I don't know, Mel. But it needs to be sooner rather than later. I don't know how much longer I can last here."

"Really? Is your mom being that horrible? I know she gives the Wicked Witch a run for her money, but I thought that since she was with a hottie and probably getting dick on the regular, that she'd lost a little bit of the stick that's shoved up her ass."

Groaning into the phone, I plead with all I have left. "Mel. Please. Do not, under any circumstances, reference Catherine's sex life."

"Shit, babe. You have it bad, don't you?"

"No?" My answer comes out more of a question, because even I'm not sure.

"Girl, we've been ragging on your momma and her extensive man-whoring since we were practically babies. You not wanting me to reference it now, when it's clear that the new baby daddy is giving you the taco tingles, speaks volumes."

I fling myself back onto the bed and whine. "Ugh. Whyyyyyyy, Mel? Why, out of all the men in the world, does my body have to react to *his*?"

Melissa blows out a long breath. "I wish I had an answer for you, my friend. But when you find *the one*, it's impossible to deny."

I choke on my saliva and sputter. "*Hold up.* Nobody said anything about him being the one. He can't be the only one I ever feel this for, can he?"

Even as I say it, I know it's the truth. This kind of earth-shaking connection is too much to hope for twice in a lifetime, and my best friend just confirmed it.

"Anything is possible, but I haven't seen it. You and me, we're just destined to be old cat ladies. Pining after men we could never have."

I roll my eyes. "You and I both know that Maverick would fold if you got him alone. The way he stares at you while you dance, that isn't brotherly love."

"He isn't my *brother*," Melissa snaps.

"No, but he's your brother's best friend. And no matter how hard that man tries to act like he's just looking out for you, there's a lust that runs deep in his eyes. I see it every time he comes around."

"And how did the conversation get turned around to me? I know your aversion tactics when I see them. Don't think you'll be able to skirt around this, missy."

There's a pause, and I know she's waiting for me to come forward with my struggle. But as always, asking for help is and will be my downfall.

"Fine, Mila. Just know that I'm here. If you need to vent, hatch an escape plan, or plot stealing that fine specimen of a man from your mother. I'm your girl. Ride or die, bitch."

"Ride or die." I chuckle, the lightness of our conversation helping to take off an immense weight off my shoulders. "Have I told you how much I love you?"

"No. But you can show me by leaving me the Civic when you head to Montana."

"Was already planning on it. Actually, I—"

"Mila, lunch is ready!" Catherine's voice trails in from the hallway, cutting me off.

"The witch summoning you?" Melissa asks.

"Yup. Gotta go, but I'll call you soon. You're my lifeline. Keeping me afloat through this suicide mission."

"Yeah. You're a better person than me. I would've left her high and dry when she called asking for help."

"I know, but it's not really for her. It's for the peanut."

Catherine's shrill scream cuts through, "Mila!"

"Coming!" I answer before sighing into the phone. "Hey, keep your phone on you at all times. Never know when I might need an intervention."

"Ha! You got this, babe. Love you."

"Love you, too." Ending the call, I get up from my woeful position on the bed and head toward a family lunch I'm dreading more than a colonic.

Breathe in. Breathe out. I've got this. If I can survive a night with Jason Crown and come out relatively unscathed, I can face Catherine Kournikova.

Chapter Eleven
MILA

"Oh my god. This all looks so good. Did you make this, Catherine?"

"Heavens no. Jason spoils me and has food brought in because he knows I suffer from nausea. It's a miracle I can keep anything down." Catherine smiles, placing a hand on her abdomen and looking lovingly toward Jason who's approaching the kitchen now.

My breath halts as I take him in. He's in another pair of cream linen pants and shirt—the epitome of Miami *chic*, with his slicked back hair and bronzed skin. How is he so gorgeous? It isn't even fair.

"Ladies, are you ready to eat? I hope you don't mind Cuban food, Mila. I was craving some *pastelitos*." He motions toward a container full of strudel looking pastries and I instantly drool.

"Oh, no. Those look Amaz—"

Catherine's phone rings and she interrupts me once again. "Excuse me, but I have to take this. Be right back."

She looks flushed, and dare I say panicked? But that's crazy. My mother never panics. Catherine is always cool, calm, and calculating.

And as I watch her step out of the kitchen, Jason reaches around me and grabs one of the pastries, splitting it in half right in front of me.

"Have you ever tried these?"

My mouth waters at the gooey jam filling. "Can't say that I have, but I'm definitely excited to try. After all, you still owe me my dessert."

Jason's eyes twinkle as the corner of his mouth tilts up in a smirk. "That's right. I do."

Just then, he takes two of his thick fingers and slides them inside the strudel's slit, coating them both in that rich filling. *How can him poking a pastry seem so obscene, or get me so wet?*

And if I thought my lady bits were on fire because of his little show, they outright combust with what he does next.

While maintaining eye contact, Jason lifts his sugary fingers to my face, swiping my bottom lip before nudging them forward.

"Open."

And because I'm in a lust induced trance, I do, taking him in and reveling in the sensation of his thick digits invading my mouth.

Instantly, I'm hit with an explosion of flavor unlike anything I've ever tasted before.

It's almost too much. The heady combination of this man feeding me paired with the tangy sweetness of this dessert has me ready to melt into the floor. *Heaven. This is sheer fucking heaven.*

Jason's nostrils flare, his mind clearly on a similar path as mine if his dark and stormy eyes are any indication.

An intense moment of silence passes between us before Jason's deep voice is ordering, *"Suck."*

That one gravelly word makes my entire body erupt in goosebumps before I'm quickly doing as I'm told.

I suck hard, swirling my tongue around his fat digits and reveling in every note of sweet tangy goodness.

"Fuck." It's almost a whisper, but I hear him.

As if overwhelmed, Jason's eyes close and his body shudders. I'm about to give his fingers another swirl of my tongue when footsteps in the hall have him quickly withdrawing, taking a full two steps back in the process.

Guilt is visibly riddled over his masculine features, and it takes everything in me not to step up to him and hold him. He can't feel guilty when what's between us seems so impossible to ignore.

"I'm sorry, Mila. That was out of line." Jason clears his throat and starts serving up a plate just as Catherine walks in.

"Did you two save me some dessert?" She's pointing at the *pastelito* on Jason's plate, the one he'd violated in my honor, giving me my first taste.

"There's plenty here, Catherine," Jason answers without looking up from piling food onto his plate.

"Oh good. You really should try these, Mila. They're to die for." Catherine beams up at me with a smug satisfaction and the devil on my shoulder dares me to speak up.

"I have, and they're fucking orgasmic." I'm staring right at Jason when I say it, the angle letting me catch his fork freezing midair.

"Mila Kournikova. I taught you better than that. Have some manners, *please*."

My gaze switches over to my incubator and I see she's staring daggers at me. Bet she didn't expect this side of me to come out and play while I acted out the role of her dutiful daughter.

Well, too bad. She may get the perfect man in the end, but I'll be damned if I'll let her recreate my childhood into something it definitely wasn't.

I'm about to call her out on her bullshit when Jason cuts in, saving us from having to face the ugly truth the past seventeen years hold.

"Ladies, why don't we go sit down? There's something important I need to discuss." He's already walking past Catherine and toward the kitchen table, the massive oblong shape facing another picturesque window with views of the aqua sea.

"Perfect!" Catherine coos. "I have something I've been wanting to discuss with you too."

At this, Jason looks back from the table, his brow raising and face blanching. Both a sign that he isn't all too thrilled with mother's announcement. "Really?"

"Oh, yes." Catherine takes her plate and sits next to Jason as I walk to the other side, not caring that I'm missing out on the amazing view. At least I won't be near my mother's reach. At this point, God knows what else will fall out of my mouth.

I've never been the jealous type, but with Jason, it seems like I'm having a plethora of firsts.

Upon closer inspection, Catherine looks unsure of herself. *That's another first.* She reaches up to his forearm and squeezes. "I was thinking… It's going to take time to get the baby's room ready, so maybe it's best if I move into your room this week. That way I have more than enough opportunity to handle my business as well as plan for everything that baby Crown will need."

The room spins at the mention of baby Crown—assigning him or her a name making it all too real. The man I've been lusting over is going to have a baby… *with my mom.*

I can't breathe. I need air. There's no fucking air.

"Mila." Jason's voice echoes in my head as if we were inside of a tunnel. "Mila. Are you okay? You look sort of pale."

The room is closing in on me and I feel like I'm dying. I'm in no state to answer.

Next thing I know, I have broad hands pressing down on my shoulders. "Mila. Talk to me, baby girl. Tell you're okay."

"She's fine, Jason." Mother's voice cuts in just as her palm not so gently taps my cheek. "I told you to eat more, Mila. You know starving yourself won't make you any more appealing to the boys."

Lies, lies, lies. She's never told me that and I would never do such a thing. I love food too much to skip a meal, and if she really knew me, she would know that.

I want to yell, but I'm still in this fog. I just want her to stop touching me. For everyone to back the fuck up and give me some space.

Suddenly there's a large hand rubbing slow circles on my back, all the while a deep voice urges everyone to leave me alone. *Armando.*

"Please, sir. I think she's having a panic attack. My sister gets these sometimes and crowding her only makes them worse." He's lifting me by the arms and carrying me away from the table, away from the toxic woman and her perfect lover. "I think some fresh air might do her good."

"Perfect. Thank you, Armando." I hear feet shuffling and a chair scraping hard against the marble floor, but my vision is still shrouded in darkness. "You're in good hands, Mila. Jason and I are going to finish talking and then I'll come and check on you. Okay, sweetie?"

As if I'd answer, even if I could. No. What I need to do is to get the fuck out of here. I'm already hyperventilating at the mere idea of them sleeping in the same room. I won't last here much longer. With every step, visions of a little brother or sister with Jason's eyes and perfect lips assault me, making me stumble.

"Miss, are you okay?" Armando's strong arms hold me up and the knowledge that we are now a good distance away from Catherine and her plotting makes me breathe a little easier, allowing me to really take in my surroundings for the first time since the kitchen.

"I'm so sorry, Mando. I don't know what got into me." I'm hanging on to his forearms, his sturdy frame keeping me upright.

"Don't worry, Miss. Family has a way of bringing that out in us sometimes." Looking up into his eyes, I see that there's a hint of recognition. *Just how much did he hear, and how much can he tell?*

"Mando, call me Mila. Miss sounds so proper, and the thoughts I've been having as of late are anything but." I groan into my palms, leaning back against the exterior wall. "I'm sorry. I shouldn't have said that."

"It's okay, Mila." Armando's soft tone has me looking back toward him and I'm able to see the genuine pity on his face. *Oh, he knows.* "It isn't my place, but if it's any consolation, he hasn't shared a bed with her since her arrival in Florida."

Yup. He definitely knows. My throat goes dry and it's impossible to swallow what feels like a lump full of sawdust. "Am I that obvious?"

Armando shakes his head. "No, Mis—Mila. I'm trained to notice details and that sort of thing. Especially on all of those who surround my employer."

I nod, not really knowing what else to say.

"Like I said, don't worry. Everything will work out the way

it's supposed to. Life is funny that way." He intertwines his arm in mine and steers me toward the beach. "Now, how about we go for a stroll? I think the fresh air will do you well. You'd be surprised at how uplifting digging your toes into the sand can be."

I throw my head back and chuckle. "Oh, you don't need to ask me twice. I've been dying to get out there since I arrived."

"Well, then. Your wish is my command."

SINFUL CROWN

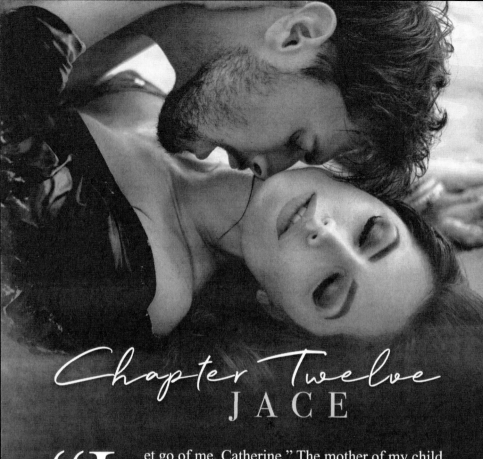

Chapter Twelve
JACE

"Let go of me, Catherine." The mother of my child is digging her nails into my forearm as I'm about to go after Mila and Armando. No way I'm letting her out of my sight when she isn't well.

"Really, Jason? Pining after a child doesn't suit you." She squeezes my arm with the word *child* and my entire body stills.

I turn ever so slowly, my eyes narrowing into tiny slits as I stare at the woman that is trying my patience. "What the fuck are you implying, Catherine?"

"She's barely eighteen, and you're doting on her like she's the one who's pregnant with your baby instead of me." She's raising a brow now, and I swear it's taking everything in me not to pop a blood vessel.

"Are you serious right now? She's your daughter, for fuck's sake. Show a little more empathy." I jerk my arm out of her grasp and shift my entire body to face her. "I don't know what you're getting at, but Mila was having a damn panic attack and you're over here acting as if it's no big deal."

She blows out a breath and rolls her eyes. "I never said I wasn't concerned. I'm simply saying you're acting a little above and beyond for having just met my daughter." She purses her lips, that brow of hers raising once more. "You even called her baby girl."

My chest tightens, and I know she's right. I let it slip. But hell, that's what she is. Mila is, and forever will be, my baby girl. Still, I can't let her mother know that. Not when she's staring at me like the cat that ate the canary.

"So what? I called you sweetheart when you fainted, and you've yet to grace my bed since Colorado." Catherine's eyes turn downcast, and I know that was a low blow, but I couldn't help it. Not when she was threatening to expose what I truly feel for her daughter. "Truth is, you're both mine to protect, and I'm not okay with anything happening to either of you."

"I guess that makes sense. You're so protective of me, I should've rationalized that you'd be the same with my daughter." There's a spark of hope back in her eyes and it threatens to crush me with guilt.

I might not love this woman, but I couldn't bear anything happening to her and by proxy my child. If she thinks I feel the same about Mila because of their familial relationship, then so be it. I won't correct her.

I'm about to turn back and find Mila when Catherine places her hand on my chest. "Now that that's cleared up, can we go back to talking about my moving into your room?"

Shit. It will look terrible if I put her off once more, just to go in search of the daughter I said I felt nothing for.

"I'd rather—" Just then, my cell goes off, the loud vibration cutting into my sentence and saving me from this massively uncomfortable moment. "Hold on."

I raise a finger as I pull my phone out of my pocket and look down at the screen.

"This is my brother. I have to take it." And I'm not lying. Hunter never calls me. Hell, he typically goes months without contact, so this must be important.

"Of course." Catherine drops her hand, making me feel like I can breathe again.

Damn. That's no way to feel about the woman you're supposed to spend the rest of your life with. "Please come find me when you're done."

I nod, knowing that our sleeping arrangement is definitely something that needs to be discussed. I was just hoping it would be later rather than sooner.

Clicking the line open, I press my phone to my ear. "Talk to me. Everyone okay?"

I'm giving Catherine my back as I walk toward my office, needing to have this conversation in private. Whatever it is, I'm sure I'll need to be sitting down.

"Jace. We've got a problem." Hunter's gruff voice comes across the line, confirming my suspicion.

"I figured as much. What's going on?" I'm stepping into my sanctuary and closing the door behind me as my brother lets me in on something I'd prayed would never happen.

"Austin. He's planning on taking one more trip down south in an effort to uncover what *they* wanted." He's being vague, but I'm getting what he's putting down.

"Dammit! Why can't he leave well enough alone?"

"Hey, if your loved ones were being targeted and tortured, I know you'd do the same. Yes, they were involved with our pops, but it's no secret his wife and children were the primary focus of the deception."

I run a hand through my hair, tugging at the ends. What he's saying makes sense, but I don't like it. "So, what are you thinking? I'm assuming you're calling me because you have an action plan."

He grunts. "I'm thinking you should head down south and cut him off. Tell him you'll deal with it since he should be focusing on his upcoming nuptials instead of dealing with difficult psychopaths." There's a pause, but he continues. "Just… whatever you do. Stop him from finding out."

My stomach churns and heart beats over time. "You know?"

Hunter chuckles dryly. "Yeah. I know."

"Did Dad tell you? I thought I was the only one. Fuck. He swore me to secrecy."

"No. He didn't tell me. I found out on my own—and don't ask me how I know. I won't say."

I clear my throat and blink away this revelation. "Okay

then. I guess I'm just grateful that you do."

"I've arranged for the WRATH securities jet to pick you up tomorrow. Head down there and offer Austin assurances. Say whatever you need to. Just make sure he doesn't come face to face with our *old friend* Raul."

I'm nodding, mapping out everything I need to do to get that situated. "Alright. I've got this. Thank you for giving me the heads up. I couldn't stand to see Austin get caught up in this before he finally gets to marry the girl of his dreams."

"If only we were all so lucky." Hunter's tone comes off bitter, making me wonder if he has someone he's set his eyes on but can't have. Much like my predicament.

"I hear ya, brother."

"Alright. Call me when you're down there and keep me posted. I'll have the SAT phone on me at all times."

"Ten-four. Talk soon."

I cut the line and throw my head back. In a wild turn of events, it seems I'll be heading down to Mexico once more. Not something I'm looking forward to, given the circumstances.

Shoving the phone into my pocket, I head to the French doors leading outside. Never have I needed a stroll on the beach like I do now. With so much going on, I could sure use a dose of vitamin D and fresh air.

The strong, salty breeze envelops my senses, covering me in a cocoon of comfort that only the ocean can bring. I've just about returned to my natural state of Zen when I see it. *Them* more like it.

Mila is laughing, the light playing on her naturally glowing caramel skin, all while Armando has his arm across her shoulders, pressing her body into his in an all too familiar embrace.

Red. It's all I see as I charge forward, determined to break whatever this is. I vowed to keep this girl safe from all men, and that includes the head of my security. I'll gladly fire his ass if he's stepped out of line, and the closer I get, the more it seems that he has.

This realization is making my blood molten, my heart thumping wildly in my chest.

"Armando!" His name comes out in a growl. It's a miracle it sounds like English at all.

Instantly, he drops his hold on Mila, but the rage does nothing to subside.

"Sir. Is everything okay?" He's staring at me with such concern it makes me take a step back and ask... *is it?*

"Oh my god. Is Catherine okay? The baby?!" Mila is shrieking next to Armando, her face going pale.

It's enough of a sight to shake me out of my temporary jealousy fueled insanity.

"Yes. They're fine. Everything is fine." *If you don't count my losing my shit whenever another man touches you.*

I don't say that last bit because I don't need to be institutionalized. Not yet anyway. At the rate I'm going, I'll be landing there soon.

"Did you need something, Sir?" Armando is looking at me, and if I really were to assess his gaze, I'd know I've been caught. Not much slips past him, and I have a feeling he's already suspected I have feelings for the girl to his left.

"Yes. I need to talk to Mila, and then later, at some point, we'll need to have a conversation." I plan on fully detailing just how *off-limits* Mila is to him, in case my actions now weren't clear enough.

With the way I'm staring at him and positioning my body between the two, I might as well be pissing a circle around the girl.

"Understood. I'll head back to the house. See you soon." And without fanfare, my right-hand man leaves me alone with my biggest temptation.

A beat of silence passes as both Mila and I stare at Armando's retreating frame, neither of us willing to break into this awkward moment.

"So, is everything really okay?" Mila looks up at me with her big eyes that threaten to make me fall even deeper.

"Yes." I need to come up with something, anything, just so it doesn't seem like I was being a possessive caveman. In my defense, I do need to talk to Mila, but it definitely could've waited until tonight. "I'll be leaving for business tomorrow afternoon." Something akin to panic crosses Mila's eyes and I can't help but feel the need to soothe her worries. "But I'll be back soon."

"Okay. Is that everything?" Her eyes are narrowing, and I swear it's as if she's looking into my soul.

"No. We'll be taking a family trip back to Colorado within the next two weeks. I wanted you to know so you could prepare."

"Back to Colorado? Is that where you're from?"

That's right. I forget that despite this mounting attraction and sense of belonging, we really know little about each other.

"My brother owns a ranch out there, and one of my other brothers is taking it over. He's the reason for the trip since he's getting married and can't do it without his favorite kin." I smirk, knowing full-well that he's closest to Matt, but I'm not admitting that.

"Oh, wow! It must be beautiful." A melancholy look floats across her face and it takes everything in me not to pull her into an embrace. "But as much as I'd like to go back home, I don't think I'll be able to join you."

Something pinches in my chest, and I don't fucking like it. "Oh? And why is that?"

I'm raising a brow, waiting for her to tell me what can be so important that she needs to be kept from my side, especially on such an important occasion.

She's rolling in her lips now, and her pace back to the house slows. "Uh, well. I have some business to handle and I don't know exactly where it'll take me."

My skin prickles and I have a sneaking suspicion I know what business she's talking about. "And what does this *business* entail?"

Mila's face flushes red and I know I've hit the nail on the head. *Over my dead-fucking-body.*

"It's personal and I'd rather not say."

"Whatever business this is, it can wait. You're not staying here by yourself. I won't allow it."

She scoffs. "You won't allow it?"

"That's right. And I want you to tell me about this business you're needing to handle. Being that you're under my roof, you're my responsibility and I want to make sure it isn't anything that's going to get you into trouble."

Oh, I've done it now. The little spitfire looks like she's about to spout plumes of smoke from the top of her head, and as she opens her mouth to speak, I know I'm in for one hell of an earful.

Chapter Thirteen
MILA

O h, this is rich. I've never had a real father before, and if this is what it's like, then I'm not sure I'd ever want it.

"Who do you think you are, telling me what I can and cannot do? If I'm under your roof, it's because I'm here as a guest, not a burden or obligation." Just then, his face falters and I see a hint of that vulnerability I've been able to catch on rare occasions. It almost makes me stop my rant. *Almost*. "If I have business to handle, it doesn't concern you, nor do I need your approval to handle it."

Before I know what's happening, Jason is lifting me by the waist and throwing me over his shoulder.

"The fuck it doesn't, Mila. I'm your *daddy*, and it seems

like you need reminding."

"Jason!" I'm squealing, knowing I should tell him to put me down, but I don't want to. I'm enjoying the way his big hands feel on my thighs, his fingers digging deep into the fleshy muscle.

"What, baby girl?" Jason swats my ass and I almost groan. *Focus, Mila.* He's pissing you off, not turning you on. *But everything he does feels so good.*

"Put me down. I'm not a child." I'm huffing as we round a dune, the tall grass serving as a cover of sorts, blocking us from on goers.

"No, baby girl. You're most definitely not a child." Jason lowers me onto the sand but quickly turns me around, facing me away and shoving me down on my knees. "You're all-fucking-woman."

My breath hitches at his words, loving what they imply and effectively distracting me as he presses his palm between my shoulder blades, pitching me forward.

I'm in front of him, doggy-style with my arms behind my back, his fingers wrapping tightly around both of my wrists and holding me captive.

This entire situation has my body tingling all over from excitement. *What's happening? What's he going to do? Is he going to spank me like he'd promised on the boat?*

"Jason?" My voice comes out breathy and low.

"No, don't you Jason me." His free hand rips down my yoga pants and he hisses. *"Christ."*

I'm panting heavily now, knowing that he's staring at my

bare pussy. Never have I been more grateful to go commando than I am now, aching and wanting him to touch me in my most private of parts.

"What's the matter, *Daddy*?" Like a wanton woman, I wiggle my ass just a little, tempting him with a forbidden fruit I know he shouldn't want—but clearly does if his hooded eyes are a sign. "Don't you want to spank me? Your baby girl?"

"Fucking hell, Mila." Jason groans as he stares down at my exposed slit, the thing dripping with want as I wave it in his face like a red flag tempting a bull. I'm about to say something enticing when all of my flutters come to a screeching halt at his next words. "Or should I call you *Jessa*?"

My world tilts and I stop moving. *He knows. He fucking knows.* Oh god. The business. He knew full-well what the hell I was talking about!

I'm fuming, trying to pull free from his hold on my wrists, embarrassed as all get out. "Let me go, Jason!"

"Oh no, baby. Not until you've had your reminder." And without warning, his calloused palm strikes my right cheek, mere millimeters away from my aching pussy.

I still, a mixture of emotions flowing through me as I try to catch my breath.

"I'm your daddy, Mila, and it'll be one fucking cold day in hell before I let you give this ripe cherry away." Another loud smack lands on my left cheek and my body jolts as a pleasure unlike any I've ever felt washes over me. "*Fuck*, baby. I see your little cunt clenching for me, clenching for her daddy."

"Yes!" I moan as he lands another blow to my right cheek

before rubbing the smarting flesh, all so damn close to where I want him, but never actually touching. The entire process leaving me restless for more.

"Say it, Mila." He's lowered himself over me, his fully clothed slacks pressing against my exposed rear as he whispers into my ear. "Say what I am."

He's positioned himself perfectly behind me. If I push back, just a little... *oh fuck, yes. That feels sooo good.* I'm pressing myself into him, grinding my slit against the ridge protruding from his pants and coating the thick material with my arousal.

"Answer me, Mila. Who am I?" Jason growls, his body unmoving despite his labored breathing.

"My daddy," I answer on a mewl. "You're my daddy."

"That's right, baby." Unable to help himself, Jason gives me one quick thrust before retreating, that single action making my eyes roll back in my head. "I'm your daddy, and don't you forget it."

He's pulled back now, allowing him the space to land the last slap right between my quaking thighs—the pad of his fingers pressing into my swollen nub and detonating the coiling pressure that had been building in my body, spiraling me into the most intense orgasm since the last.

It's earth shattering and I've lost all sense of space and time as I bellow my release.

Thankfully, Jason quickly places a hand over my mouth, muffling my moans and keeping us from being discovered, the simple act allowing me the relative privacy to enjoy every second of this unsurmountable pleasure.

I've never come so hard in my life, and it must be my nearly touching Nirvana that has it all clicking into place.

He's *my daddy.*

The one who knows about my alter ego, the one who's been watching me and bid two million dollars just to take my virginity.

Holy-fucking-shit. This new revelation has my orgasm extending, making me oblivious to the fact that Jason is now pulling up my pants and righting me. All while the world goes on as normal around us.

Jason Crown, the man who's supposed to be my stepfather, has been watching me. *Watching me and wanting me.*

I turn around, dumbfounded by this knowledge, but knowing exactly where I want to go from here. *I want him.* He might be my mothers now, but it's obvious there's something between us, and he's even admitted that he was only with Catherine out of duty.

Maybe, just maybe, there's a way we could be together. But as my eyes land on the man I've been lusting after, I can see that it was all just a pipe dream.

"I'm so sorry, Mila. That was out of line." He's quickly standing to his feet, all while I'm still sitting there half dazed from a pleasure-induced stupor. "I should never have touched you that way. It's wrong. *So fucking wrong.*"

"What? No, don't you dare take that back." I'm pointing at him from my spot on the ground and he takes that moment to pull me up by my arms.

"That was unacceptable behavior from a man that's supposed to be your protector. But I couldn't help myself. Not when I knew what you were planning on doing." He drops his hold on me, his eyes shuttering closed as he tilts his head toward the heavens. "Never again, Mila. Tell me you will never auction off such a privilege." He drops his head forward, his eyes meeting mine in a piercing gaze. "Nobody deserves that gift, Mila. Nobody."

I'm blinking, unsure of what to say. I can't promise him that. I need the money for college, and I'm sure as hell not asking him for it.

Jason huffs out in frustration, as if reading my thoughts. "Talk to me, baby. We can't get through this if I don't know why you felt the need to hang a for sale sign on that perfect pussy of yours."

My jaw hangs open. How can he offer a compliment laced with an insult, all in one sentence? *But isn't he right? Isn't that what I was doing?*

"I'm sorry. That was crass." His hands find my arms once more, gently rubbing up and down. "I'm not good at this. I've never had the need to talk to a woman before, not one who wasn't family. But I'm trying. I want to try. For you."

He's looking at me with those caramel laced eyes and I'm melting. "Yeah, well. Say something like that again and you'll get smacked upside the head."

Yes, I might be melting inside, but I'm not about to let a man be rude to me.

"Done. Now you promise me that those legs will stay

closed and that you'll be shutting down that Jessa profile on *OnlyFriends*." His fingers dig into me ever so slightly, the pressure more of a plea than a demand.

"I want to, but I can't. I need those funds."

"Baby, I don't know why you need the money so badly, but I'm sorry. I can't let you do it." Jason crushes my body to his as one of his hands goes to the back of my head, his embrace reverent. "I bid two million, and if you need more, then I'll give it to you. But please… I beg you. Don't fucking do it."

His voice cracks and I feel his chest vibrate beneath me, making me wonder if it's from rage or fear. Maybe a little of both. But what is he afraid of?

Pulling back, I'm able to see his anguish riddle face and it breaks something inside of me. "It's for school, Jason. And I could never ask you for that money. I would've returned it by now, but you didn't leave any contact info. Hell, it wasn't until just now that it all clicked into place. That it was you. That you're *my daddy*."

Something taps against my stomach and I know it was his manhood. *Holy fuck, that was hot.* My words alone have the power to turn him on.

Jason quickly steps away from me, dropping his hold on my body and making me instantly miss him. "Know that I wasn't planning on following through with claiming you, Mila. You aren't some prized cattle, having to be collected."

His words make me balk, they might as well have been a slap straight across my face.

"I don't mean that to offend you. I just want you to know

that you're worth more than that." He turns, giving me his back. "You're worth everything, Mila, and I'd gladly give it all up for you if I had to."

Is he still talking about the bid? He must be.

"Jason." I step forward, placing an open palm against the tight muscles of his back. "I promise, I'll think about it."

His back tenses at my words, displeased with them for sure, but it's the best I can do right now. Yes, I was doing this for college, but I was also doing this just for me. Gaining my independence on my own terms, never needing to rely on another person to get me through anything ever again.

That money was going to set me up, and that's a lot to give up. *But didn't he just say he'd do the same for you?* A tiny voice whispers, but I shut it down. I can't afford to listen. Not when people with money and power have always had control over me, one way or another.

Moving out of Catherine's home was the first step to gaining my freedom, and this next step? It was supposed to be the end of having to rely on them.

"I see." Jason clears his throat as his body pulls away from mine. "Since there's nothing left to discuss, I'll be heading back to the house. See you there."

I don't respond. He's right. There's nothing left to discuss, and no matter how badly I want to reach out and have him hold me, I have to let him go.

He doesn't belong to me, and he never will.

SINFUL CROWN

Chapter Fourteen
MILA

I slept like shit last night. Tossing and turning, unable to quiet my mind when all that kept looping in my head was what happened on that dune.

As the first streams of light seep in through the glorious wall of windows, I wonder if I handled things wrong. Should I have promised him I'd drop the bid for my virginity? I know I definitely can't accept the two million from him, and he would never claim me, even if I did. It would be like taking something for nothing, and it would make me beholden to him for life.

Two million isn't exactly chump change.

Ugh. I need to get out of this bed, out of this room.

Coffee. That will set my brain right. Maybe after I've had some caffeine in me, I can try to decipher where Jason's true intentions lay.

My mind is a jumbled mess all the way to the kitchen, stopping its erratic thoughts only once I've laid eyes on the man in question.

Even with everything that he is to Catherine, Jason's broad, muscular back makes my body light up like a switchboard. He's in nothing but sleep pants, facing away from me as he pours himself a cup of liquid gold.

"Great minds think alike?" I awkwardly chuckle as I step around the island and see his muscles go taut.

"Mila." He greets me with nothing more than my name, the one word coming out cold and forced. Inexplicably, it's like a dagger to my chest.

"Jason," I return, but unable to leave it at that, I step up beside him. "So, that's it? I don't do or act the way you want, so you're going to be callous toward me?"

He rears his head, a look of shock and disgust playing across his features. "Mila, this isn't a game." Jason hisses but keeps his volume low. "It's your virtue you're auctioning away and you're throwing away my offer as if it's nothing."

Jason slams down his mug and paces away from me before quickly spinning on his heels and stopping just a breath away from my face. "I'm giving you an out. Hell, a shoulder to lean on and an ear to lend a listen. I don't know why you feel the need to give such a precious gift away when I'm right here." He stops, tilts his head back and sighs before returning his gaze to me and I swear I see him break inside. "I want to be the one that gives you what you need, the one that takes care of you. *Not some fucking stranger.* I can't bear the thought." He takes my face in his hands as his eyes search mine. "Baby, why won't you let me?"

Heat builds behind my eyes, and I feel them fill with tears. "I… I can't. It's not like you'll take me, anyway. It's not an exchange if it's just you giving me money." He drops his hands from my face and I feel something inside me crack.

"You know why I can't, Mila. I owe that much to your mother and our unborn child." He turns, unable to face me while he speaks a truth so sad it threatens to destroy me where I stand.

Unwilling to give up so easily, I walk up to him and place a hand on his exposed flesh, reveling in the tiny current of energy his nearness brings.

"Jason, it's not fair. Can't you see? This is me, trying to have control for once in my life. And if you just give me the money with nothing in return, it'll be one more thing and one more person hanging over my head. I just can't accept it."

At this, he violently swings his face toward mine with both eyes narrowed. "No. Don't you dare think that. Everything I will ever do for you comes with no strings attached. I want to see you thrive. I want to see you blossom into the amazing woman I know you are inside."

His words are like a bucket of ice water to the face. "How can you say that? You barely know me!" I hiss, feeling my volume escalate despite trying to keep it down.

Jason lets out a deep sigh. "I've been watching you for a while, Mila. Since *before* I met your mother. I didn't know who she was, but do you think it's a surprise I would bed someone who looked so much like you? My fucking obsession?"

I'm gasping for air now, trying to piece together what he's saying. Is he admitting to bedding my mother while thinking of *me*?

Jason is pressing his body into mine, my back digging into the edge of the counter and making it tinge from pain—but I don't care. I'm too dumbstruck at his admission to fully realize he's now caged both arms around me, his face mere millimeters from my own.

"That's right, baby girl. You're the one I pictured while I slid in and out of that willing hole. And you're the only one I've dreamed of ever since."

I'm standing beneath him, my breath coming in ragged and fast. How is this real life? How can his sinful words about him and my mother make my pussy ache so bad?

"Jason." It's all I can manage as my eyes bounce back and forth between his.

"I know, baby. I know. It's so messed up."

I'm slowly nodding as I feel him pulling away, and it takes everything in me not to wrap my arms around him and hold him to me.

"And no matter how much any of that is true, my actions have led us to where we are now." Jason pinches the bridge of his nose. "We could never be together, Mila, and for that, I am sorry. But please, don't let my mistakes keep me from helping you. I promise you; I will never hold that money against you. I can't. I care for you too much to do that."

Tears stream down my face at his words. Nobody has cared

for me so unconditionally, that I don't know how to take it as truth. My brain is shooting up all sorts of system error warnings that I have absolutely no words to say.

Jason must take my silence as a refusal, and he simply nods. "Alright. Well, I've said all I have to say." He turns, giving me his back once more as he leaves the kitchen, his black coffee a foregone conclusion. "I'm leaving today but call Armando if you need anything."

Think Mila. Think. Say something. Anything.

"When will you be back?"

His body stills, giving me one more second in his presence. "I don't know."

But with those three paltry words, he exits, leaving me a crumpled mess of emotions—all of which are my own undoing.

Jason

It's been three days and I'm itching to get home to her, even though she isn't mine. Three Days and all I've managed to do is make sure that Raul won't say jack shit to my brother when he arrives because he's physically unable to. Despite how much I tried to bargain with the man, he kept spitting the truth in my face, something that could never happen in the presence of Austin. So I did what I had to do.

No, I haven't killed him. But I damn near did.

Just then, my phone rings and I see that it's my brother,

Hunter. "Hello?"

"Did you handle it?" Not a man of many words, I'm not offended by his lack of greeting.

"For now. I'm not sure how long I can hold him off, and for some reason, Cardenas is hesitant about finishing the job completely. I think he's trying to keep the package as a bargaining chip."

"Greedy bastard," Hunter mumbles under his breath, and I can't say that I'm shocked my older brother would be so open to having Raul *permanently handled.*

"Yeah, well. It's not our problem right now. At least not for the next month or so. That should give us enough time, and maybe after a mind blowing honeymoon, Austin will forget about what's happening here."

"I highly doubt it, no matter how many amazing blowies he gets from Anaya." Hunter snorts. "One good thing on our side is that Jack is the one who'll be taking over Cardenas' estate. Although, that leads me to believe that we should probably let him in on the secret."

My stomach knots. The more other people know, the more we risk it all blowing back up in our faces.

"I don't know, brother. But that's something we can discuss when we're all there for the wedding."

"You still bringing your *guests?*" Hunter's amusement is evident in his tone.

"I see you've been chatting it up like a couple of old biddies." Shaking my head, I sigh into the phone before answering. "Yes. And I don't want to hear any *I told you so's* or

I swear, I'll pack up and leave. I'm on my last nerve."

Silence descends and I know I've really done it if Hunter is worried about me. "Jason, you know you can talk to me about anything, right? I'm here for you."

Wow. Yup. I've done it when he's calling me by my birth name.

"Thank you, brother. I appreciate it, and I might just take you up on that. But for now, I just want to get home."

"To your *guests*."

"Yes." More like one guest in particular, but I'm not ready to share that right now.

"Alright. See you soon, then."

"See you soon." And with that, I cut the line and pull up the number to my private charter.

I need to get out of here and back to my girl as soon as possible. The bidding on her virtue ends tonight, and there's no way I'm letting her accept anyone other than me.

Fuck it if she thinks me a Neanderthal. I'll drag that girl kicking and screaming from any man she tries to give herself to.

Her, giving that ripe cherry to anyone? Yeah. Not happening. Not while I'm alive.

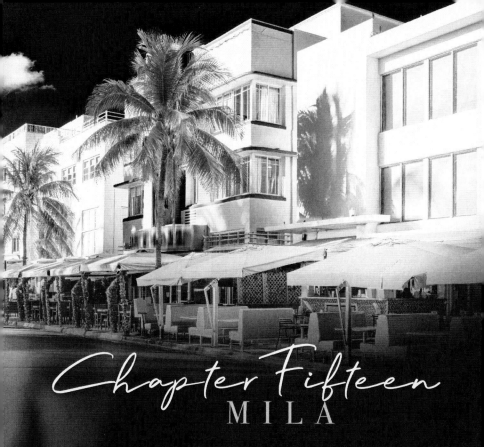

Chapter Fifteen
MILA

"Seriously, Mila. I don't even know why I asked you to come here. All you do is mope around all day, and if I knew any better, I'd say it was almost as if you were pining after someone." Catherine throws me side-eye as Armando drives us from the Cafe we just had our working dinner at.

"I don't know what you're talking about, *Mother*. I do everything you ask of me." My gaze falls on Armando and I see he's staring at Catherine as we come to a red light, and it isn't exactly a friendly stare.

"I'm talking about you spacing out during my client call this morning. I needed you to bring me my files full of the options I'd pulled, but you were off in la la land."

It's true. *I was.* Tonight is the bid cutoff and I'd been wondering if Jason would be back in time. I've yet to decline his offer, making him the winner when the clock strikes down. I know I'm fucking myself over because I won't accept his money, but I just can't bring myself to reject him. My stupid heart won't let me, and don't even ask me when she got involved, but she's fully invested in Mr. Jason Crown.

"Well, I have a lot to plan. I'll be leaving soon and I need to make sure I have everything ready. I'm sorry if I was a little preoccupied. It won't happen again."

"Yes. It's probably best if you leave soon, anyway." She's checking her lipstick in a compact as awkward silence descends in the SUV. I'm thinking she's going to leave well enough alone, but with the snap of her cosmetic, she makes her resentment of me that much clearer. "But since bringing you here was a mistake, the least you can do is help me find your replacement before you leave."

A lump forms in my throat at the thought of leaving. Not because I'll miss her, but because I won't get to see Jason anymore. As much as I'd hate to admit it, these past eight days have been sheer torture, and my mother was right. I was pining after someone. *Her* someone.

"Sure. I can help you with that." *Even though I'd rather shave my head and eat nothing but lettuce for the rest of my life.*

The SUV slows to a roll in front of the house and as soon as it comes to a full stop, I bust out yelling behind me. "I'll start on that tomorrow. Heading to my room now."

I'm about to open the front door when Armando comes at

me from the side, pinning me to the floor as he speaks into his earpiece. "Cover Big Momma and secure the perimeter."

Big Momma? Is that Catherine? Oh, she won't like that one bit.

I'm snickering beneath Mando, about to ask him what my code name is, when he shoots me a lethal glare and it finally dawns on me, he really thinks we're in danger.

My brows furrow. "Armando?" I'm whispering, wondering if there's someone inside the house. Is that why he didn't let me go inside?

He doesn't answer, simply presses a finger to his ear and responds to whoever is on the other side of the line. "You better make sure it's clear, because if it isn't, Mr. Crown will have your ass."

Shit. He does think someone was inside.

Where's Catherine? The baby!

My head flings to the side trying to find my mother, but I see nothing. Pressing my palms to Armando's chest, I push with everything I have. "Catherine. I have to go to her. She isn't good in these types of situations."

"No can do, miss. One of the other men has her. She's fine, but my orders were to keep you safe. *No matter the cost.*"

Wow. His words hit deep. I'm left blinking up at him in disbelief.

Jason asked the head of his security to guard *me*. To keep *me* safe instead of his baby momma, putting my safety above hers, and I just don't know how I feel about that.

Before I can further process this, the front door is flinging open and one of the other men I'd seen on the property before comes walking through.

"All clear, sir." He's directing his words at Armando, the massive beast of a man finally lifting off of me and letting me breathe freely as he extends a hand, lifting me so effortlessly.

"Okay. I'll need a full debriefing, but before we do, we need to take the ladies to the penthouse. Make sure they sweep the house for anything the intruder could have left behind."

"Penthouse?" Of course my mother's ears would perk at that.

"Yes. One of Mr. Crown's properties. It's heavily guarded and uncompromised, unlike his beachfront residence."

Mother is nodding, her eyes growing as big as saucers. I know what she's seeing. Dollar signs and how much she'll have as soon as she and Jason are married.

My stomach turns and I want to vomit. Needing a distraction, I focus on the situation at hand. "Armando, who do you think broke in? Did they take anything?"

"We don't know that yet, but we have our suspicions. For now, we need to get you somewhere safe." He's talking as he's ushering me back to the blacked-out Escalade, but my mind is still back with the intruder.

"Is there anything I can do to help? I'm pretty good at digging up dirt when I put my mind to it."

Armando lets out a hearty chuckle. "Thank you, but we've got it. Although I don't doubt your skills for one second, Miss."

"Mila. I've told you over a million times." I'm looking right at him when I say this, so I catch the glance he gives my mother before he answers.

"I understand, Miss. But I've been instructed not to."

Oh, hell no. That glance he just gave my mother says it all. "Really, Catherine? Not only do you require me to act all prim and proper, but now you're asking Jason's team to do your bidding as well?"

She rolls her eyes as she slides in next to me while Armando circles the car. "Don't look at me, sweet child. That was all Jason's doing."

My face instantly flushes with heat—a mixture of embarrassment, betrayal, and rage washing over me. "What? Is that true Armando?"

He closes the door and starts the car but doesn't respond.

"Answer me, Armando. I thought we were friends." My voice cracks, and I'm unsure if it's from the hurt of his refusal to talk to me, or from the fact that Jason is controlling the situation from however many miles away.

As the car moves and not a word has been uttered by Armando, I know pushing him will be futile. At least in front of my mother. She obviously knew something had been discussed between my former friend and soon-to-be stepdaddy. That alone is telling, and I wonder if she had anything to do with prompting this change in protocol.

Whatever it was, I intend on getting to the bottom of it. I haven't let my mother control my life since I was thirteen and I'm not about to let a man do it either.

Jason

"Where is she?" I'm ripping through the penthouse elevator like a bat out of hell and Armando is the first face I see. *Perfect.* He can lead me to her. And yes, the look in his eyes tells me I don't need to elaborate on who the *she* is.

"Yeah, I wouldn't go to her right now." He's staring at me with contempt. Something I've never seen from my right-hand man before.

"Oh? And why is that?" I'm downright glaring at him, demanding answers with my tone and posture as both arms cross over my chest.

"She's upset with you." He raises a brow as if I should know exactly what he's talking about.

"What? Is it the car?" I'd ordered her a G-wagon for her to take to school in the Fall, and I figured she'd be a little upset, but to be so bothered that she isn't talking to me is absolutely ridiculous.

"No, Jace. It's not the car. She hasn't even seen it yet because of everything that went down at the house."

"Well then, what is it?" I'm getting irritated with Armando, needing him to spit whatever it is out already.

"She's upset because of your direct orders for me to respect professional boundaries with her." He's staring at me blankly, but I see the smirk starting at the corner of his mouth.

I roll my eyes. "You're here to protect her, not to be her friend. Getting close to her will only cloud your judgment, and I need you to be as sharp as possible when it comes to her."

Everything I'm saying isn't a lie. I want her protected at all costs, but I'm not going to add in the fact that jealousy might have played a minor role in that request, and by the smile on Armando's face, I bet he knows it already.

"And speaking of safety, I need you to tell me everything you have, and if you've contacted the men of WRATH securities. They have a bigger database to work with and can help us narrow down our search for the perp."

"Yes, sir. They've been notified and are already working on tracing his features against their network. There were no distinct markings that would identify him as cartel."

"What the fuck?" My brows push together and I'm at a loss.

"I know. But don't worry. We'll get to the bottom of it."

I tap Armando on the back. "Of that, I have no doubt. In the meantime, I'm going to check on Mila."

"It's your funeral," Armando mumbles under his breath, and I know he intended me to hear, but I don't give a fuck. It feels like ages since I've had my fix of caramel skin and I won't let her soured mood stop me.

Stepping through the modern space, I'm taking long strides and practically speed walking all the way to the room next to mine. I'd instructed the men to place her there, not that she's in any danger while here—it's a venerable Fort Knox. I just wanted her as close as possible without actually having her in my bed.

Unfortunately, visions of me slipping into bed and having a willing and waiting Mila has my cock standing at attention—not something I want happening right before I see the girl in question.

I count to ten and will my dick to stand down, finally knocking when it's at half mast. *Hey. It's better than it was ten seconds ago.* That shit would've scared her.

There's a shuffling behind the door and then I hear it. The sweetest voice to grace this earth.

"Coming." Mila pulls open the tall door and reveals her slight frame clad in nothing but a silk nude-colored robe. Well, there goes my half-mast. It stood no chance with her standing before me looking like a fucking goddess.

As soon as I've finished perusing her body, my eyes land back on hers and she isn't amused.

"*Jason.*" My name comes out of her lips sounding like an accusation, but I'm not deterred.

Taking liberties that aren't mine to have, I step around the door and into her room, putting my body right next to hers.

"Mila. I just wanted to make sure you're okay. This afternoon was eventful, but I promise you you're safe now."

Her eyes narrow further, if that's even possible. "I'm just peachy. Just ask your head of security. Oh, that's right. He wouldn't know because he isn't allowed to talk to me." She pokes a finger in my chest, and even this somewhat aggressive touch sends a jolt of pleasure through me. She feels it too because her face softens a tad before she resumes her glaring. "Honestly, what bullshit is this, Jason? You aren't my keeper and you can't determine who I'm friends with or what they call me."

I hold both palms up in defense. "Hey, I never said he couldn't talk to you. All I said was that I didn't want him distracted. You're too precious for me to lose, Mila." I lift a hand to her cheek, cupping her angelic face, memorizing the feel of her soft skin.

"But I'm not yours to lose in the first place." Mila's face falls, losing all the hard edges of anger and taking on softer ones of sadness instead.

There's a silent acknowledgement between us. *We know.* We know that we'd rather be with one another, but it isn't possible. And toeing the line between the relationship we're supposed to have and the one we want is becoming increasingly harder.

"You're mine where it matters, Mila. Let me in and let me take care of you." My thumb strokes her cheek, once, twice, before she's pulling back and walking to the wall of windows. It's displaying the setting sun over the ocean, making the water reflect glorious shades of oranges and reds—its beauty still paling in comparison to hers.

"I already told you, Jason. I can't." She won't face me, and I'm not having it.

Reaching her in two long strides, I press myself behind her and let one of my arms slide around her torso. I slide it up her body and her breathing hitches. This is wrong. We both know it, but neither of us moves to stop.

I'm moving at a snail's pace, allowing her time to push me away if she doesn't want my touch, but she does nothing. Nothing except drive me wild with her ragged breathing as my hand glides up the valley between her breasts.

Her nipples are poking right through the thin silk material, and I want nothing more than to take one of those delicious peaks into my mouth and suck—suck hard until I hear her moan my name.

"Jason, what—?"

"Shhh, baby. Daddy's making a point."

"Mmm. And what point is that?" She pushes herself back onto my lap and my cock is more than ready to take, the fucker jerking against the crevice of her ass, begging for entry.

Finally, my hand lands at its intended destination, fingers wrapping tight around the delicate column of Mila's neck while my lips brush against the shell of her ear. "That you're mine in every way that matters."

She gasps, unable to refute me. Because if what she feels for me is a tenth of what I feel for her, we're both fucked—destined to live a life of two star-crossed lovers, never finding solace in the arms of another, and only finding peace in each other's embrace.

I feel the vibration of her next words travel up my fingertips and into my soul. "What does it matter? It's not like we can act on any of them. They're all just pretty words, none of them carrying any weight."

My fingers flex, the tips digging in a little deeper, wanting to claim her the way my body never could. "Don't say that. My heart, it will only belong to you, Mila."

She sucks in a sharp breath as I feel a cold tear drip down the back of my hand, and on a hiccup, this angel delivers the words that sends my soul soaring.

"My heart. It's yours too."

I let out the breath I didn't know I was holding, pressing my lips to the back of her head and sucking in her scent like it was my lifeblood.

"Fuck, baby. I needed to hear that." I wrap my free arm around her waist, letting the hand travel to her mound while never dropping my alternate grip on her throat. "Now, there's something else I need to hear."

"And what is that?" She's shaking against me as I let my fingers drift softly over her lace panties, stopping my movement only once I'm fully cupping her heat.

"This pussy belongs to no one. Not even me." I give it a squeeze, holding back from doing more even though I want to. "Nothing's been inside that tight little hole, and nothing ever will be. Is that understood?"

Mila makes a strangled sound before she's whirling out of my hands and whipping around. "How dare you ask for my body and my heart, when you can't give me the same?"

I'm blinking in surprise. Doesn't she know I could never touch another woman for as long as I live?

"Mila—"

"No. Don't look at me like that with those big honey-colored eyes." She marches over to the door and swings it wide open, lowering her voice to a harsh whisper. "Do not ask me for something you can't give in return. It isn't fair, and despite what my stupid heart feels for you, my brain is still functioning properly."

She motions toward the open door and it's clear she wants me to leave. I'm about to say something when she holds up her hand. "Stop. I need you to go."

Her emotions are painted clearly in her eyes. There's a hurt mixed with anger that I'm not sure I should touch when I have nothing more to offer than my heart. Yes, it belongs to her, but she's right. What good is it, really?

Wishing with all that I have that things were different, I drop a small red box on her vanity before walking past her and out the door with a whisper, "Happy belated birthday, baby."

Mila's eyes fill with tears, but I don't get to see the first one fall because she's shutting the door in my face, sending my heart free-falling into a pit of sorrow.

How fucked is this life? Depriving me of heaven on earth, only after having shown me it's real.

Chapter Sixteen
MILA

"Cheer up, Mila. You're acting as if I've stolen your summer. You'll be leaving soon enough." Catherine takes a sip of her mimosa, which is mostly champagne, and definitely not something she should drink while pregnant. *So much for her making mocktails.*

"Should you be drinking that?" I'm raising a brow, thinking that can't be good for the baby.

"French women drink all throughout their pregnancy, Mila. I'm not over here getting drunk. It's just one little glass. And honestly, most girls your age wouldn't be concerned with what their mother does. They'd be jumping for joy, getting to vacation in South Beach on their daddy's dime."

Truth is, I've been in a sour mood since my last encounter

with Jason, and her shoving her relationship with him isn't making it any better.

"He isn't my father." I glare at her, wishing more than anything that he really was my special kind of daddy. But he's not. "He's your soon to be husband, *mother*. And I know why you brought me here. It isn't so I could have an awesome summer. It's so you can parade your maternal instincts around him, suckering him into putting a ring on it."

Catherine brings her hand to her chest, acting wounded when I know she's anything but. "It hurts that you think so poorly of me, Mila, but I like the way you think. I don't have a ring yet, but I'm working on it. And would having a new parental figure be such a bad thing? He's already taken with you, accepting you into his fold and calling you *baby girl.*"

She's raising a brow at me, begging me to dispute the fact. I know he's called me that plenty, but when was it said around her?

Needing to shift the focus, I steer the conversation back to the topic at hand. "It's a bad thing when the only reason you're marrying him is so your financial support doesn't run dry like the child support with my father just did." I take a sip of my orange juice, wishing that it had a little booze in it to soothe the sting of reality.

The more I've thought and reflected, the clearer it became. It may have taken me years to figure out, but I now understand.

Mom never really wanted me. I was a means to an end. A child to secure the funds she needed in life. And I know it's the same for the baby she squeezed out of my soon to be stepdaddy's cock.

Unbiddenly, Jason's toned body comes to mind, imagining him in the throes of passion, about to fill a pussy with his seed.

I quickly shut my eyes. These are not the type of thoughts a girl should be having of her soon to be stepfather. *Her very handsome and sexy stepfather.*

Stop it, Mila. I clench my thighs together, hoping the friction will ease my throbbing core, but that only makes it worse. *Jesus.* Maybe I should excuse myself and go take care of this. Lord knows I'll just embarrass myself, drooling all over the table as soon as Jason walks in, because my lady bits don't listen to logic.

I'm still reeling from our last exchange, something that never should have happened, but I'm not regretting for as long as I live.

I've come to terms with the fact that we aren't meant to be. And even though he was selfless in offering me the two million, expecting nothing in return, I just can't tell him what he wants to hear. Even with us admitting that we have feelings for each other, I know nothing will ever come of it. He has his virtue and I have the knowledge that growing up without a father's presence is hard—something I would never wish on the little peanut.

It is what it is, but expecting me to become a nun in exchange for his empty words is just another gilded cage. One I'd rather die without than live in.

No. I promised myself I would do this for me, and that's exactly what I plan on doing. Just like he's given his word to my mother, upholding whatever sense of duty he deems necessary, I have to do the same for myself.

He'll be busy making a life with Catherine, and I need to have the freedom to escape that whenever I want. I won't be able to do that if I'm relying on my mother's lover for support.

"Ugh. What's taking him so damn long? He knows how I hate to wait on breakfast. Even with my morning sickness, I get crabby when I don't eat."

"Is that the only time?" I mumble under my breath.

"Why don't you go see what's taking him so long? This view is just too good to pass up." She motions toward the ocean just over the balcony's edge but keeps her eyes on the guy cleaning out the rooftop pool.

"*Sure,*" I huff, getting up from my chair.

I haven't talked to Jason since last night, and to say that things are strained would be putting it mildly. I'm definitely dreading this next encounter without the buffer that Catherine provides.

Walking back into the home, I let my thoughts drift back to the first time I laid eyes on him.

Thick head of hair paired with the most intense hazel eyes I've ever seen. He was wearing a white linen button up, with the top buttons undone, exposing his tanned muscular chest beneath.

Instantly, my mouth went dry and I was at a loss for words—only to be interrupted by the horror my mother bestowed upon me with her introduction. I'd been drooling over *her* man.

Rolling my eyes at the memory, I trudge inside and stop only once I'm in front of the master suite. The door is cracked open and I can see that Jason is still sleeping. Still sleeping and fully hard.

He's on his back, only a thin sheet covering his body with his member standing proud, tenting the fabric around him. *Fuck. He's big.* My pussy clenches at the thought. I've never been with a man before and the thought of something that big going inside of me both thrills me and scares me all at once.

Unsure of what to do, I lift my hand to the wood frame and knock. Surely, this will wake him up.

He kicks his feet at the sound, throwing the sheet to the ground but remaining asleep.

Damn it. What now...

I try to avert my gaze, but I can't help it. Even though his body isn't mine, I still have eyes. And damn, he's just so big and so beautiful. Sure, I saw his tip the other day, but that in no way prepared me for *this.*

Even from this distance, I can tell his cock is regal. It sticks straight up, the thick member bobbing as if waving me closer— and I oblige, curiosity and lust getting the best of me.

I've already racked up the sins when it comes to this man. What's one more? It's not like my mother deserves him.

I'm at the foot of the bed when his hand reaches down, squeezing the object of my rapt attention. He slowly strokes himself up and down, mumbling to himself, "Just put it in your mouth once. *Fucking once,*" he growls, his eyes still closed.

My stomach flutters and rolls. *Does my mother not give it*

attention?

Something Armando said earlier comes to mind. *He hasn't shared a bed with her since her arrival in Florida.*

Wow. Does that mean it's been a while since he's had a woman suck him off?

Driven by lust induced insanity, I find myself crawling onto the bed on all fours, inching closer to his needy dick.

My face is mere inches away when I see the tiny bead of liquid forming at the head of his cock, crying out for attention. Without thinking, my tongue pokes out, licking the salty pearl away and moaning at the way it tastes in my mouth.

A mixture of shame and pleasure washes over me as I relish knowing his *very* forbidden flavor. This is wrong. *So very wrong.* We said as much yesterday, and I've already stepped way over the line.

I'm about to pull away when Jason's big hand reaches out, his thick fingers lacing behind my head and gripping onto my hair.

"That's right, baby. Suck Daddy off." He's gripping my head tight, so I can't move, but I fling my eyes up to his and see that they're still closed. *Is he dreaming? Does he know it's me he's asking for?*

His hand pushes my head closer to his throbbing member and I have no choice but to comply or run… so I comply.

The fat bulb of his cock hits my lips and it's all I can do not to moan. Who am I kidding? I know I want to taste him again. *Just this once.*

Opening my mouth as wide as I can, I take him all in. He's

172

so big I have to use my hands to work the base of his shaft as I suck and swirl from his tip and back down. *He tastes so good.* His skin is velvety soft, so at odds with the hardness underneath.

I must be doing something right because Jason's breathing grows ragged as grunts emanate from deep within his chest and the grip on my hair gets tighter, his hand pushing and pulling my head against him so hard I'm gagging.

That's when it happens. The sound wakes him from his dream, a smile spreading across his lips as his eyes begin to open.

"You suck Daddy so good, baby. I knew—" His words die on his delicious mouth as soon as he sees this is real life—that it's really me bobbing up and down his big rod.

Jason's eyes turn feral, but to my surprise, he doesn't stop me. His hand remains gripped onto my hair, his amber eyes flaring with something unknown.

I watch his jaw clench as he continues to push me up and pull me out, over and over again. Our eyes locked on one another, never looking away.

Feeling emboldened. I cup his balls with my hand, massaging them as I continue to suck and lick.

"Fuuuuck." He throws his head back and moans, my eyes traveling up his chiseled body and up to the vein throbbing on his neck.

He looks so good. I feel myself drooling even more than I already am.

Like a magnet, his eyes lock back onto mine, seeing the appreciation in them. As if in response, his dick pulses in my mouth, making me hum with pleasure. I feel myself getting wetter, turned on by the fact that I make his body come to life like this.

He likes it. Likes what I'm doing to him. Something apparently only I'm giving him.

"Naughty little girl." Both hands grip my head as he holds it still, his body going rigid as a darkness clouds his honey-colored eyes. "You wanted Daddy's cock? You're getting Daddy's cock." He grits out before pumping up into my mouth, thrusting hard and fast before unloading his seed.

Hot spurts of cum flood my mouth as he growls, our eyes locked on one another, daring the other to look away.

His taste is heady, making me willingly swallow. God, I could do this forever. Watching him come at my hand is intoxicating. Knowing that I, Mila Kournikova, can make this beast of a man fall apart, is a drug all its own.

Grabbing the base of his cock, I lap up the last of his cum, licking it like it was the most delicious popsicle in the world. *And damn, it definitely is.*

"Mila." His gravelly voice comes out strained, and that's when the reality of what I just did hits me. My future stepdaddy's dick is in my hand, the taste of his cum still in my mouth.

My eyes flash from his member up to his eyes and then back down. *Oh my god. What have I done?!*

Yes, he's yet to marry my mother, but that's semantics. *This was still wrong. So wrong.*

Panic fills me, knowing my mother could've walked in at

any point during my blow job on her man and my stomach rolls. I think I'm about to puke.

Scurrying off the bed, I don't look back. I can't.

"Mila!" Jason growls and I hear the rustling of bed linens, but I'm not sticking around to find out.

Rushing into the hallway, I run past one of the men I'd seen on the property before—*security*—and beeline it straight to my room, shutting the door behind me and sliding down the backside until my ass is flat on the floor. God, they could've seen me too!

Of all the dumb shit I've ever done, I think this has got to be the worst. Jason has made it more than obvious where we stand, and I've yet to secure another bidder or book my flight back home. *What the fuck am I going to do now?*

Chapter Seventeen
JACE

What in the ever-loving hell just happened? I'm not sure how or when we crossed that line, stepping into the physical. But now that it's been fully breached, I don't think I could ever go back—not after seeing what her mouth feels like sucking on my cock.

That shit was otherworldly, making everyone before her seem like a joke.

How did I ever think sex was gratifying? I didn't know the meaning of the word until her lips graced my flesh.

I don't know how I'm going to do this, but I need to find a way to make us work. Knowing what I do now, I don't think I could ever live without her, and I sure as hell will die before I let another man experience what I just did.

Call me selfish, but I don't share.

I'm just pulling up a pair of slacks when Catherine's voice rounds the door. "Jason? Is Mila here?"

Jesus Christ. "No, she isn't." But had she been three minutes sooner, she would've found her, and I highly doubt she would've kept the smile she has on her face.

"That girl. She never listens." She's saying this while softly laughing, and it takes everything in me not to call her out on this bullshit charade.

Unable to hold back completely, I start a conversation I'm not sure she's ready to have. "She never listens to what, exactly?"

Catherine's eyes widen just a tad, and had I not been watching her closely, I would've missed it. "You know, teenage girl things. Chores and such. Like just now, I'd sent her to come get you, but she clearly went off and did her own thing."

"Hmm. And what chores are you having her do? While this isn't the home she's used to living in, we don't want her slacking on any of the tasks you've given her, do we?" I'm so full of shit right now, knowing that Mila hasn't lived at home for some time.

Regardless, I need to see how Catherine responds. She must sense something in my tone because she dials up her smile and, without skipping a beat, walks right up to me, placing both of her palms on my bare chest.

"You know, she takes after me so much that there really isn't much I could ask of her. She's so independent."

I raise a brow, amused at the sudden change in her tone.

"So, there are no chores, then?"

She shakes her head. "Not really. Just little things like making sure she calls her father."

This makes my stomach turn, knowing full-well how absent Mila's father has been. I'm about to pry her for more answers when she's dropping her hands as if I were a hot potato. "Oh god, that reminds me. It's time for their monthly call!" She's about to whirl around when I grab her wrist, only easing once her questioning eyes are back on mine.

"Her father. Who is he?"

Something flashes in her eyes, but she quickly shuts it down, replacing it with her Stepford Wives stare. "John McComb."

My eyes narrow and my mind spins. *Where have I heard that name before?*

Catherine tugs at her wrist, but I fail to let her go. "How come he's no longer in the picture?"

"Really, Jason. Now is not the time. I'm starving and Mila needs to call her father."

At this I drop her hand, scoffing at her ridiculous statement. "I'm sorry, but now is the perfect time. We're going to have a child together, yet I know so little about you or your daughter's lives. Hell, you wanted to share a bedroom with me and I don't even know the history behind your love life."

Her face flushes as she smoothes the front of her dress. "Is that what this is? A little bit of jealousy?"

I'm so dumbfounded by her assumption that I don't respond. And thankfully, Catherine continues without needing confirmation.

"Well, you have nothing to worry about." She snakes her arm around my waist, and it takes everything in me not to make a face of repulsion. Not only am I not attracted to her anymore, but the very thought of physical contact with anyone other than Mila makes me physically ill. "John was a mistake from my youth. I didn't know what to look for in a partner—someone whom I could stand beside and not behind."

Needing to get some distance from her, I walk toward my closet, but she quickly follows.

"Is that why you didn't work out? Because you felt he overshadowed you?" I'm putting on my dress shirt and reaching for my cuff links when I turn back toward her. "I'm sorry to break it to you, sweetheart, but I'm no wallflower."

She giggles, the act seeming so unnatural coming from her. "Oh heavens, no. It's just that he was so much older than me. A good two decades, and that never works out. Not when he was so set in his ways and I was nothing but a budding flower."

My brows raise at this. "If he loved you, he would've made it work. Would have torn down the moon and the stars so they could bathe you in their light, letting them help you grow."

"And *that* is why you're the right man to be by my side." She's beaming up at me as if she's taken the cake.

Unfortunately for her, she's the last person I want to shower with presents and bathe in ethereal light. Nope. That would be her daughter.

"I don't know about all that, Catherine. You're now established in *your* ways, and by your theory, we shouldn't

180

work. There's an age gap of over a decade."

She blushes profusely and I know it was a dick thing to bring up her age, but she's the one who mentioned it making a difference to a relationship in the first place.

"But that's a little different, Jason." She fidgets with the hem of her blouse before her eyes drift up to mine. "You aren't a baby. You're established, and I'm sure you already know what you like."

Yes. Your daughter.

But of course, I don't say this. What kind of monster would I be? I'm staring at the woman who's carrying my legacy in her womb. The woman that should for all intents and purposes be my wife, but God help me, all I want is her daughter.

"I don't know, Catherine. Those things might be true, but I'm not sure we fit together." I walk toward her, holding her hands in mine, trying to soften the blow I'm about to deliver. "How about we hold off on moving forward with our relationship, just until the baby is born?"

Catherine narrows her eyes at me, her lip forming into a thin line. "You mean until paternity can be determined."

It's a statement, not a question. She isn't stupid and knows only a fool would be willing to commit to something when they aren't sure of the child's DNA.

I'm about to offer some sort of assurance when a welcomed yet ill timed interruption breaks the tense moment.

"Ja—." Mila's words are replaced with a blank look I can't quite decipher. Her eyes drift from me to her mother and then to our joined hands, and no matter how much I want to drop them,

I can't. Not if I don't want Catherine to ask questions I can't answer.

"Did you need something, Mila?" Catherine wraps an arm around my waist as she turns to face her daughter, whose face has gone a pale shade of green.

"Yes. One of the security guys came to my room."

My body tenses, but I hold myself back from reacting anymore than I already have. Catherine can sense my body next to hers and she undoubtedly felt that response. Instead, I clear my throat and urge Mila to continue. "And?"

She raises a brow, enjoying the evident jealousy on my part. She already knows I don't want to share, that I want no other man near her. Yet here I am. In her mother's embrace.

After another tense moment of silence, Mila looks away and answers. "He said he was there to get my luggage, but I have no fucking clue what he's talking about."

"Mila! Language." It's now Catherine who tenses beside me, giving me the opportunity to break away from her.

Stepping toward Mila, I place my hands on her shoulders and feel her body release a small shudder under my grip. Even now, with all the turmoil around us, our bodies still react to one another.

"Yes. Get your things ready. I was supposed to tell you both at breakfast." Reluctantly, I drop my hold and turn back toward Catherine. "We're going to Colorado for my brother's wedding. It isn't for a couple of days, so you'll have time to go into town and do whatever you need. As for the dresses and such, they have you covered."

Catherine is gaping at me while Mila's face is turning a pretty shade of red.

"Oh, Jason! But I'd much rather have done the shopping here than in some small town in Colorado." Catherine is down right pouting, and it irritates me to my core.

"Like I said. They have you covered. Cassie Moretti, a stylist from Dallas, will be there. She's come prepared from what my brothers have said, so there's no need to go traipsing around town, especially when we've yet to figure out who broke into the beach house. It isn't safe." I'm glaring, begging her to be ungrateful despite everything I've given her without reproach.

I've taken this woman into my home, covered all of her medical and living expenses, and all without a shred of evidence that the child she carries is mine. Nothing more than the fact that we laid together once. A fucking mistake I wish with every fiber of my being I hadn't made.

Guilt. It hits me fast and deep.

If that child she's carrying is mine, then it was meant to happen, and regret should be the last thing I feel—regardless of this pull toward Mila.

"I just can't believe it. Cassie Moretti? *The* Cassie Moretti?"

Catherine's squealing breaks me out of my guilt induced stupor. "Yes. I believe she was a Martinez before she married Ren Moretti."

"The men of WRATH," Mila whispers behind me and I can't help but feel another pang of irrational jealousy.

"You know the men of WRATH?" I narrow my eyes as I face her, just in time to catch her eye roll.

"Of course I do. They were the most eligible bachelors in the country, up until they all got taken a couple of years back. They were all girls ever spoke about in school." She's staring at me as if I should know this, but I'm fucking clueless.

All I know is that they're the security team my family has hired for longer than I care to remember. But thankfully, they've managed to get us out of dodgy situations each and every time.

Still. This does nothing to quell my jealousy, and knowing I shouldn't but do anyway, I ask a completely inappropriate question in front of her mother. "And you? Did you talk about the men of WRATH?"

Mila is staring at me with something akin to disbelief in her eyes, and it isn't until her mother breaks the awkward silence that Mila finally reacts with a snort.

"No, Jason. Mila is an innocent *little girl*. She doesn't have time for boys and unfortunately doesn't have time to come with us to the wedding. She's promised to help me find her replacement since she's leaving for Missouri soon."

My cheek is ticking as I focus my gaze back on the mother of my unborn child. "Montana. She's going to school in Montana, not Missouri. And she's coming with us to Colorado."

Catherine's mouth has gone slack, but I can't find two fucks to give. I don't care if she now knows that I've already accepted her as family and memorized her school of choice. It is what it is and we'll just have to find a way to deal with it.

"Mila. Say something." Catherine's shrill voice pierces my

ears as she turns toward her daughter, and that's when I see it. Mila's tear-brimmed eyes.

She doesn't answer, and I fear that if she does, it might set those tears loose—my very undoing. I can't stand to see this girl cry.

Stepping in, I answer for her. "There's nothing she needs to say. It's been decided so you better get your things in-order. We leave in a couple of hours."

And without giving her an opportunity to reply, I walk past both of the women in my life, needing some serious air and perhaps a tumbler of whiskey or two.

Chapter Eighteen
MILA

I'm staring at the open suitcase, wondering what in the world my hands are doing. As if under a spell, I just walked back to my room and pulled out the black duffle that housed my belongings on the trip that forever changed me.

I'm a different woman than the one who got on that plane in Colorado. Somehow, Jason Crown has pulled out a side of me that is selfish and needy. One that doesn't care what the cost is, and that wants something for her and her alone. *For once in her goddamn life.*

It's like she'd been locked up, always trying to do the right thing and play the right role. But for once, she's been set free—stealing moments with a man that doesn't belong to her. And god, how I want to see more of her. But the real question is, *should I?*

I'm about to throw the duffel across the room when my phone rings. Needing the distraction, I practically run to it and answer on a rushed breath. "Hello?"

"Girl! Please tell me you sound winded because that daddy of yours just finished giving you a workup."

"Mel. It's good to hear from you," I droll, unamused by my best friend's rhetoric.

"Seriously, Mila. What's up?"

"What do you mean?"

"My bestie Spidey sense was tingling." I can practically hear her brow arching from here.

"You do know you aren't normal, right? How do you even do that? Like that one time I'd broken down on the side of the road. You were dead asleep and somehow you knew something was wrong."

"Yup. I remember. I called you and then my brother."

I let out a throaty chuckle. "God. Poor Erickson. He looked like he was in the middle of a date."

"Don't you worry about him. For a guy who spends all his time in the woods, he sure does see a lot of action."

"Oh my god, Melissa! How can you talk about your brother like that?!"

"Easy. He's way older than me so we didn't grow up together. He's more like a friend. Anyway, don't change the subject. What's going on? And don't lie. Remember. I'm a human lie detector."

"That's for sure." I snort. "Ugh, so you know how I have my business transaction?"

"Yes. We texted about it last night and you still hadn't rejected Your Daddy. Did the two million not go through?"

"I haven't checked..." I fidget with a strand of hair, letting awkward silence descend before Mel breaks it with her dramatics.

"You haven't checked? You. Haven't. Checked. Girl! That's two-fucking-million! What is wrong with you?"

"Nothing. Well, Jason came into my room last night and it sort of made me forget everything else."

"He what?! Mila, you better start spilling the tea or I'm coming through this line and pulling you all the way back to Colorado so you can tell me that in person."

"About that... I might be leaving for Colorado in a couple of hours."

"Woman! You're killing me!"

"I know. I know." I blow out a raspberry, gathering the strength to let her in on the past twenty-four hours. "Okay, so a lot has happened, but long story short—Jason and I have admitted to each other that we have romantic feelings for one another."

Sharp squealing on the line has me pulling the phone away from my ear, only placing it back once the sound has died down. "—have to explain everything from the start!"

"I'd be here all day if I did, but I'll give you the cliff notes. Even though we admitted that to each other, we are both in agreement that nothing could ever come of it. Well. He is. *Or*

189

was." I stop breathing. I can't believe I'm about to say this. One—Two— "I-gave-him-a-blowie-and-he-let-me."

Full-on screeching has commenced, and I definitely have to remove the phone from my ear. It isn't until a full minute later that the noise dies down enough for me to see if Melissa is still coherent.

"Mila, I swear to god you better have not hung up on me!"

"No, girl. I'm still here. Just trying to preserve my hearing, that's all."

"Ahhh! I can't believe you gave your first blowie! How was it? How was he? Did you like it? Is it huge? I bet it's huge. He looks like he's got that big dick energy." She's talking so fast, it's a miracle she can breathe through it all.

"He's blessed, and that's all I'll say on that front." I fight a giggle as Mel lets out a noise of frustration. "Anyway, things got complicated after that."

"Naturally. So, what are you going to do? Does he want to take things further? Is he going to stop dating your mom?"

I groan, throwing myself back onto the bed. "Ugh. What a mess I've made of things. I shouldn't be making him choose, and I'm not going to. Even though I want him with every fiber of my being, and he clearly wants me too, it isn't right. And technically, I don't know what he wants now. I sort of ran out of the room after the deed was done. I mean Mel, he was pretty clear with what he wanted, and it was to keep me as his eventual stepdaughter."

"So how does all this play into you possibly coming back home?"

190

"Well, get this. About thirty minutes after I did irreversible damage to our relationship, one of his security guys came into my room and told me we were leaving and asked if I had any luggage he wanted me to load. So I go to ask Jason what he was talking about, and I walk into him with my mother looking all cozy."

"Oh, hell no. That trifling ho!"

"No, Mel. *I'm* the ho." I groan into a pillow. *How is this my life?*

"You are most definitely not a ho. You are the embodiment of chastity. Or you were, up until you ran into Daddy Dearest." She cackles uncontrollably, making me openly glare at the receiver.

"Excuse me. But I don't think any of this is hilarious."

She's catching her breath and slowing her hysterical laughter. "No. No, it isn't. It's just the irony. You know why I picked your alias name, right?"

"You mean Jessa?"

"Yes, Jessa. I chose it because you'd undoubtedly be paired with an older guy. One who'd love to take your cherry. Well, Jessa Kane is one of my favorite authors of all time. And get this… all she writes is age gap daddy kink novellas!" She cackles again. "Oh god. I did this. It was my doing!"

I'm rolling my eyes and shaking my head. "Did what, Melissa? I'm not following here."

"I gave you the name and now you have your real life Daddy. Duh. All you need is your happily ever after. It's called manifesting, Mila. Look it up."

I'm still shaking my head, wondering how in the heck I became friends with this basket case I love so much. "Aaaaaanyway. I walked in on them all cozy. I got mad and almost walked back out, but I needed confirmation about this trip we were supposedly taking. Turns out his brother is getting married in the next town over to ours. Jason practically demanded I go, and get this—even stood up to Catherine when she tried to say I wasn't going." My voice quakes on that last bit, and I know Mel doesn't miss it.

"Oh, Mila. Get your ass home. And if you need a rock, I'll be there for you. No questions asked. You said it's the next town over, right?"

"Yes, but I don't know if I should be going. He belongs with my mother. She's carrying his child, and I still need to figure out how to return the two million if it did in fact go through."

"Just because two people have a child together doesn't mean they have to be together romantically. Co-parenting is very much a thing now." She's saying this like I don't have a clue, but I'm the product of co-parenting and I can safely say, it sucks donkey balls.

"I know they don't have to, Mel, but I want to give my brother or sister a fighting chance at a normal childhood. The one I never got."

"I still think you should go and see what happens. Everything is so new, and last we spoke, you said they weren't even sharing a room yet. The way I see it, he's still up for grabs."

My mouth is hanging open now. "You're talking about him like he's the last pack of Little Debbies on the shelf."

"No, girl. He's the last box of Godiva, and you're a damn fool if you don't scoop it up for yourself."

I clutch the phone tighter, knowing she's right. What I feel for Jason is special, and I know that if I let this go, there's a very real chance I'll never get to feel this again. On a whispered breath, I make the choice. "Fine. Guess I'll be seeing you soon."

More squealing ensues, but thankfully she keeps the outburst short this time, saving my poor eardrums. "I cannot wait to see you two together."

"We *aren't* together, Mel."

"No, I know. I meant in the same room. You know how good I am at reading people. Anyway, send me the addy when you get a chance. Good thing you left me the Civic, although I'm not sure it'll make the trek over the mountain."

"She'll be good to you. Just make sure the water levels are good before you leave." Butterflies stir in my stomach at the idea of seeing Melissa. Being with both of them in the same room almost makes it more real.

This whole time it has felt like a dream. An unreal situation that I've landed in but will somehow wake up from.

Being around Melissa is like looking in a mirror. She lets nothing slide, always telling it like it is.

"Got it. Full tank of fluids." Another squeal, before she's blowing air kisses. "See you soon, girl. Got to go shopping. Can't meet my future brother-in-law in the same ol' rags I've been wearing, you know."

I chuckle. "You know you don't need an excuse to go shopping. I swear, you alone could sustain Hailey's boutique."

"You know me. I have to shop local! Well, that and Amazon Prime doesn't have same day delivery up in the boonies." She groans into the line. "One of these days I'll leave and never come back. Okay, maybe only to visit you and the beautiful babies you and that daddy will be popping out."

"Oh my god, Melissa! I'm cutting the line. I swear, you say the craziest shit."

"That's why you love me, babe!"

"You'd like to think that." I roll my eyes and end the call, unwilling to hear any more salacious comments from my friend.

Yes, they may be crazy, but if I were telling myself the truth, I like the way they sound.

I'm rolling over, putting the phone on the nightstand when my eyes land on the small red box sitting on my vanity.

The memory of Jason placing it there last night replays in my head and I swear my heart beats overtime.

I haven't opened it. I'm too chicken shit to.

Gathering some of Melissa's enthusiasm, I walk over to the offending box, pushing it with my index finger as if it were to suddenly come to life and attack me.

Of course, it just sits there. It's an inanimate object.

Finally sucking it up, I reach out and undo the gold latch keeping it closed, my breath hitching with what I see.

It's the Cartier love ring. *It's the love ring.*

His meaning couldn't be clearer. But still, what does this mean for us? He didn't say things would be different when we spoke last night.

You didn't give him a chance. Your ass kicked him out, then blew him and ran.

Ugh. The devil on my shoulder makes sense. Or maybe it's the angel, pointing me toward the happily ever after Mel was talking about.

Fuck it. As I slide the gold band onto my index finger, I tell myself that I deserve this. I deserve to at least try. Whatever comes of this, fairy tale ending or fall out from hell, I'll deal with it then. But for now, I'm taking the leap.

Chapter Nineteen
JACE

"How much you wanna bet I can shoot this into her mouth?"

Mila's eyes go wide as I hold a cashew in my hand, pointing it in Catherine's direction.

We're on the WRATH jet on our way to Colorado and Catherine is sprawled out on a loveseat next to Mila, her mouth hanging wide open as she saws logs. *First trimester and all I want to do is sleep.* Catherine's words replay in my head. Seems she wasn't kidding.

"You wouldn't." Mila is narrowing her eyes at me as I sit back in the captain's chair across from her. "She could choke!"

I feel the corner of my eyes crinkle at her reaction. "You're right. I wouldn't. But I needed to say something to break you out of whatever mood you're in."

"Mood? I'm in no mood." Mila's face contorts and I chuckle, the noise making Catherine snort-snore in her sleep.

"Maybe we should move her to the bed. Sleeping in that position can't be comfortable."

Mila raises a brow. "There's a bed on this thing?"

"Yes, there's a bed." I make a face of disgust. "And thankfully it's been sanitized. The last time Austin and Anaya used it… let's just say we had to play extremely loud music—*for two whole hours*. And had the flight been longer, I'm sure the music would've been playing longer too."

I'm whispering now as I bend down to scoop Catherine up, a necessary step if I want her in the bedroom and away from Mila. I'm lifting her up when I feel Mila's eyes searing into mine, and a quick glance over shows me she's staring a look I can't quite decipher playing across her beautiful face.

Without another word, I whisk Catherine to the back of the jet, pressing open the panel that leads to the bedroom. Just then, she nuzzles her face into my neck. "Mmm, Jason."

My stomach sinks as my eyes drift back to Mila, the undeniable look of jealousy evident on her face. *Fuck.* Can I blame her?

We've all but declared our feelings for each other, yet here I am, playing the role of her mother's lover as I tuck her in.

I'm lowering her onto the bed when Catherine stirs, her eyes still closed as she reaches out for me. "Stay, baby. Come cuddle with me."

Bile crawls its way up my throat. There isn't anything in

this world that could make me lie with her, and it's then I know that I'll have to find a way out of our relationship.

"You rest now. The baby needs it." I place a hand on her abdomen and that appeases her.

I may want nothing to do with her romantically, but hell will freeze over before I ever give up on that baby.

Catherine mumbles something before she's rolling away from me, her hands tucking under her pillow in support of her head.

Without delay, I make my exit, but the sight that greets me is crushing.

Mila is chatting it up with one of the pilots and I just about lose my shit on them both.

Clearing my throat, I move to stand between the looming man and the girl who's stolen my heart.

"Jeff. Is there something I can help you with?" I'm narrowing my eyes and obstructing his view of Mila. My intention is crystal-fucking-clear. *Hands-off.*

Jeff's eyes narrow as he looks at me and then back toward the closed door. No doubt he thought I'd do like my brother and take my woman back to give her a proper shagging. Problem is, he's paired me with the wrong girl.

"No. Everything is all good. We'll be landing shortly. Please let us know if there's anything we can do for you." He gives me a solemn nod, not daring to look behind me because the look in my eyes speaks of violence and knows I'm all bite with little bark.

I'm not one for second warnings.

"That's rich." Mila scoffs behind me as I watch the pilot retreat with his tail tucked between his legs.

Slowly turning back toward the girl who's upturned my world, I can't help but raise a brow at her bratty behavior. "Excuse me?"

"Your jealousy. It's so damn obvious, and so inappropriate." Her eyes drift back to the bedroom and the reference to her mother isn't lost on me.

A switch is flipped and I bend over, my fingers wrapping firmly around her neck, giving it a gentle squeeze.

"What's inappropriate is you selling that pussy of yours." I'm whispering into the shell of her ear and the shiver that spreads across her body is undeniable.

"It's *my* body and I can do with it as I please." Her hot breath on my cheek has my cock standing at attention, not caring that her mother is just a few feet away.

"You're wrong. As of midnight, it's now *my* body." Mila sucks in a sharp breath as my grip around her neck tightens just a fraction. "That's right, baby girl. I noticed you failed to reject my bid."

With one of my legs I kick her thighs open, making her pant, her eyes falling to my knee as it slowly inches toward the juncture of her heat.

"So what? I was going to return it. Find a new bidder once I leave Colorado for good." Her chest is rapidly rising and falling, but her words serve like a cattle prod to my soul, turning me into a ball of actions and emotions.

There's no time for slowing down or logic. I need to claim

this woman and make her mine before she vanishes as quickly as she arrived.

"Like fuck you will." Without thinking, my knee grinds into her apex, the soft mewl that falls from her lips urging me to keep going. Like a bull seeing red, my free hand rips open the button of her jeans and I hiss, finding that she's once again gone without panties.

"Jason!" she whisper-shouts. "What are you doing?!"

"Taking what's mine, baby girl. Now be a good girl and be quiet. We wouldn't want mommy to hear." I slide a hand down the inside of her pants and let my middle finger glide up and down her drenched slit. *Oh, she wants this.* She's dripping wet.

Mila bucks against my hand, her body jolting at the contact, but the rolling of her eyes and the moan she's let out lets me know she's enjoying my touch.

I find the engorged little nub and give it a swirl, making her next mewl loud enough to give us away, but I'm too far gone to care. *Let them find us.*

Her hands find perch on my shoulders as I continue working her little slit, her hips now rotating, the action making her pussy press harder into my hand.

"Tell me, Mila. Were you really going to give this precious cunt to someone else?"

At this, her eyes pop open, a defiant look in her eyes as she stares me down.

"Yes."

Fire. It consumes me as I throw all caution to the wind and pump three fingers into her virgin hole, thrusting so far up I'm sure to break her barrier—all while growling, "*Mine.*"

Mila lets out a piercing whimper, burying her face into my forearm, the action doing little to hide what I've just done, and have yet to regret.

Without slipping out of her warmth, I continue to pump deeper before pulling almost all the way out and pumping back in. Each thrust of my fingers punctuating the following words. "All. Fucking. Mine."

Wet squelching sounds are co-mingling with Mila's whimpers that are now transitioning into louder moans as I press up against the spongy wall of her g-spot.

"Shhh, baby. Keep quiet and let Daddy take you."

A strangled sound escapes Mila's pouty mouth before her next words have the world fading around me. "Yes, Daddy. *Please.*"

Before I know what I'm doing, I'm carrying her to the small bathroom just outside her mother's quarters.

I need her like I need air. *Fuck the consequences.*

"Tell me now if you don't want this Mila, because there's no going back and I can't promise that I'll be gentle." I'm lowering her onto the small vanity as I reach back and click the door closed. "This is far from romantic and the ideal spot to take you for the first time, but I can't fucking wait."

Mila's small hands find my face, turning me back toward her mesmerizing eyes. "Please. You're all that I want."

Well, fuck if her words don't slay me where I stand. This girl was made for me and I'm more than willing to fight this uphill battle if she's what's waiting on the other side.

Closing my eyes, I touch my forehead to hers. "You're all that I want too, baby girl. God, I need you so bad."

"Then take me."

My eyes open to find that she's staring straight at me. No bullshit. Just her and her raw emotions.

Like a man starved, I do as she says and take—ripping the shirt from her body and marveling at the perky tits behind a white lace bra; the dark rose of her nipples calling to me, begging for a suck.

Finally taking what's mine, I lower my face and wrap my hot mouth around her aroused peaks, teasing the hard nipple through the delicate fabric and enjoying the little buck Mila gives.

"Fuck!" Mila hisses, and my hand flies to her mouth in a flash.

"Baby, you've got to be quiet." My eyes find hers and she nods, an understanding that what we're doing—despite it being what we both want—carries a lot of repercussions.

Mila's hands drop to my slacks, and I watch in awe as her fingers deftly undo my belt.

My breath hitches as her hand reaches in and her grip finds my fat girth. *Fuuuuuuuck.* My knees threaten to buckle. Her touch is better than the last and that's saying something since her mouth is nowhere near my dick.

"That's right, baby. Stroke that cock."

Mila whimpers, her body moving closer to the edge of the vanity as she points my swollen head right at her entrance.

"Is this what my girl needs? Is this what she wants?" I

bump the tip against her hole, stopping myself from fully penetrating.

She's whining now, lifting to wrap one of her legs around my waist as her body inches closer, making the mushroom head sink in the slightest bit. "Yes. Please, Daddy, yes. Give it to me. Give me that big cock."

Her words drive me to my breaking point, and with both hands on either side of her hips, I grip tight as I plunge my thick shaft into her wet heat, the slurping sound it makes echoing in the small cabin of the room as she buries her face into my chest, a muffled shout cut off only by my heavy breathing as I settle inside of her, begging whatever gods are out there for the strength not to bust in her already.

She's so damn tight, it's a wonder I was able to make my way through her narrow channel—the ability speaking volumes as to her desire for me.

Lord. I don't know how much longer I'll last.

"You're mine. All fucking mine. My little girl. Mine to protect. Mine to take care of." The realization that she's finally in my arms, my cock buried deep inside of her as her tight walls choke all nine inches of my length—it's almost too much. "Tell me, Mila. Tell me you want this—need this—as much as I do."

Just then, Mila's fingers dig into my lower back, her body pressing hard against mine as she grinds on me. "Yes. Oh god, yes. I need you. I need you more than life."

Her face looks up at mine, and I see it—the truth in her glittering eyes. She's as deep in this as I am. Two fools in love without a hope of happiness.

Well, fuck fate. I'm doing whatever it takes to feel this, whatever this is, for the rest of our lives.

And with our eyes locked on one another, I pull out slowly before sliding back in, doing my best to wordlessly convey this promise; that I'm hers, fully and completely.

She must understand, because the look on her face as I plunge back in is one of pained relief.

Mila's head tilts back, her body arching as her legs wrap tighter around me. "Oh, god. Yes. Don't stop, please."

"Never, baby. Never." And that's the damned truth. Not even if her mother walked in on us at this very moment would I stop.

I can't. I'm too far gone into everything that Mila is.

As I grip her hips and pump in and out of her swollen heat, I fall deeper and deeper into this sick obsession. *She's perfect.* Giving, smart, driven, and fiercely independent.

And, *Christ*, hot as hell. My balls ache as I look down at her tight little body, perky nipples visible through the saliva soaked bra and I can't help but let out a feral growl, pumping harder and faster into her virgin body.

Mila whimpers, a reminder that this is her first time taking in a man, and that knowledge has my fingers digging in deeper—an inner drive to claim her and mark her overwhelming me with urgency.

Never have I wanted to fill a woman before, fully claiming her and making her mine. The thought is so wrong—defiling Catherine's daughter—but I can't help it. I want it. Need it. To tie myself to the woman of my dreams.

My hand drifts to the back of Mila's neck, my fingers digging into the base of her thick hair, pulling as my lips find hers and swallow her whole.

Mila moans into my mouth, her sounds muffled by the intertwining of our tongues. Our first kiss, and it's fucking glorious. Being this close to her, our bodies joined in the most primal of ways, our tongues pushing and pulling as I breathe her in. It's all perfect. *Just like her.*

As if hearing my inner thoughts, Mila's walls start to contract around me, milking the seed that was made for her.

"Baby, you keep doing that and you're going to make me come." I pull back enough to see her hypnotizing eyes smiling back at me.

"That's the point, Daddy." Mila claws her fingernails down my back, stopping at my ass and making me thrust hard into her wet slit. On a hiss and a grind, Mila shocks the hell out of me once more. "Come in me. Come in your little girl."

Fuuuuuuck. A hot spurt escapes and I know there's no going back. Whatever happens, I welcome it with open arms.

"My dirty baby." My fingers yank back on her hair, giving it a sharp tug. "You want this, don't you? Daddy fucking you raw and hard, marking you with his cum."

Mila clenches around me and I know my words have hit their mark. She's nodding now, unable to form words as her mouth gapes open, panting hard as her lower body undulates around my girth.

Never have I seen a more beautiful sight.

I'm about to fuck her hard and fast, releasing every bit of

juice I have, when there's a knock on the thin bathroom door.

"Sir. It's Lisa. Catherine is awake and asking for you."

There's a pause as I stare into Mila's eyes, and what I see in them takes me by surprise.

Determination and possession dance between them, her small hands cupping my backside as she pumps me in and out of her. *Holy fuck.* She's taking me, not caring that her mother's awake or that there's someone right outside.

I don't answer the stewardess. She's delivered her message, and if Mila's soft moans and the sound of slapping flesh aren't enough to give her a hint as to what's transpiring in here, I don't care to clue her in.

I've got my baby to take care of. She's hungry for Daddy's cock, and that's just what I plan on giving her.

Mila pulls my face toward hers, her mouth clamping down hard on my bottom lip and sucking. "Take me. *Now.*"

"Yes." I reach down and pinch one of her erect nipples, my hard flesh pumping hard and fast into her heat. "Whatever my baby wants. Whatever my baby needs."

Mila arches into my touch, the pain an obvious trigger, releasing a moan that has my lips crashing into hers in an attempt to muffle her cry.

The sounds our bodies are making are only growing louder and more obvious, but I can't stop, not when I feel Mila's tears spill onto my forearm and not when I hear the bedroom door open next to ours.

I'm thrusting in as deep as I can, Mila's tight virgin walls squeezing me and sucking me in farther, as if wanting to swallow my cock whole.

"Mila?" There's a knock on the door, but neither of us stops before Catherine's voice seeps in once more. "Jason?"

I'm staring right at her daughter, my thick shaft slurping in and out as Mila's palms grip tightly around my ass. She's shaking her head at me, the look in her eyes lethal.

"Don't stop." She's whispering to me before raising her voice and answering her mother. "I'll be out in a minute, mom. Jason is with the pilot. I'm sure he'll be out of the cock—" her walls contract around me just then. "—pit soon."

Holy shit. My eyes roll back in my head. This is so damn hot. She wants me and doesn't give a flying rat's ass that her mother is right outside the door.

It's the spark that sets me off—one hand digging in deep into her hip as the other holds onto her neck—and with two sharp thrusts, I'm blowing into her, rope after rope of hot sticky cum flooding her womb and praying with all that I have that it takes. *She's mine. This glorious creature is mine, and I'll do whatever it takes to have her.*

Mila is whimpering around me, her body vibrating, her walls pulsing over and over again as her mother is saying something in response—her words muffled by the culmination of our pleasure hitting its peak.

Wanting to prolong this moment for as long as possible, I let my hand trail down her body, my thumb swirling her little clit as she bites back another moan—one I gladly swallow with my mouth, letting both of our orgasms dance together the way they were meant to.

It feels like time stops; the world fading around us as we enjoy these last moments of bliss. *This is it.* What life was made for. Feeling a pleasure like this is the peak of my existence. Hands down, the best thing I've ever experienced.

And as Mila's hands slide up my back, her body melting into mine, I know that this is something I want to experience over and over, until the day I die.

Chapter Twenty

MILA

I'm sore, but I welcome the pain. It's a reminder that this was real, that Jason Crown took me, all while my mother was a few feet away.

Regrets? None.

As Jason slowly pulls out of me, our mutual release coating his thick shaft, I can't help but stare. It's glorious. Being connected, having taken his body in mine. There's nothing like it in this world.

"Fuck, baby. Are you okay?" Jason whispers as he notices the tinge of pink on his distended flesh.

"It hurt a little, but I'm okay. I promise." Looking up at him I give him a reassuring smile, unable to help the wince as he fully withdraws.

"I'm a savage." Jason presses his forehead to mine, his lips brushing softly against my own. "You deserved better than getting fucked on a counter your first time."

I'm shaking my head softly, not wanting to dislodge his connection. "Don't. It was perfect and I wouldn't change a thing."

His eyes squeeze shut, and he takes in a deep breath before his nose is rubbing against mine. "What now? I'll do whatever you want, Mila. Just tell me what you need."

Wow. The realization that he's willing to go out there and come out to my mother just now is overwhelming. Do I want that? To tear them apart? That's a dumb question. If I'm being honest with myself, sleeping with him and taking his dick into my mouth already did that.

No. I need time. Time to figure out what the hell I want. I mean, I know I want him. But is taking him the right thing to do?

Guilt finally rears its ugly head and I feel like a massive triflin' ho. Catherine is outside this door, waiting on her man and her daughter. She'd be distraught if she knew of what had just transpired.

Coming to a quick decision, I softly push Jason away, getting off the vanity and regaining my composure.

A thick wetness drips down my leg, and I swear I see Jason's eyes gleam with delight.

"Here, let me get that." I'm thinking he's about to get some toilet paper, but he's taking two of his fingers and swiping up. I'm baffled, staring at his hand when he brings it back to my slit, shoving the cum coated fingers in deep.

"What the fuck?" My face is flying back toward his and I see that he's wearing a mischievous grin, unashamed of what he's just done.

Oh god. He wants this. With me.

My thoughts go back to my mother, the visuals floating in my head bringing tears to my eyes. How is this all going to work? Will I have a child with Jason, just like my mother?

"Shhh. Baby. We don't have to figure it all out now." Jason is pulling up my jeans and bringing my shirt over my head as he soothes me. "Why don't you take your mother to the back bedroom, tell her you want to see it. Once you're there, I'll finally come out."

I nod as Jason swipes tears from under my eyes. "Okay. That's a good idea."

"Don't worry, Mila. Everything is going to be okay." With a kiss on my forehead, he turns me toward the door, but not before giving me a soft swat on the ass.

I'm not going to lie. That felt good. All of it.

Jason's strength is so refreshing. For once in my life, I feel like I'm not having to handle everything on my own.

Knowing that he's got my back, I step out into the main cabin, being sure not to open the bathroom door too wide and give Jason's presence away.

As I step closer to the captain's chair Catherine has commandeered, I see that she's busy typing away on her laptop.

"Always working," I mumble under my breath.

"What was that?" Catherine turns to face me, her eyes

quickly scanning me from head to toe.

"Oh, nothing. How was your nap? I can't believe there's a bed on this thing."

She purses her lips and rolls her eyes. "Of course there is, Mila. An aircraft of this size and caliber typically does." Her eyes rake over me once more and her brow arches. "You were in the bathroom a long time. Is everything okay?"

"Actually, no. I'm not feeling too well. Maybe you can show me that bedroom? I'd like to lay down for a little." I'm hoping she takes the bait, because I don't know how else to distract her and give Jason the out.

Thankfully, Catherine groans but makes her way toward the rear of the jet. "Yes. I'll even show you how to work the lights. If it's one of your migraines, then you should probably turn off all sensory distractions."

My brows shoot up, surprised at the extremely thoughtful gesture. Thoughtful for Catherine, at least. "I didn't think you remembered I had those."

Mother scoffs. "What do you think I am, a monster? I'm your mother for goodness' sake."

Another pang of guilt hits me as we walk past the bathroom and into the small bedroom. I'm too ashamed to fully enjoy the amenities being shown to me, too at turmoil to be able to actually relax when she leaves.

It doesn't matter. I need to keep her from going back out into the cabin, at least for a minute. Catherine and I might have our differences, but I in no way wish to hurt her by having her finding out about Jason and me this way.

Thinking on my feet, I quickly reach out and grab her hand. "Mom. Can I have a word with you?"

Catherine blinks back in surprise. "Of course. What is it?"

I pull her down onto the bed, our outer thighs touching. "I know I was a *surprise* pregnancy, just like this one. Do you, or did you ever regret getting pregnant with us?"

She's gaping at me, staring at me as if I've just asked the most absurd question.

"You're my daughter, Mila. I love you by virtue of that alone."

I'm shaking my head, my hand gripping harder onto hers. "I've honestly never felt that. I've always thought I was more of a burden to you than the child you loved."

Catherine's face is turning a bright shade of red, and I now know that having a heart to heart with my mother probably wasn't the best idea.

"What is this? Are you trying to make me feel bad for working hard and having the career of my dreams? Because let me tell you something sweet child, there will come a time where you become a mother and I'd like to see you throw everything away and devote yourself to that kid." She scoffs as she pulls her hand from my grip. "I bet your bottom dollar that you won't. Come and judge me then, you ungrateful little girl."

My face contorts into one of disgust as my hand flies to my abdomen. If by some chance I were pregnant with Jason's child, I would do things a hell of a lot differently than her. "No, I never expected you to lose yourself in me, *Mother*. But I did expect you to be present and loving. I know for a fact that isn't too much to ask for."

I know that because as I sit here and think of my hypothetical baby, I know I'd do that and more. And all without reproach or resentment, but instead, gratitude and humility— humbled by the fact that I'd get the chance to raise a little soul, despite my shortcomings and misgivings.

"Yeah, you'd like to think that. Just wait until you're in my shoes. I'd like to see you throwing all of this in my face then."

I'm about to retort with something nasty when there's a knock on the door. "Ladies. We're landing in a couple of minutes."

Jason's voice cuts through the door, and I can hear his concern. *Shit.* If the walls are so thin that he heard us arguing, then what are the chances Mother heard him and me in the restroom?

"We'll be out shortly," Catherine answers as she stares daggers at me before lowering her voice. "You'll be on your best behavior while we're in Colorado, or so help me, I'll be shipping you off to Missouri myself."

I roll my eyes and huff. "Montana. The school I'm going to is in Montana."

"Whatever." She goes to turn but looks back as she reaches the door. "And call your father. It's the last one in the agreement. After this, you'll talk to him whenever you want to… *that's if he'll take your call.*" She mumbles that last part, and it cuts right through my heart.

I was born to two parents who never wanted me, neither of which played an active role in my life. As I hear mother

216

question Jason about Cassie Moretti, I vow to never become the same. I couldn't. Not having lived what I did.

More of that treacherous guilt seeps into my gut, turning it sour. That's what I would be doing to my little brother and sister if I took Jason away.

There's no way Catherine would be okay with sharing custody if Jason and I were together. I'd essentially be ripping my siblings' chance at having at least one decent parent—*more than I had.*

I can't do that. I just can't.

Flinging myself onto the bed, I wrack my brain with possible scenarios where we could all come out winners, but nothing sticks. The only thing that makes sense is for me to stay in my lane and let them be in theirs.

It might tear me up inside to see them together, but no new casualties will be had, and at least I'll always have the memory of having had Jason Crown. Something I'll cherish until the day I die.

"Oh my god, this is stunning! When you said family ranch, I pictured something much more…" Catherine makes a face of disgust before regaining her composure. "*Rustic.*"

Jason shakes his head and I swear I see him roll his eyes as we step out of the SUV and onto the gravel leading up to the gorgeous farmhouse. Its white panels are accentuated with warm wood trim throughout, a row of rocking chairs lining the wrap-around porch that just begs for sunset viewings and sweet tea.

"It's beautiful, Jason," I'm whispering next to him as we make our way up the porch steps.

Just then, a woman with long black hair steps out from behind the screen door and beams at me. "Thank you. I thought so too when I first arrived, and now I'm lucky to call this home." She's wrapping me in an embrace, her pregnant belly bumping into me before I can respond. "Welcome to Crown Ranch, I'm Penelope." She pulls back enough to give me a once over, her hands bracing on my biceps. "But you can call me Pen."

I'm speechless, never having had such a reception before. "Um, thank you, Pen. I'm—"

"Mila," she finishes my sentence, her eyes quickly flitting over to Jason before coming back to me.

"And I'm Catherine, Jason's girlfriend." I nearly hurl at my mother's declaration as she inserts herself between Pen and me, extending her arms out and pulling the shocked woman in an embrace she's clearly not feeling.

Pen clears her throat. "Uncle Jace, should I show the ladies inside, or did you want to stop at your cabin first?"

Catherine pulls away, realizing she's getting the cold shoulder and I wonder why? Pen has never met us before, but clearly she's already formed some sort of opinion.

My eyes narrow on Jason, a million questions racing through my mind. But when I really look at him, I see that he's glaring at my mother.

"Take them inside, please. I'd like for them to meet the rest of the family first." We're about to step through the door when Jason's fingers wrap around Catherine's forearm, preventing her from moving forward. In a hushed voice, he harshly whispers in my mother's ear. "Please refrain from calling yourself my girlfriend. Our re—"

He keeps talking, but Penelope is pulling me into the foyer and keeping me from hearing the rest.

My slight annoyance drops as soon as I step into the wide open space, a beautiful table sitting right in the middle with the most beautiful arrangement. "Oh my god. This is breathtaking."

"Thank you. The flowers are from our cut garden." She's practically bouncing on her toes. "I'll have to show you on the way to your cabin."

"I'd like that." Pen continues to tug me through the house, and I just have to ask. "Penelope, how did you know my name?"

At this, she stops, giving me the brightest smile I've ever seen. "Uncle Jace called. He said he wanted to make sure you were treated like family, because you're ours now."

My heart squeezes and the back of my eyes tingle. God, that man. Looking out for me when he doesn't have to. "Oh." It's all I can manage as Penelope keeps moving us forward.

"He said you're from Colorado too but didn't say where exactly."

"Oh, I'm from Bainbridge."

Pen stops so abruptly I run into her, making her brace against the wall.

"What?! That's like right over the ridge! How could you've

been here all this time and we never have met?"

"That's wild, right? To be honest, I never made it out this way because I've kept my world small. Intentionally."

A look flutters across Pen's eyes. One of recognition as she nods, her small hands squeezing my own. "Well, no more of that. You've got us, and we're so lucky to have you."

I'm laughing a full-bellied laugh. "No. I think I'm the lucky one."

"You will be once you've had my cobbler." An older lady with graying hair comes into view, with a gaggle of people positioned throughout a grand room.

There are children's toys splayed throughout and a massive entertainment center and sectional anchoring everything.

"Mary, this is Mila." Pen is walking me toward the older lady. "Mila, this is Mary, our house manager and surrogate Nana."

"Pleasure to meet you, Mary." I haven't finished my sentence when she's pulling me into a firm embrace.

"No, sweetie. The pleasure is all mine. Welcome to the family."

I'm still reeling from Mary's greeting when a new booming voice comes from behind me. "Quit hogging the new sister!"

New sister?

A broad man with green eyes and neck tattoos is pulling me from Mary and into another hug.

But there's a grumble behind me as the man holding me squeezes tight.

"You better drop your arms if you want to keep them."

Jason growls as the man holding me chuckles.

"So, it's true then?" The man drops his hands, his deep green eyes floating over to Jason's.

Just then, a petite woman with flowing blond hair enters the room, two young children at her side. "Relax, Jace. Austin isn't making a play for your gir—"

"*Stepdaughter.*" Catherine's voice cuts in before the blonde woman can label me something I could never be.

This makes the blonde's eyes go wide. "*Stepdaughter?*"

Jason bristles next to Catherine. "She isn't my stepdaughter." He pulls at his collar, his eyes landing back on me. "I didn't imagine introductions going like this, but I guess now is as good a time as ever, since everyone is here."

Everyone's eyes are trained on Jason, hanging on his every word. "She's Catherine's daughter. And Catherine is pregnant… with my child." He's walking mother forward, his hand braced on her lower back as everyone's mouths are hanging wide open.

All except for Pen. My eyes narrow. *I wonder how much she knows.*

The blonde is the first to clear her throat, breaking the tense silence. "Well, Catherine. Welcome to the family. My name is Anaya. And this is my fiancé, Austin Crown, and our children, Amanda and Alex." She points toward the man with the neck tattoos and the two small kids. "I'm sorry if I assumed incorrectly. I'd just never seen Jace so poss… um, protective of someone before."

Catherine's eyes narrow a bit, but she splashes on a smile, contradicting the apprehension in her eyes. "Yes. Jason is very *protective* of Mila and me. We're so lucky."

"As he should be." Another strapping man speaks up from the massive u-shaped sectional, his strong nose and jawline so similar to that of Jason's. "You're carrying his child, and Mila. Well, she'll be of your loin too." He's raising a brow, his eyes assessing Jason.

"Catherine, Mila. Meet Jack. The eldest Crown brother."

"And my baby daddy." Penelope sits on the man's lap, her arms wrapping around his thick neck. *God*, these guys are built like linebackers.

"Ugh. What did I say about the PDA?" The man with the neck tattoos, Austin, is throwing his head back and groaning.

"Get used to it, brother. She's carrying my child, and that sight alone makes it impossible to keep my hands off her." Jack is staring at Pen, his eyes roaming over her body while more groaning ensues to my right.

Anaya, the blonde woman tugs at my hand, her voice barely above a whisper. "Penelope is Austin's stepdaughter from a previous marriage."

My mouth hangs open. *I can't help it.* "She what?"

Anaya just nods, my mind going a mile a minute. That would mean that Jack was her uncle. She's pregnant *with her uncle's baby.*

Anaya must see the horror on my face before she's squeezing my hand and shaking her head. "They aren't blood related."

"What are you two whispering about over there?" Pen purses her lips as she playfully glares at Anaya.

222

"Just giving her the family low-down." Anaya is beaming back at her stepdaughter? Wait, if he's no longer married to Penelope's mom, then is that still the case?

Pen answers, as if reading my mind. "Oh, we'll have plenty of time to catch up when the ladies of WRATH arrive."

Just then, the two kids who'd been by Anaya hoot and holler. Anaya smiles back at me. "They're excited because that means the WRATH kids are coming too. They're little enablers, those kids."

"*Staaahp.* Those kids are sweethearts." Penelope is waving away Anaya's concerns when Catherine cuts in.

"Ladies of WRATH? As in Cassie Moretti and her possie?"

Pen's narrowed eyes land on my mother. "So you've heard of them?"

"Of course! Cassie styles some of this country's elite. And her friends, well, they aren't slackers either." She's practically salivating, thinking of the social ladder she's about to climb.

"Right. Well, you'll be meeting them because they're part of the wedding party." Anaya is raising one solitary brow, assessing my mother as if questioning whether she's safe to be around.

"And they've yet to meet Hunter and Matt, the other Crown brothers," Jack cuts in, but his eyes are trained on Jason. "They're off making the rounds on the property."

"Are they still doing that? I thought we kept security on the ranch." Jason's brows furrow and I'm wondering why security would be needed out here.

"We're having a conference call as soon as they get back so

be sure to stick around the main house when Pen takes the ladies out to your cabin," Jack answers, his expression solemn.

Jason nods, the look in his eyes severe. What exactly is going on behind the scenes? The break in at the house in South Beach, the penthouse fortress, and now the security at the ranch?

Something tells me not all is well in the Crown Family's business. But as I stare at all the love in the room, between the children, the Crown brothers and their women—I know that whatever it is, it's worth it if it means I get to call this bunch my family.

Chapter Twenty-One

JACE

What the fuck was I thinking, giving Mila an out? As soon as I entered her tight young body, I should've told her she was mine and there was no backing out. Because she is mine and the thought of her as anything else fills me with nothing but furious rage and desperation.

"So… You going to fill us in on what's really happening?" Jack asks as soon as we step into his study.

"I don't know what you're talking about." I'm playing dumb because I'm not ready to assess what's really going on between Mila and me. *Not until I know what she wants.*

Despite how badly I want to claim her and keep her, I won't do it against her will. I may be a Neanderthal when it comes to her, but I still have a heart, and it could never be happy knowing I've dimmed the light that shines so brightly in my love.

Fuck. *My love.* Yes, there's no doubt in my mind that I love her.

"Leave him alone. He'll talk when he's ready." Austin's assessing gaze is searching my face. For what? I don't know.

"Ready for what?" Matt asks as he steps through the door, followed by Hunter. The pair may be twins, but they look nothing alike.

Where Matt is polished and very opinionated, Hunter is all mountain man and brawn, rarely giving his two cents.

"Nothing, just that our little brother is lusting over his baby momma's daughter." Jack is snickering while I'm shooting him daggers. *Am I that obvious?*

"Oh, come on, brother. Don't fault Jack when you practically ripped my head off for hugging your girl."

"She isn't my girl." *Yet.*

"That's right. She's your future stepdaughter." Jack smirks.

"Ahh, that makes sense then." Our eyes land back on Matt. "Crown men apparently have something for stepdaughters, don't they, Jack?"

A clear dig at our eldest brother, Matt earns himself a series of groans and hisses.

"Leave Pen out of this," Austin growls at Matt, making Matt raise his hands up in apology.

"Sorry, brother. The joke was just out there, ripe for the picking."

Jack and Austin release a threatening snarl toward Matt,

and he finally drops it.

"Anyway, do any of you care to fill me in on why we need to personally patrol the ranch?"

"*El Jefe*," Jack answers, but leaves it at that.

"What about him? Last I knew, he was holed up in Mexico with the Cardenas cartel." I know this because I'd just left there, and the fucker had been sharing a cell with his brother, Raul. The very same man I'd beaten to near death.

Jack and Hunter share a look and I wonder if Hunter's already filled him in on our secret.

"He's dead," Hunter adds, his voice holding no emotion.

"*What?*" That can't be right. "But Cardenas was keeping him alive. Wouldn't even let me question him when I was down there."

"You were down there?" Austin's eyes push together and I know I need to come clean with at least that much.

"Yes. I just came back from Mexico. Paid our friends a little visit."

Austin's head cocks back. "What were you hoping to get out of it?"

"Probably the same thing you were." Hunter cuts in and saves me from sticking my foot further down my fucking throat.

"Yeah. Well, it doesn't look like I'll be getting that chance now." Austin runs a hand through his hair while blowing out a frustrated breath. "Why the fuck did Cardenas off him?"

"He didn't." Jack raises a brow, his eyes going back and forth between me and Hunter. "Raul did it."

"What?!" Matt, Austin and I all balk at Jack's revelation.

But it's then I notice Hunter remains quiet.

"Did you know?" I turn my gaze toward the savage brother in his flannel button up and unruly hair.

Hunter stares at me for a beat before nodding. "Spoke with Pen's father this morning. Confirmed as much, then told Jack."

My eyes narrow, wondering why the fucker didn't tell me he'd been in contact with Cardenas first.

"So, what now?" Austin is looking toward our eldest brother and I now more than ever wish I would've filled him in on the secret I've been keeping all these years.

"We leave it be. It doesn't concern you anymore." Jack is looking at Austin, his eyes narrowing. "You're supposed to be focusing on your wedding, and then on keeping the ranch running while I prepare to take over Cardenas' empire—not that I want to, but a deal's a deal."

"I still want answers, brother. You can't deny me that." Austin's crossing his arms over his chest, a look of defiance taking over his features.

"You can take that up with Cardenas. He'll be here for the wedding in a couple of days." Jack is looking right at me and the look on his face says he knows more than he's letting on.

"I just don't understand why Raul would kill his older brother. He was trying to free him, for fuck's sake." I also don't understand how Raul did it. When I left him, he was more dead than alive.

Hunter snorts. "Was he? Or was he trying to get to *El Jefe* himself, do the honors of snuffing his light with his bare hands instead?"

230

"Shit, brother." Austin is clapping Hunter on the back. "Everything okay? I know you're all dark and broody, but that's even darker than usual."

"I'm fine," Hunter responds quickly. A little *too* quickly.

"Seriously, bro. What's crawled up your cranky hole?" I'm holding back a smile, trying to be serious while I give my brother shit.

"If you're going to pry into my business, then I'll pry into yours. How's that love triangle you've got going on? From what Austin said, you've got it bad for your fiancé's stepdaughter."

"She isn't my fiancé. And Mila isn't now or ever will be my stepdaughter." I'm throwing daggers at Hunter when Jack cuts in.

"No, but she will be your child's sister."

Hunter chokes on his saliva, his closed fist tapping forcefully on his chest. "Holy shit. You got a girl pregnant?"

Austin snickers. "Not a girl. A cougar."

Hunter's mouth is hanging wide open, his eyes filling with something I can't quite describe. Definitely more emotion than I've ever seen on my brother before.

"Ha. Ha. Laugh it all up now. I'd like to see you the day you fall for the wrong woman. It seems to be a Crown brother curse."

Hunter's features turn dark—and it dawns on me—the stick up his ass is about a girl. "Holy hell. Hunter's got it bad for a girl. *The wrong girl.*"

"No. I don't."

Matt's face transforms, his mouth hanging open as he stares

at his twin brother in disbelief. "Damn. How did I miss it? I'm supposed to be your other half, brother."

Hunter rolls his eyes. "You're not my fucking soul mate, Matt. It's not like we were even in the same sack."

Matt's grabbing at his chest in mock indignation. "You wound me, brother. And as compensation, I demand you tell us all about this girl."

"There is no girl, and you better drop it or I'll be heading back to my cabin."

"Ohhhhh, he's definitely got it bad for a girl. Wouldn't be threatening us with his retreat if he didn't." Jack's eyes are dancing with mirth as he stares at Hunter. "But we'll drop it. We know how you get, and it isn't worth it. Not when we have a wedding coming up and a cartel murder to decipher."

"Can't we leave well enough alone?" Dead men can't leak secrets. It's no sweat off my back that the old man is dead. "Cardenas is still in possession of Raul, right? Seems to me like he handled business for us. Saved us the trouble."

Jack scoffs. "You'd like to think that."

"No. The reason he killed his own brother is important. I can feel it." Austin is scrubbing a hand over his face, and it's just my luck that he refuses to drop it.

Needing to steer him in the other direction, I mention the only thing that would sway a man. His woman.

"That might be the case, but it's nothing you need to be worried about right now. Think of how upset Anaya would be if something happened to you right before your wedding."

Austin huffs out a breath but nods. "You're right."

"Of course, I am. When have I ever been wrong?"

Matt snorts. "I remember that one time you tried to teach Jack how to pick up a woman at a bar."

Austin is laughing so hard he's wheezing now. "Oh. My. Fuck. How could I forget that?"

"Yeah, well, I don't think it's funny." Jack is glaring at Matt while Hunter comes to his defense. At least that's what it seems like at the beginning.

"Leave the poor man alone. He takes on a lot for this family. How was he supposed to know that telling a woman that he'll 'give her a nickel if she tickles his pickle' is the wrong thing to say?"

"You motherfuckers. I was drunk off my ass. None of you should have let me talk to a woman in that condition. I was coming off of heartache from losing our parents. The least you assholes could've done was keep me away from women."

I'm laughing so hard; tears are coming out of my eyes. "Oh, man. But we were all grieving, and seeing you make a fool of yourself helped raise our spirits."

Matt's wiping away at his own tears of laughter when he pipes up. "Yeah. Didn't you want to be our rock? Make us feel better?"

"No. You jerkoffs could've all fucked right on off. Just like now." He's standing from his desk, his knuckles pressing firmly onto the dark wood. "Get out. This family meeting is over."

"Oh, man. We have to tell Pen." Matt is clapping Austin on the back, his words making Jack growl behind us as we all file out.

"You better not, or so help me, I will beat your asses! All of you!"

We're all laughing hysterically as we exit his office, not that we'll actually tell Pen.

Hell, I believe in karma, and if life has taught me anything, it's that that shit is real. That's one thing I'm not willing to risk. Not right now when things between Mila and I are so fragile.

I'll do anything to protect what I have with that girl, and that includes being on my best behavior when it comes to my brothers.

Mila

"So this is it." Pen opens her arms wide after we've all entered the moderately sized cabin. "What do you think?"

We had to ride out here on a side-by-side, so it's a good distance away from the main house. The property is nestled between a thicket of trees with a small creek running alongside it. It really is quaint, but my mother looks like she's about to lose her shit.

Wanting to cut her off before she says anything stupid, I quickly answer. "It's beautiful, Pen. Thank you for setting us up here."

Penelope beams back at me. "I'm so glad you like it. This place holds so many sweet memories." She points a thumb toward the back. "If you follow the creek, it will lead you to a waterfall a couple of miles down. It's the perfect spot for a picnic."

Her cheeks tinge pink and I wonder just how many *picnics* she's had there with Jack.

"Right. Well, I won't be making that trek. You know, because of the baby and all." Catherine places a hand on her abdomen as if that explains everything. She's forgetting one little thing. Pen is pregnant too, and a whole lot more pregnant than she is.

"Oh, that shouldn't be a problem. I take my little brother and sister out there once a week, and I'm due to pop any day now. Fingers crossed the peanut holds out for the wedding. I don't think Anaya will forgive me if I go into labor during her nuptials." She's laughing, but something tells me her sister-in-law, *err*, stepmother... would be fine.

This family loves each other fiercely. That's something I've been able to see from the moment I stepped into their home.

"Okay. Uncle Jace is in the master and then your bedrooms are on either side of his. Let me take you there now." She's begun walking, but my mother cuts her off.

"There's no need for that. Jason and I will share a room." She's staring at Pen as if this is a done deal. Something that was discussed between her and Jason, the thought souring my stomach and making my heart hurt.

Pen snorts, oblivious to my inner turmoil. "No. I'm sorry, but Jace was very clear with his request that you be put on either side of the master." She walks around my mother, continuing down her path toward the hallway. "If he wanted you with him, he would have made it abundantly clear in his message."

She's giving Catherine her back, so she misses the feral look of rage simmering beneath my mother's cool facade.

Not wanting to stick around to see more, I quickly follow behind Penelope toward the rooms, briefly peeking into the master as we pass by. It's gorgeous. A four-poster bed anchors the middle of the room, the tall dark posts making an explicit statement that this is where the master of the castle sleeps.

A shiver runs through me, imagining a naked Jason laying between the luscious bedding, but it's quickly cut off by Penelope's words.

"And this is you." Pen opens a door, motioning me inside before turning back toward my mother. "Catherine, you're on the other side."

She's clearly giving Catherine different treatment to mine, and I can't help but feel a little guilty for it. As soon as my mother ducks into her room, I have to ask Pen why that is.

"Hey, what did Jason tell you about Catherine?"

"Why do you ask?" Pen's eyes are glittering with knowledge I can't wait to divest her from.

"I get the feeling you're not my mother's biggest fan, that's all."

She smirks. "Well, let's just say I'm really good at reading my uncle Jace, and he's very fond of you. Whereas your mother... *she stresses him out*." She pauses, her hands absently going to her belly and rubbing. "Can I ask you something?"

"Of course!" She's been so nice to me. I'd be horrible if I denied her any answers.

"How sure is she that the baby is his? I know my uncles,

and one thing they've stressed for as long as I can remember is the importance of protecting the family name. A.K.A. *no glove, no love.*" She makes the last statement in a deep masculine voice, no doubt imitating a line she's heard multiple times if her face is any indication.

Suddenly, my thoughts drift back to the jet. The jet where Jason took me raw. No glove, and definitely lots of love.

Penelope's eyes are going wide, her lips curling up into a wide smile. "Oh, girl. You and I have some dishing to do, don't we?"

I feel my face flush further, my head vehemently shaking no. "I don't know what you're talking about. And as far as the baby. My mother's baby. I don't know."

"Your mother's baby? Is there another baby in question?" Her eyes narrow on me, scrutinizing every breath and every flinch.

Holy hell. That was a definite slip up on my part. "Nope. No other baby, aside from yours, that is."

And that isn't a lie. Doesn't it take a couple of days to get pregnant? So it can't be a lie, right? Heck, Jason's seed might not even take. Don't women try for months before getting pregnant?

No. Not at all. Not if my mother's experience is anything to go by. Based on what Jason said, it was a one-night stand turned into forever.

A pang of jealousy hits me strong and fast, the air threatening to leave my lungs.

"Hey, sweetie. I'm sorry. I didn't mean to upset you." Pen

takes my hand and walks me back toward the bed. "You don't have to answer anything if it makes you uncomfortable."

I shake my head, clearing it of the envy laced fog. "No, that's fine. I just… I'll be fine."

"Hmm. Before I forget, the ladies of WRATH get here in the morning. Anaya is having a fitting for all of us then. Be sure to get there early enough for mimosas and catching up."

"That sounds like fun."

"Oh, it is. And I just know that they'll love you as much as I do."

Her smile is contagious, and I instantly feel welcomed into the fold. Something I never want to lose. Aside from Mel, I have had nothing resembling a tight-knit family, and now that I've experienced it, I don't want to be without.

This only adds more credence to my needing to stay in my lane. If I mess things up between my mother and Jason, it will only muddy the waters, making them feel like they need to take sides. Yes. Dividing a family is a surefire way to lose that tight-knit feeling.

Not something I'm willing to do. I care too much for Jason to put his family through that. And as that realization hits, I add one more tick to the '*I shouldn't be selfish*' tally, even though I really don't want to.

"Okay, then." Pen gets up from the bed and walks toward the door. "Family dinner is at seven. You won't want to miss out. Trust me." She winks at me then, reminding me so much of my best friend and her antics.

Ugh, I wish Melissa were here. I know I need to ask if it's okay for her to visit, so better now than never.

"Hey, Pen." I stop her before she leaves. "Is it okay if my roommate comes over for a visit? I haven't seen her since I left for Florida, and I really miss her."

Pen scrunches her nose and smiles. "Of course. You don't need to ask for permission. This is as good as yours." She's waving around at the cabin, but even despite her assurance, I can't help but feel like an interloper.

"I just didn't want to assume, with the wedding and all."

"Oh, don't worry about that. In fact, since she's your roommate, she's practically family. I'll run it by Anaya, but I'm sure she won't mind if she sticks around for the wedding festivities, too. The more the merrier."

My heart soars knowing that I'll have my best friend by my side, helping ease the sting of seeing my mother and Jason together once I let him know of my decision. I know he said he's leaving it up to me, but it doesn't make this any easier.

"Thank you, Pen. It means the world to me."

"It's nothing, babe." She's waving me off as she turns and heads into the hallway, but not before calling out. "See you soon!"

Chapter Twenty-Two
JACE

"Something smells good." And it does. The scent of garlic and rosemary permeates the air, and my mouth starts its Pavlovian response.

I'm stepping into the kitchen at the main house when I'm greeted with Mila's index finger pointed in the air, asking me for a minute as she presses a cell phone to her ear.

"Uh-huh. That's right. Montana." There's a pause, and it's a good minute before she responds to whomever is on the line. "Sure. I'd really like that."

I look over at Mary who's at the stove, silently asking her who Mila is talking to, but all she does is raise a brow, wordlessly chastising me for being nosy. *Do I care?* No.

This girl belongs to me, even if she hasn't realized it yet.

"Okay. See you soon, Dad." Mila's words have my stomach churning, giving me the urge to rip the phone from her hand and give that man a piece of my mind.

I've taken two steps toward her when Mila is pulling the cell from her ear, ending the call with the asshole who's bailed on her since birth.

I'm raising a brow as I close the distance between us. "Was that your *father?*"

Mila nods, but the smile on her face doesn't correlate with what I'd be feeling after speaking with an estranged sperm donor.

"Yes, but I don't want to talk about him. I want to say thank you for all of this." She's opening her arms wide, encompassing the kitchen that's decked out with balloons and homemade banners the kids made in honor of Mila's birthday. "I know it had to be your doing."

"It was, with the help of the kids and Pen." I rub my palms up and down her arms. "Happy belated birthday, baby. You deserve this and more." I'm whispering that last bit, but I know I've caught Mary's ear. She's peeking over at us, a curious smile playing on her lips.

Fuck. I don't think I'll be able to hold back from showing Mila affection much longer.

"Jason." Mila bristles, but the biting of her lip lets me know she likes this—my touch and words of adoration. Still, she clears her throat and takes a step back, the action making my heart clench.

How much longer until she accepts that we're destined to

be together? I'm ready. Willing to tell her mother what's what and set clear boundaries.

I've realized that denying myself Mila's touch is for the birds. It's absolute horseshit and no way to live.

Just because I'm having a child with someone else doesn't mean I can't be with the woman I love. I refuse to deprive myself of everything that she is, knowing she would make an amazing partner in life.

Unfortunately, it's not looking like Mila is feeling the same way. *I'll need to convince her.* For now, a change of subject is in order.

"What did your father say?"

Mila's demeanor shifts, her smile dropping and eyes dimming. "He wants me to visit him once school has started. Said he wants me to be his intern. Maybe take over for him once I'm done with school."

"Does he have a design firm?" I ask, remembering that's what Mila wants to major in.

"No, he—." Mila is interrupted by loud crying.

"Nanna Mary! Nanna Mary! Alex said I'm not allowed to have any birthday cake!" The little blonde girl is wailing with her brother in tow.

"That's not what I said." Alex is rolling his eyes, his face one of deep annoyance. "I said she can't have any cake until the birthday girl blows out the candles."

"There's a cake?" Mila's face is flushed, clearly not having expected as much.

"Of course there's a cake. What kind of birthday dinner

would it be without one?" Mary is rounding the kitchen island before lowering herself to Amanda's level. "Now, sweet child. Your brother is right, but that doesn't mean you won't get a *huuuuge* piece of cake with ice cream."

"Ice cream?" Amanda's eyes go wide.

"Yup."

Just then, my niece turns to her brother and blows a raspberry at him, the sight making Mila chuckle and my heart warm.

I can't help but take Mila's hand in my own, giving it a quick squeeze. "Are you happy?"

Her eyes meet mine and I see the wonder and joy dancing behind them. "Very. I can't believe you planned all this… and there's cake!" She whisper-shouts, making me chuckle.

"What's all the commotion?" Catherine walks in and Mila quickly pulls her hand from my hold, her retreat only making me want to pull her in harder. *Fuck who sees.*

I will always offer my support to Catherine, and I will be more than an active parental figure in my child's life, but I'm done trying to deny my feelings for her daughter.

"We're waiting on birthday cake!" Amanda shouts in answer to Catherine's question.

"Birthday? Who's… oh, wow." Catherine's eyes land on Mila and then on me. "Jason, you really are something else, aren't you?" She's speed walking toward me, her arms wrapping around my waist before I even have time to respond. "But I thought I'd told you she'd already celebrated."

"Mila is celebrating her birthday with family today. Albeit, not on the actual date. But it's still important that she sees she has family now." *Family that cares.* Clearing my throat, I slowly pry her hands from my back. "Had she stayed back in Florida like you'd wanted, this wouldn't be possible."

Looking toward Mila I see her eyes are as big as saucers, meanwhile Mary's mouth is hanging wide open. *That's right.* What kind of mother wants to leave their child behind? Not a very good one.

"Oh, Jason. But she's so independent. She enjoys her solitary time." She looks up at me sheepishly, but I have no sympathy.

"Is that right? Have you asked her that yourself?" I'm ready to go toe to toe with her, unwilling to back down, when a boisterous greeting cuts into the tension.

"Happy Birthday, babe! Again! It's like the Groundhog Day of birthdays." A young blonde strolls into the kitchen like she owns the place and instantly I know this must be Melissa. One of my birthday surprises for Mila.

I know how much she means to her and I couldn't have planned a surprise birthday dinner for her without her close friend and roommate.

Looking toward my girl, I know it was the right move. Her previously soured expression is replaced with one of sheer joy as she runs toward the blonde.

"Oh my god! Mel! What are you doing here?!" She's pulling her friend into a hug, practically mowing her over where she stands.

"Jason called, wanting to know what you'd done for your

birthday. So I told him, but he wasn't having it." Melissa looks over toward Catherine just then. "Although I love our pajama days and Gilmore Girls marathon, this sounded like a lot more fun. Thank god for your new daddy, *am I right?*"

Wow. I know Mila and I play, but I didn't think she'd openly tell her friend about it. Guess I was wrong. Not that I mind. I just hope her friend is team Jace, urging her to drop whatever hesitation she has with us moving forward.

Catherine, not having missed the dig, narrows her eyes on Melissa. "Yes. Jason is so sweet. Even after I told him Mila enjoys her private celebrations, he planned all of this for our baby's big sister."

The reminder of our connection is like a dark storm cloud coming over us. Not that the thought of a child is a bad one. Just a child with *her.*

I shake my head, needing to clear it of the negativity. It isn't the baby's fault it will be born to a mother who evidently lacks compassion and warmth.

Taking a step toward Mila's roommate, I extend my hand in greeting. "Melissa. Thank you for coming. I'm glad you found the ranch okay."

"I did! It got a little hairy on the crossing, but the Civic delivered me in one piece. And now here I am!" The tall blonde releases my petite Mila and pulls me into an embrace next. "Come here, big guy. We're practically family, aren't we?"

My cheeks are flushing with heat at the surprise greeting when I hear a growl to my left. *What the fuck?*

Before I can fully assess the situation, my eyes are drawn

back to Mila who is making a strangled sound, her pouty lips falling open with one lone word falling out. "Maverick?"

My brows are pushing together when I feel Melissa's hold on me stiffen. As if in slow motion, she's prying herself from me, her body ever-so-slowly turning toward the direction of the growl.

Taking in the scene, I see Melissa's bright blue eyes go wide as she stares at Hunter, his gaze fervently set on hers as his chest rises and falls at a pace that's rapid for our normally stoic brother.

Wow. My face splits into a shit-eating grin as I piece it together.

My girl and her roommate live on the other side of the mountain. The very mountain Hunter lives on. *Oh, this is just too good.* He has been pining after the wrong girl, alright. The girl who's standing right in front of me.

Hunter's chest makes a rumble before he's choking out his next words, a clear strain as evidenced by the chords in his neck going taut. "*Baby doll.*"

What in the ever-loving-fuck am I witnessing? My brother, Hunter, calling someone by a sweet term of endearment? *Yeah.* I'm clearly in the twilight zone.

But as I look back at my girl, seeing the glee in her eyes, I know that this is real. Very real if Hunter's shaking fist is any indication.

"Brother. Everything okay?" I'm walking over to him, clapping a hand on his shoulder while Melissa remains quiet behind me—the previously boisterous woman having gone as silent as a mime.

Hunter gives me a sharp nod before he's finally ripping his gaze from Melissa and acknowledging everyone else in the room.

With a clearing of his throat, my brother finally starts contributing full sentences. "What is *she* doing here?"

"I was invited, thank-you-very-much." Melissa finally comes to life at what appears to be Hunter's hostility.

"By whom?" Hunter has gone back to staring at Mila's roommate, but the look on his face speaks of anger instead of lust and possession like before.

Melissa steps forward, coming toe to toe with my brother's looming height. She might be taller than average, but Hunter still has a good head on her at his six-foot-three.

She's glaring up at him, not caring that he's staring daggers at her. "Mila's stepdaddy invited me."

"I'm not her stepfather" and "He's not my stepfather" are uttered simultaneously by Mila and me, neither of us wanting such a damning title being tied to one another. Not if we want a chance of us ending up together, that is.

There's a beat of silence before Catherine reaches for Melissa, pulling her into a tense hug and interrupting the awkward moment. "Melissa. Such a pleasure to see you, dear. You're like crabgrass, aren't you? Always popping up everywhere."

"Did you just compare me to a fucking weed?" Melissa is bristling as she pulls away from Catherine, her eyebrows dropping dramatically.

"Did you?" Hunter follows up in defense of Melissa and I'm suddenly in need of some popcorn, wanting to see how this plays out.

There's no way in hell I'm coming to Catherine's defense. That was damn rude of her, and no doubt it was intentional based on the look of annoyance she's giving her daughter.

"Mila, please explain to your friend that I was just making a statement. There's no need for everyone to get up in arms about it."

"She's standing right in front of you, *Mom*. You can tell her yourself." Mila raises a brow, urging her to do as she said.

"Apologize. Now." Hunter is growling at Catherine, her face suddenly going flush.

"Jason?" She's turning toward me now, as if I were going to fight my brother on this.

"What? I believe you did liken Melissa to a weed." I'm staring at her blankly, feeling only a slight sense of pity since she is carrying my child. "Look, it's clear my brother feels offended on this young lady's behalf. The sooner you clarify you meant no ill will, the sooner we can go back to the birthday festivities."

"So you invited her?" Hunter's narrowed gaze is on me as I nod in confirmation.

"She's Mila's roommate."

"I know." Hunter's eyes fall on Mila, and I see that she's shifting nervously on her feet.

"You two know each other?" Catherine is looking back and forth between Mila and Hunter, but it's my brother who answers first.

"Yes. Now apologize to Melissa," Hunter grunts, and I feel the need to step in at his harshness. Yes, she may be an ice queen, but she's still the mother of my unborn child.

"Hey. Watch your tone." I nudge my brother. "Let's keep things light, for Mila's sake. We don't want a brawl ruining her surprise dinner, do we?"

The girls' eyes go wide as Mary speaks up. "Wouldn't be the first time."

"I meant nothing by it, Mel," Catherine quickly adds, not wanting to see exactly what a Crown brother brawl entails.

"Mhm." Melissa makes a non-committal sound, but thankfully drops it.

As much as I'd like to see how this plays out for my brother, I want nothing tarnishing Mila's dinner.

"Good. Now that it's handled, how about we make our way into the dining room. Dinner is ready!" Mary is carrying a huge dish out of the kitchen and into the other room that is equally decked out in birthday decorations.

As we all shuffle behind her, I can only hope and pray the rest of the night is uneventful. But if the introductions were a foretelling, *I'm not holding my breath.*

SINFUL CROWN

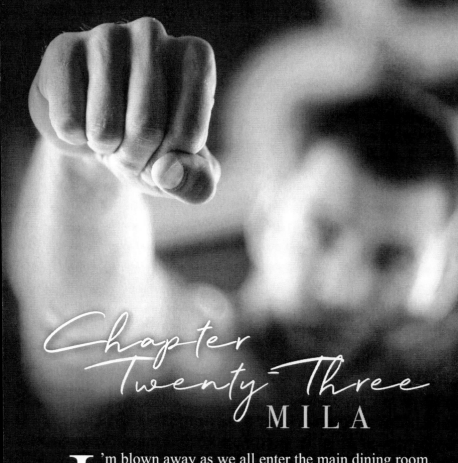

Chapter Twenty-Three
MILA

I'm blown away as we all enter the main dining room, most of the family having already taken their seat at the table.

"Here." Jason pulls a chair out for me as I take in all the details.

"*Jason.*" I feel my eyes well up with tears of gratitude. I honestly don't remember ever having such a thoughtful birthday. Mel has done an amazing job of celebrating with me every year, but it's just been us two since we were fifteen.

This. This is just so much more.

"Happy belated birthday, baby." Jason is pushing my chair in, his thick fingers gently caressing my arm before he pulls away.

appearances' sake, but no. He sits his fine ass right next to mine.

"This is amazing, Mila! *Yes*. It definitely beats our birthday tradition of takeout and T.V." My best friend is sitting across from me, looking all bright eyed and I can't help but sniffle, a lone tear crawling down my cheek.

"I love our birthdays together, Mel. But, yeah, this is special." Turning back toward Jason, I give him a massive smile. "Thank you. So much."

"Don't thank him until you've tasted the cake. It's my mother's specialty," Penelope calls out from the end of the table at the same time a strange man's stomach lets out a grumble, the sound making everyone chuckle.

"Ladies, this is Matthew Crown. I believe he's the only one you haven't met yet." Jason's deep voice sends shivers down my spine as he introduces his brother, a very inappropriate response on my behalf, but I can't help it.

My voice shakes as I give my greeting, "H-hello, Matthew. It's a pleasure to meet you."

Jason leans in, whispering in my ear as Catherine greets his brother. "Those goosebumps better be for me, little girl."

My thighs clench and I feel a throb under my panties. *Jesus*. This man is lethal to my libido. It's as if it'd been dormant my entire life, but upon meeting him, it's nonstop in a state of want and need.

Turning to the man in question, I bite my lip and smile before whispering words I know will affect him. "Yes, *Daddy*."

Jason's eyes flare and I know I've hit my target, only

remembering where we are when Catherine's voice cuts into our bubble once more.

"So, how do you all know each other?" Mother's eyes are on me, narrowing a bit before dancing over to Melissa and then Hunter.

My stomach sinks, knowing there is no way in hell this will end well if any one of us answers in earnest.

"Melissa is my best friend's little sister." Hunter's answer is innocent enough and I thank the gods that be for this small miracle.

"Erickson?" Jack, the eldest Crown, asks.

Hunter nods as Mel answers. "That'd be the one."

Mother's eyes furrow, clearly needing more information, and I wish she'd just drop it. Isn't she the one that said she didn't want Jason knowing where I work? The more she digs, the more it's liable to come out.

"Okay. But how did you not know of the Crown brothers, Mila? If you two knew of Hunter, then clearly, you'd know about his family."

I feel the color drain from my face. What exactly is she implying?

"She didn't know he was a Crown," Mel hisses, coming out in my defense. "We know *Hunter* as Maverick. Always have. Whenever I would ask him for his real name, he'd say '*it doesn't matter.*' So Maverick he remained."

My friends' tone took on a tinge of resentment at the end, and I know she's fully justified in feeling it. She's had it bad for this mountain man to her left for as long as I've known her, and despite him clearly feeling something for her as of late, he's always kept her at arm's length.

"I could see that. They *are* Crown men, after all," Mother adds, oblivious to my friend's heightened emotions.

Penelope chortles. "Yes. They've had thirsty women after their deep pockets for as long as I can remember." She's openly glaring at my mother as she says this, the implication not lost on any of us as the table grows quiet.

Until Mel pipes up, sheer disgust written all over her features. "Is that it? Is that why you refused to give me your name? Even when I danced for you, agreeing to no more private lap dances for anyone else, you *still* didn't give me your name." Mel gets up from the table, clearly upset and not realizing what she's just dropped on everyone. "I can't believe that's what you think of me. That all I'd care about was your money instead of who you really are. My *hero*." She says that last word with deep sarcasm, throwing down her napkin on the table before speeding out of the dining room.

I'm getting up and rushing after her when a hand on my wrist stops me cold. "Lap dance? What the fuck, Mila. Is that what you two do for work?"

The look on Jason's face is one of horror, but I don't have time to answer questions, not while my only friend for the past three years is in visible pain and in obvious need of her sister.

I make a quick exit, ripping my arm from Jason's hold before uttering an apology to the room. "I'm so sorry."

"Fuck. I'm the one who's sorry." I hear Penelope mumble as I cross the threshold in search of my friend.

What a wild turn of events.

I'll eventually go back and apologize to everyone, but now I need to find Melissa and get this all sorted out. I can't imagine what she's feeling. But after everything she's done for me, skipping out on a surprise birthday dinner is the least I could do for the one person who's been my constant shelter in the storm.

Jason

"Hunter. Hallway. Now." I'm pulling away from the table, not caring that everyone's eyes are on me. I need fucking answers and I need them now.

My brother grumbles something under his breath but follows. What I'm not expecting is Matt to follow too.

"What? You didn't think I'd miss out on this, did you?" Matt's eyes are dancing with dark humor.

"Let's take this into Jack's office," I'm muttering loud enough for both of them to hear. The last thing we want is having this discussion in front of the rest of the family. Not when I don't know what's going to come out of Hunter's mouth.

"Matt, you don't need to be here. This is between Jace and me." Hunter is narrowing his eyes on his twin brother, but Matt isn't having it.

"Oh, yes I do. I want to know everything about the girl who's had my brother tied up in knots for over a year."

Hunter's mouth hangs open as I shut the door behind us. "How'd you know?"

"I'm your fucking twin. I felt it, though I couldn't quite place my finger on it, and I knew asking you would've been pointless. Squeezing words out of you is like trying to squeeze blood out of a turnip." He sits his ass on the chase before propping his feet up on the coffee table and crossing his hands behind his head. "But I knew it was only a matter of time before it came out."

"Yeah. Well, out it came. At *my* girl's birthday dinner."

"Doesn't seem like she's really your girl if you didn't know where she worked." Matt's smirk is irritating the shit out of me, and it takes all that I have not to slap it off his face right at this moment. "And besides, isn't it her mom that you got pregnant? Seems like she should be the one who's your girl."

That's it. I'm lunging at my brother, intent on hurting him real good when Hunter's hands are gripping onto my biceps from behind, his hold preventing me from moving forward like I want.

"Stop." Hunter's command does little to stop me. That is until he's uttering his next words. "If you want answers, you need to stop."

"Fine, but Matt, you better keep your mouth shut. One more unsolicited piece of commentary, and I'm not letting Hunter save you."

Matt is making a zipping motion over his lips, his fingers flicking away an imaginary key.

Once Hunter is finally satisfied that I won't be attacking our brother, he finally releases me, his large frame retreating to a wingback chair.

"Go on. Ask away." He's motioning for the chair next to his, having enough forethought to direct me as far away as possible from Matthew. *Smart.*

"Have you seen her naked?" I don't know why this is the first thing that comes out of my mouth, but it does. And I need to know now like I need air.

"Yes."

I'm flinging myself from my chair and over to Hunter in two seconds flat, wrapping my wide grip around his neck and squeezing before I've given him a chance to explain.

"Not Mila." Hunter ekes out through my hold. "Only. Mel."

Fuck. I drop my hold so fast, all while shaking my head of this blind rage. "I'm sorry, brother. Damn. I'm so sorry."

"Don't. I should've worded that better." Hunter shakes his head, his hands pushing me off of him with force. "I'd have done the same if I thought you'd seen Melissa that way."

"So, what? The girls are pole dancers?" Matt interrupts, his eyes as wide as the tumbler now in his hand. *When did he get that?*

"Melissa is, but her roommate is just a waitress." Hunter's eyes land back on me, and I think I see envy reflecting back in them. *If he only knew.*

At this moment, I'm just glad he isn't aware of Mila's *OnlyFriends* account. I'd be just as murderous as I was two minutes ago.

Crown men aren't serial daters. But once we set our eyes on the woman we want, there isn't much holding us back. And unfortunately for them, possessive ownership seems to be part and parcel of our claiming.

Sucking in a sharp breath, I make my way over to the bar, pouring Hunter and I both a tall tumbler of Tortured Crown. *How fitting.*

"How do you do it? Deal with her shaking her shit in front of others?" Matt is asking as I hand Hunter his glass.

"Not well, brother. Not well." He takes a giant gulp of the amber liquid before continuing. "I've been at my wit's end. Especially with that fucking bouncer eying her the way he does… I swear, what I'd give to meet him in some dark alley."

"Woah. You've got it bad, don't you?" Matt looks at Hunter with something akin to awe.

Yeah, it's safe to say we never thought we'd see the day that Hunter Crown would fall for a girl. He's the most cynical man I know, always saying that women are only heartache and trouble.

"Was Melissa right? Did you not tell her our family name because you thought that's all she'd care about?"

Hunter groans, rubbing his calloused palm over his face. "She's Erickson's little sister. I hadn't seen her that way, as a woman—*one I'd like to fuck*—until about a year ago. At first, it was just out of habit. Not saying my name. But then as time went on, and I saw the hunger in her eyes… I wanted it all for myself. Just for me. Because of me. Not my name."

My head rears and brows furrow. "Hey, if what Mila says about her roommate is true, then she's a good girl. Don't think you'd have to worry about her taking you for a ride."

"Wish the same could be said about your baby momma,

brother." Matt is rolling in his lips as he mentions Catherine and her perceived intentions. *Shit*. I'm glad I'm not the only one who was getting the gold-digging vibes.

Makes me feel like less of an ass.

"About that. You know you don't have to be with her just because she's carrying your child, right?"

I keep quiet, knowing that what they're saying is true, but refusing to commit to anything until Mila tells me what she wants.

If I'm forced to live a life without her, then I'll make the sacrifice and tie myself to her mother. For the baby's sake.

But if she gives me the green light, I'll do whatever it takes to make her happy, all while being the best father I can be to the child Catherine carries in her womb.

"What are you two going to do now?" Matt cuts into my thoughts, bringing us back to the present.

Hunter is throwing back the rest of his drink as he gets up from his chair. "I'm going in search of Melissa. Apparently, I have some shit to clear up."

"You mean some groveling to do?" I snicker but am cut short with Hunter's next words.

"You wouldn't be snickering if you saw what your girl was wearing while serving up horny old dudes, all trying to grope her any chance they got."

Yup. He's right. My snickering stops short and all I see is red.

There's no way in hell I'm letting Mila go back to that job. *No fucking way.*

Chapter Twenty-Four

MILA

I 'm hugging my best friend who's been crying since we found our way into this spare bedroom. At least I hope it's a spare bedroom.

"Shhh. Mel." I'm rubbing slow circles on her back as I hunch next to her on the bed. "Everything is going to be okay."

She buries her head into my neck, her tears trickling down my shirt and joining the rest as they form a wet spot on my silk blouse.

"It is. You know why?" She pulls away from my hold as her swollen red eyes find mine. "Because I'm leaving this hell forsaken state and never coming back."

"Like fuck you are," a deep voice calls from the doorway, making both of us startle.

Hunter is standing there, his chest heaving in obvious rage... or is that panic?

"Excuse me?" My friend regains her composure, wiping away her tears as she stands.

"You heard me, *baby doll*. You aren't going anywhere." The way he says it, with so much command and possession, sends shivers running through me.

One quick look at my friend and I know she felt it too. "And why is that? I don't have any reason to stay. Not when my best friend is leaving for college and my brother is always working."

Hunter takes two steps into the room, closing the distance between him and Melissa. "Because I said so."

Melissa throws her head back and cackles. "Oh, please. The man who wouldn't even trust me with his name? That's hilarious."

Hunter's eyes narrow as his face lowers to hers, their lips a mere breath apart. "I'm not joking, Melissa."

Something flares in my friend's eyes, determination running through her as she stands tall, never wavering under his stare. "Neither am I, *Hunter*."

A clear shiver runs through the Crown brother as he stands over my friend, the image almost indecent for me to witness. It's clear her saying his name has some sort of effect on him— one that I have no business witnessing.

I'm getting up to give them their privacy when Mel is calling out to me. "No, Mila. Stay. It's Maverick who needs to leave."

"You're out of your goddamn mind if you think I'm leaving you alone right now." Hunter spits out more words than I've ever heard him utter.

"And why is that?" Mel looks up at him, unwavering in her stance.

"Because you're hell bent on punishing me, and god knows what you'll do."

I'm rolling in my lips, trying hard not to smile. But damn. Hunter knows my friend well.

Mel narrows her eyes at him. "Yeah? And you'd deserve it too. Whatever it is I'd do."

Oh, this is just too funny. It's clear Melissa doesn't know what exactly she'd do in vengeance, but she'd do it, and have a hell of a time doing it too.

"I have a better idea." Hunter picks Mel off the ground and throws her over his shoulder before she's even had a chance to answer. Not that it stops her once she's bent over his strapping body.

"Put me down, you fucking caveman!" she hollers as he carries her out the door. "Mila! Stop him!"

"Oh, no. I'm not getting involved." *And I'm not.* Not only because I know he'd never hurt a hair on her body, but because despite her putting up a fight, I know that this is what she's always wanted—that beast of a man finally claiming her.

"Traitor!" Melissa yells down the hallway as I make my way to the door, only to be stopped by the other Crown brother. The one I wanted to avoid at all costs.

"Going somewhere?" Jason walks me back into the room,

his hand going to the door and shutting it closed behind him.

"Yes." I swallow thickly, the sudden lump in my throat making it impossible to breathe. "I need to apologize to everyone."

"They're fine. I promise." He keeps walking until the back of my knees bump against the bed.

"But—but the birthday dinner." I'm stuttering, trying to find an excuse that'll get me out of this room.

"They're probably done eating. Don't worry. We'll have a do-over tomorrow." His hand cups my face as my mouth falls open in wonder. He says this as if everything that transpired in the last hour could just be shoved under a rug.

"You must be out of your mind if you think we can all go back to acting as if Pen didn't call out my mother on her true intentions and Melissa and I didn't get outed as adult entertainers to the entire family." My scoff is cut off as Jason's fingers grip my jaw with force.

"You're *not* a fucking entertainer, baby. You're a waitress."

My eyes shoot up at the realization that Hunter has filled him in. But really, did I expect any different once the cat was out of the bag?

"Does it matter what position I worked? I'm still an employee of the Sapphire." Jason's fingers clench tighter around my neck while his body presses harder against mine, the clear bulge in his pants pressing firmly against my belly and making my knees go weak.

I know what that snake feels like inside of me, and the memory of it is making me tingle all over.

266

"Not anymore, you're not." Jason's guttural whisper brings me back to reality, one where our intimate encounter was just a fluke. Something that could never be repeated.

"Oh? And why is that? Because last I checked, your name isn't Mila, and you can't up and decide for me like that."

"I can. I will. And I just did." Jason drops his hands to my waist, squeezing it tightly before picking me up and flinging me onto the bed like a little rag doll.

I'm panting, breathless at his sudden moves.

"Jason. I can't. I have to keep working." I'm talking as this mountain of a man crawls onto the bed, his body positioning right above mine. "Especially now that I'm not taking that money. I need it for school."

My words are a whispered plea as his hand finds my pants. And with one harsh tug, he's ripped the material clear down my thighs. "No, baby. That money is yours. Everything I own is yours. And you can't sell something that's already been taken."

My heart is beating in my throat as he grinds the palm of his hand on my clit, all while thrusting three fingers into my aching heat.

"Jason," I mewl.

"That's right, baby. Say my name. The man who owns this pussy. The man who'd do anything to keep and protect it." He pumps in and out, his palm continuing its pressure as he lowers his head to my breasts, sucking in a peak over the silky fabric. *"Your fucking daddy."*

With his free hand, Jason rips down my blouse, exposing my visibly aroused nipples through the transparent lace of my bra.

"Jesus, baby. They're fucking perfect. Like two little eraser tips. Perfect for sucking, licking and biting." He grinds hard down as he utters these filthy words, making my world go black as a rush of emotions floods through me.

He's my daddy. The man who's done nothing but look out for me, wanting to please and pleasure me at every turn. How lucky am I to be able to lose myself in his sinful touch, despite knowing that he isn't really mine?

Somehow, that makes it even more exciting. Knowing that my mother's future husband is finger fucking me in a house full of people.

"What's my dirty little girl thinking of?" Jason licks up the column of my neck before his lips are hovering right over the shell of my ear. "Does it turn you on, baby? The thought of me sucking on these perky little tits?"

My walls contract around his fat fingers, letting him know just how much I like it. "Yes. *God, yes.* But we can't."

"And why not?" He's picking up his pace, my arousal coating his thick digits and making them slide in and out easily now.

"They'll hear. They'll hear me coming." I'm biting down on my lip, trying to keep myself from moaning too loudly as I squeeze my eyes shut. "And they'll know. They'll know I'm a dirty girl."

My legs are shaking as I try to hold myself from my release, but it feels inevitable as Jason rips down my bra, his mouth suckling a perky tip and making me moan out in pleasure.

At this moment, I'm lost to him. Lost in this game we play where I'm his broken little girl and he saves me every time—making me feel good regardless of what's going on in the world around us.

"Let them hear you, baby." He's fucking me fast and hard now, every time he thrusts in, applying pressure to this blinding spot that has my entire body shaking in need. "Let them hear me taking you. Taking what's mine."

"God, yes." I'm lifting up my hips, wanting more of him, needing all of him.

"That's it, baby. Be a good girl and come for me." He's licking across my collar bone before his mouth latches onto my other nipple, giving it a good suckle and tug before he comes up for air, his ravenous eyes landing on my own. "My good girl, letting Daddy fuck your naughty little hole."

"Oh, please." I'm whining, unable to help it at the thought of his massive appendage impaling me where I lay. "I need *more*."

Jason snarls, his body lifting off of me with such force, I'm worried he's changed his mind. But upon looking up at him, I see that I have nothing to worry about. No. This wall of muscle is ripping his shirt off his body before he's undoing his belt, the piece of leather being tossed to the side as his fingers deftly undo his pants.

I can't help it. Despite knowing that he could never really be mine, I let my fingers pull down his boxers, making that massive dick of his pop out, the wide head lining up perfectly with my mouth.

I don't hold back.

I take it into my mouth and suck, swirling my tongue around the swollen tip and reveling in Jason's musky taste.

He's perfect. Never in my life did I think sucking a man off would be enjoyable, but as I bob up and down, taking Jason's length in as far as I can, I can't think of anything else I'd rather be doing than taking his body into mine—any way I can get it.

"Fuck, baby. You're going to make me blow." Jason is holding my head with both of his hands as he thrusts into me hard, his fat tip hitting the back of my throat over and over, making me gag. "You've got no idea how beautiful you look, taking Daddy's cock into that perfect mouth."

I'm whimpering around him, my eyes tearing up at his words. I love the way we play. Being cherished and used in every way that brings this man pleasure is something I could do for the rest of my life.

My entire existence, I've always been an afterthought, never someone's focus. But here, in this man's arms, I'm his everything. His entire world. I see it in his eyes.

He's absolutely perfect for me.

There's just one problem. *He isn't mine.*

Jason must see the change in my eyes because he's slowed his pace, withdrawing as he brings me onto his lap, cradling my body to his now mostly naked one.

"What's going on in that pretty little head, baby? Tell me what you need."

I'm rubbing my nose against the bare column of his neck,

breathing him in as his hard length jumps up against my slit.

It's clear he's still horny, but he's willing to stop his pleasure just to make sure that I'm okay. That alone has me melting into a damn puddle. He really is my *daddy*.

I've heard Melissa talk about these guys in her books but always thought it childish to think that there are men out there who would baby you, making sure you were cared for in *every* possible way.

Never had I found it appealing until now. Now that I'm in Jason's embrace, his thick cock slowly sliding up and down my drenched slit as I uncontrollably rock on him.

I feel a sense of peace settle over me as I promise myself that I'll have him one last time—fully and completely, playing our little game without holding back.

He may not be mine in the long run, *but he's mine right now and I plan on enjoying every second of it.*

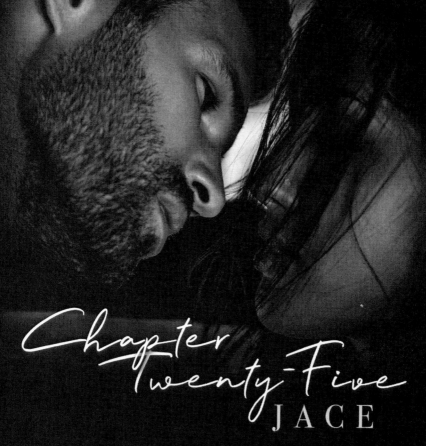

Chapter Twenty-Five

JACE

"Talk to me, baby." I run the palm of my hand up the smoothness of her back, stopping only once my fingers have gripped onto the nape of her neck, squeezing it in a possessive hold. "Come on, sweetheart. Tell Daddy what's wrong so he can make it feel better."

Mila whimpers, her sopping pussy flexing against my hard length, and I swear it takes everything in me not to ram it up into her tight hole. *Shit.* She loves this as much as I do. This power play where she's my baby and I'm her strong daddy. God, how I fucking love it.

It gets my dick painfully hard just thinking of it, and having her here, sitting in my lap, whimpering at my use of our special words is almost too much for me to bear.

"Baby, you're killing me. I don't know how much longer he can hold off." My cock taps against her slit once more, begging for entry. "Be a good girl and tell me what's wrong."

Mila blinks up at me, her eyes going big and round as her bottom lip quivers. "I'm sorry, Daddy. I've been a bad girl."

Oh, fuck. She's going all out and the alpha in me roars to life, needing to play along, so I do. "And why is that?"

"I've been having these dirty thoughts." She bites her lip playfully as she bats her lashes at me, and god I swear I'm about to nut where I sit.

Never in my life have I wanted to care for a woman the way I do, Mila, and this is just another facet of it. One I enjoy very much.

"Are you going to tell me what those dirty thoughts are, or are you going to make me pull them out of you?" I raise a brow at her as I gently swat the side of her tit, my eyes unable to keep from watching her juicy breasts jiggle.

"I'm sorry. I don't mean to tease." She smirks, a mischievous look in her eyes.

"Like fuck you don't." I mumble under my breath, rolling a hard nipple between my thumb and forefinger before I give it a good pinch.

Mila lets out a little yelp which quickly turns into a mewl as I lower my head and lap at the abused nipple, reveling in her sweet taste.

"Oh, yes." She's panting, holding my head to the breast I'm suckling. "That's it. That's what I've been thinking about."

At this I grab her by the waist and fling her onto the bed

once more, my large body towering over her much smaller one. "What, sweetheart? Having me lick your sweet little cherries?" I pull her thighs open, setting my erection right over her heat and giving it a good grind on that last word. "God, baby. You make Daddy feel so good when you let me suck on them, those perfect little tits that have been invading my head for far too long."

Mila moans as I take another full-mouthed pull, flicking my tongue against the hard little nub.

"Mmmm, yessss. Just like that." She's shaking her head back and forth against the bedspread, all while her slender fingers trail down to my ass and squeeze. "I know it's wrong. I know you belong to *her.* But I can't help it, Daddy. I want you all to myself. You're mine. All mine."

"Oh fuck, baby. You're all that I want too." Unable to hold back any longer, my mouth dives for hers, intertwining our tongues in a dance of carnal lust and pleasure. She's everything I never knew I wanted, all wrapped up in one hot as hell and kinky package. "I know it doesn't seem right, and everything feels fucked up, but let me in, baby. Open up those sweet little thighs and let me take you. Make you mine. I promise I'll be good to you—to our babies." I trail an open palm to her abdomen, my heart beating overtime at the thought of her swollen with child.

There's hesitation behind Mila's eyes and I don't think she knows the extent of my love for her, but I intend on making it crystal clear.

Taking my aching cock in hand, I rub the swollen head up

and down her drenched slit, stopping at her clit and circling it once, twice. "Do you want this, baby? Do you want Daddy's cock?"

Mila bites her lip and nods, a mixture of lust laced with shame dancing across her delicate features.

"Well, you can't have it."

Her mouth hangs open, eyes blinking up at me in confusion. "But, why?"

"Because you think there's something wrong with what we have. What we feel." I release my aching member and place both hands on either side of her head, letting my nose trail up the column of her neck before taking her earlobe into my mouth and sucking. "That's the rules, baby. You can only have Daddy's cock when you realize you're the only hole he wants to be in. For the rest of his life. I'd rather die than be with *her*, or anyone else."

Pulling away, I see that Mila's mouth is still hanging open. Taking her bottom lip into my mouth, I suck, only releasing it once I've given it a little nip.

"You're it for me, baby. You're all that I want. I don't care if it's wrong or what the world will think. Least of all your mother."

"Jason." My name is but a whisper on Mila's lips, her hands cupping either side of my face. "God, how I love you."

I swear my heart swells to two times the size upon hearing her words. "Baby, I love you too. And I'll love you for the rest of my life if you'll let me."

Mila wraps her arms around my neck, bringing me down to

her for yet another kiss before her small hands are pushing against my shoulders and forcing me onto my back.

"Does this mean you accept my offer?" I'm staring up at her, my eyes roving over her exposed flesh—so much beauty, I don't know where to start.

Mila straddles me, her hot pussy sliding up and down my steely length. "It means—oh god, your dick feels so good, Daddy—it means…" She slides up and down me once more before I'm digging my fingers into her hips, grinding her on me in need of relief. "Ohhhh, fuck. *I'm coming.*"

My cock bobs up against her slit, wanting inside, but I've yet to hear her say she'll be mine. With a strength I didn't know I possessed, I halt my girl's movement, her whimpering cry one I feel right down to my swollen balls.

"Not until you promise me, little girl." My nostrils flare as Mila deliberately makes a show of playing with her tits.

"But don't you want to put it in me? Feel my tight little hole?"

Gaaaaah. "Fuck, baby. Why do you have to make this so hard?" Just then, my cock pulses in agreement. "See? Look at what you do to your daddy."

"I'm sorry." Mila's fingers scratch down my abdomen before one of her hands is trailing behind her, squeezing the very balls I'd just mentioned, the action pulling a guttural moan straight from my chest. "Poor Daddy, let me make you feel better. Let me take care of you like you take care of me."

My mouth goes dry at her words and I'm rendered speechless as she lifts her puffy slit to just above the tip of my cock. "Just say yes and let me give you what you need—*what you really want.*"

Holy fucking hell. Pack my bags and book me a ticket straight there, because that's where I'm going. *Hell.*

I'm powerless to stop her, in awe of her body as she slowly lowers herself onto the crown, letting just the tip inside and clenching her inner walls around me.

"Fuck, baby. You know how to touch Daddy just right, don't you?"

Mila gives me a mischievous grin as she lowers the rest of the way in one fell swoop, making both of us gasp as she bottoms out around my fat girth. She's whimpering, her walls already milking me in place, and I know I won't last much longer.

"Ummph, Daddy. *You're so big.*" She ripples around me, making me see stars, only to bring me back down with her next words. "Are all men like this?"

The thought of Mila with anyone other than me makes me see red, the fury it elicits making me flip her over in one swift roll. "Never, Mila. That's how many times you will lay with another man. Do you hear me?"

I'm thrusting my big cock into her small hole, over and over again, not caring that this is only her second time. She's mine and I'm claiming her good and hard, leaving no question as to who this pussy belongs to.

"Tell me, Mila. Tell me you understand."

"God. Yes." Her words are coming out staccato with each thrust of my hips, but they're not good enough. I need to hear it all. Hear that she's really mine. "Fuck. Yes. Daddy."

"Oh shit, baby." I pull my chest back, giving me enough space to watch her fat tits jiggle with every pump of my cock. "Tell me. No other, Mila. Just me."

"Yes. Yes. Yesssss." She's pulling me down with force, her hands latching onto my shoulders. "Yours, just yours. Always. Alwaaaaaays."

She's contracting around me, milking me not only with her actions, but with her words. She's finally giving me what I've been craving all of this time. A future together.

The thought alone has me releasing rope after rope of sticky cum into her womb, all while I thank the heavens that this girl is finally mine. Come what may, I know it'll be alright because we'll have each other, and that's all that really matters.

Mila

No regrets. As I remember the look on Jason's face, I know that what I said was something that had to be done.

Despite what he promised, there's no way we could make this work, not if he's having a child with my mother.

"But why, Mila? You all but swore yourself to me as we made love. Why are you going back on your word now?"

"That wasn't a lie, Jason. My heart, body and soul will always belong to you and no other. For goodness' sake, my body only came alive in your presence, and I

have no doubt that that's how it will remain for as long as I live."

Jason's brows furrow as he takes a step forward, but I take a step back—closer to the door. "If that's the case, then I don't see why we can't make this work. I already told you, I don't have a problem with declaring my intentions with the world."

"I know." A tear slips down my heated face, unable to hold my sorrow in any longer. "But just because we can, doesn't mean we should."

Jason takes another step forward, but I hold both palms up. "No. I've decided. It's better if you stay with Catherine, raise your baby together and give it at least one good parent."

"Right." He chuckles, but there's no humor in it. "So I'm just supposed to forget everything that's happened between us, and ignore the fact that the other half of my heart is going on without me?"

I close my eyes, not wanting to see the anger on his face. "I'm sorry."

There's nothing more to say, but as I'm turning to leave, Jason grabs my wrist and halts my retreat.

"And where do you think you're going?"

Turning my head back toward him, I give him the most sincere smile I can muster. "Back to the cabin, and then home tomorrow morning."

"Look, Mila. I love you enough to let you go if that's what you truly want." I know this is what I said

I wanted, but his words still slice through me like a double-edged sword, making me blink back the tears as Jason's eyes narrow and jaw clenches. "But you'll have to let me walk you back to the cabin. It isn't safe."

Yeah. That's not happening. If I'm alone with him for one second longer, I'm bound to cave, agreeing to whatever he asks of me. No. I need to leave, and I need to leave now.

I give Jason a small nod and thankfully he releases me, turning to grab the pair of pants we so eagerly tossed to the side before. But as soon as he isn't within arm's reach, I whisper my apology and run, running as fast as my legs can carry me and never braving a look back.

I'm *still* running as I enter a thicket of trees, leaving the open field behind and taking in the full extent of what I've done.

No. There are no regrets. I will always look back at the moments we had together and feel nothing but joy and peace. I'm making the right decision. *I know I am.*

But as I trek through the tree lidded path, I can't help but wonder if maybe, just maybe, I gave up on us too soon. Maybe there was a way for all of this to workout where everyone is happy.

I'm slowing my pace, unsure if I should turn back when I hear the breaking of a branch, the suddenly eerie path back to the cabin transforming into something of nightmares.

It's dark now, the only light being the one from the dimly lit moon beyond the clouds. *Shit.* Maybe I should've waited to come back here with Catherine. *Catherine.* The woman whose man you let defile you... Yeah. That wouldn't have been awkward at all.

I listen, but there's only silence, save for the rustling of leaves against the wind.

It's probably all in my imagination. Been listening to too many True Crime podcasts. Shaking my head, I continue down the trail only to stop once I hear another branch crack.

"Who's there?" I'm whirling, calling out into the darkness, begging for whoever is out there to come out.

It's an animal. It has to be. God. That doesn't make it any better. This is bear country and we are way beyond Spring.

Wanting to get out of the woods and into the cabin, I pick up my pace, practically running until I see the clearing up ahead, the warm glow of the cabin lights guiding me the rest of the way.

I'm about to step out into the open when I feel a sting on my neck. *What the fuck?* I slap at it, as if trying to swat a large mosquito, but my vision fades as I go to pull my hand. The cabin swirls before me and I lose the only light I see. It's replaced with a blanket of darkness, the hazy shroud taking me under.

"Mila!" Jason's voice is the first thing I hear as I come to. "Mila! Where the fuck are you!?"

Here. I try to answer, but no words come out. I'm paralyzed, unable to move, unable to open my eyes.

"Baby, where are you?!" *Here. I'm right here.* "Oh, fuck! Dammit!"

Suddenly I feel strong arms wrapping around me, lifting me off of the cold, hard ground.

"Shit, baby. What happened to you?" Jason is whispering onto the crown of my head when I hear more footsteps approaching.

"Damn, brother. What happened?" It's Jack, I think.

Slowly, I'm able to pry my lids open, blinking up at the man who's stolen my heart.

"She's awake!" Jason shouts. "Mila, I told you to wait. I told you not to come out here by yourself. It isn't safe."

Yeah. Well, I know that now.

Trying to speak, I move my tongue which feels heavy in my mouth. "*Sorry.*"

"Damn straight you're sorry. Never again. You hear me? You listen to me when it comes to your safety."

I try to nod, but the best I can do is blink.

"What happened, Mila? Did you fall?" Jack is asking from somewhere behind me.

"Y-yes. Something. Something was in the woods." I'm smacking my lips, trying to get some much-needed moisture in my mouth. It feels like I'm waking up from a major bender, dehydrated as hell.

"Do you think it was security?" Jason's jaw clenches as he asks his brother, but only silence follows. "*Fuck.* Let's get you inside, Mila. What was the last thing you remember before the fall?"

"I heard branches snapping. Felt like I was being watched. So I started running." My hand, finally able to move, raises up to my neck. "Then, as the cabin came into sight, I felt something on my neck. Like a bee sting, and everything sort of faded after that."

Jason stops, his body swirling and coming face to face with his brother. "Radio the men of WRATH. Tell them they'll need to bring reinforcements."

"Got it," Jack is responding, his steps carrying him away from the cabin, leaving Jason and me alone.

"I'm sorry. I should have waited." I close my eyes, ashamed that I let my emotions cloud my judgment.

"I'm just glad you're okay." His eyes rake over me as we step into the cabin. "Well, that's yet to be determined, but at least you're in my arms, where you belong."

"Jason." I'm biting my bottom lip, eyes searching his. "This changes nothing. I'm still leaving after the wedding. You belong with Catherine. She's the one having your baby."

Jason scoffs as he sits down on the leather couch, his arms still wrapped tightly around me. "That's a poor excuse. For all you know, you could be too. It's been twice now in the last twenty-four hours that I've claimed your body. Made it mine the way a man does his woman. The woman he wants to spend the rest of his life with."

I suck in a sharp breath, knowing that what he's saying is nothing but the truth. I very well could be carrying his child, but that's a bridge I'll cross when and if I come to it. "I know my body well. That's a slim chance, because I am nowhere near ovulating. Even if it were the case, it doesn't change the fact that she's definitely with child now. *Your child.*"

Jason's eyes narrow before he pulls his gaze from mine. "I don't want you to leave, Mila. I can't stand the idea of you being out there on your own without my protection." He returns his amber-colored eyes and my breath hitches at the adoration I see in them. "But I'll let you go under one condition."

I'm rearing my head back as much as this position in his arms allows. "I don't think you have a choice."

Jason chortles. "Oh, yes I do, baby. I could insert myself into every facet of your life if I so wished." His eyes seer into mine and I see his truth. He isn't lying, and a sick and twisted part of me takes joy in that. Knowing that he wants me badly enough to do such a thing. "But I love you, Mila. And above all, I want you to be happy."

God. My heart just exploded on the spot. This amazing— and gloriously hung—man loves *me*. Me. Mila Kournikova.

"So, like I said. I'll agree to let you go under one condition."

"And what condition is that?" I'm blinking up at him, having fully regained function of my limbs now, but not wanting to remove myself from his hold.

"You stay at the penthouse in Florida until we can get a safe location set up in Montana."

My mouth is hanging open at his words. "I can't live with you and Catherine! That'll kill me!"

He closes his eyes, his face turning dark. "Catherine and I will remain at the beach house." Jason's eyes shoot open, the intensity behind them almost startling me. "But she's staying in her room. Do you understand? I will not share a bed with her."

"So, what? You're going to be celibate for the rest of your life?" I'm scrunching my nose, wanting to know but not.

"That's none of your business, Mila. Isn't that what you wanted?"

I swallow thickly, knowing he's right.

I'm the one who pushed him away. I'm the one driving him closer to my mother.

"Yes," I answer, despite knowing it's not really what I want because that doesn't matter. It has to be.

"So it's settled then. You're going back to Florida where I can make sure you're safe. Once the property I've picked out is secured, then I can transfer you to Montana." He's dead serious, as if this is something he's already thought through. Just one more reminder proving to me that he really is looking out for me wherever and whenever possible.

God, am I a fool for throwing my chances away? No. You're doing this for your little brother or sister. They deserve to have an amazing father, and I have no doubt that's exactly what Jason Crown will be.

"Okay. I agree."

Jason nods as he gives me a once over. "I don't see any marks on your neck, but I'm going to have blood work drawn. Just to make sure." He's standing up, my body still cradled in his arms. "For now, get some rest and let me know if you feel anything strange. Woozy or light-headed. Things like that."

"Okay. I was a little woozy when I first came to, but I'm fine now."

"Yeah, I'll believe that when I see the bloodwork for

myself." He's lowering me onto the bed, his eyes roaming over my body one last time before he's turning. "Get some sleep. The doc should be here within a couple of hours."

"Jason, I'm sure it can wait."

"No." He's whirling so fast, he's almost a blur. "You don't know the sick fucks we're up against, Mila. There was a reason I asked you to wait for me at the house. But maybe now you'll listen."

And with those parting words, Jason slams the door behind him, leaving me in the dark like some errant child, questioning where it all went wrong.

I t's been one month since my bloodwork came back as normal. *No signs of foul play.* So when I woke up this morning with severe nausea and an aversion to the smell of coffee, I knew it wasn't some delayed side effect of whatever happened to me in Colorado.

Just as Jason had promised, a doctor came in and looked me over, claiming that I was okay. This did little to appease an overprotective Jason, but between the security at the property and the men of WRATH looking into the incident, he felt it was safe enough for me to be alone on the trip back to Florida.

And here I am, living in a massive penthouse, complete with a fully armored G-wagon. Like some sort of princess in a tower, all with my very own rotation of security guards.

Hopefully that'll change when I move to Montana next month.

But this morning, as I leaned over the toilet bowl and relieved myself of whatever I could stomach last night, I wondered if that's even going to be possible.

I'd been ignoring the signs—chalking them up to PMS and heartache—but as the second wave of nausea hit me, I knew it was time to go to the doctor.

And who did I call? Dr. Pengraff, of course.

I know it might be weird for me to seek out my mother's OB. But she's the best in her field and I know her already, having accompanied Catherine to one of her appointments in the last month.

It's hard to find a doctor you trust, let alone like. And besides, they follow HIPPA, right? It's not like they can tell Catherine about my visit unless I expressly allow it.

So, *yes.* I booked an appointment and snuck out of the massive fortress I call home.

There's no way I could have told the security detail where I was going. They'd report it to Jason in a heartbeat, and then I'd really be screwed.

As if I'm not already. I fidget with the strap of my purse, sitting in the waiting room of the doctor's office, waiting to be called. Waiting for them to tell me if my life is irrevocably changed.

Whatever happens, I'll deal with it in stride, of that I have no doubt.

"Mila Kournikova." A tall brunette in scrubs calls my name

from the door and my knees wobble as I stand.

Stride my ass. I'm nothing but a shaking bundle of nerves as she hands me a cup.

"Bathroom is down the hall to the right. Fill it up to the line and then place it in the window." She's shutting the door behind me as we step into the hall. "Once you're done, make your way into room three. Dr. Pengraff will be with you shortly."

I nod and do as she says, walking straight toward the door marked as the bathroom. God, I wonder why I didn't take a pregnancy test before coming here. Now the suspense of not knowing if I am is making my stomach turn even more than normal.

But I know, don't I?

My mind is a jumble of thoughts as I quickly fill the cup before placing it on the window as instructed, wondering how things will change if I am, in fact, with child.

But I haven't even finished washing my hands and clearing my head when the bathroom door pushes open. *What the hell?!* I thought I'd locked it.

Taking in the brunette that's just walked in, I see that she's wearing scrubs. She must work here, but this can't be normal. "Can I help you?"

"You're Mila Kournikova." Her brows are pushing together as she looks me over. "Catherine Kournikova's daughter, right?"

"Yes."

"Okay, good. Tell that bitch she still owes me my money." She's glaring at me as if I were garbage.

"What?" I'm truly confused. Jason said he'd be covering all

of her expenses, so I have no clue what this crazy woman is talking about.

"You heard me. She owes me my money." She's cracking the door open, peering out to ensure no one is outside. "She begged me to use an old ultrasound recording on her first visit. But every time she's been here since, she's ghosted me. Refusing to pay up the ten thousand she'd promised."

My eyes are as wide as saucers as the petite blonde steps half-way into the hallway. "Look, I see you had no fucking clue. But tell your mother that if she doesn't pay up, there's no way in hell I'm helping her out on her next visit. She's on her own."

And with that, she's exiting the small bathroom, closing the door behind her and leaving me with my heart in my throat.

Holy-fucking-shit. She isn't pregnant. Catherine isn't pregnant.

Oh my god. I have to tell Jason. I have to confront my mother.

I can't stay still knowing what I do now. Needing to take action right this minute, I rush into the hallway and past the entrance to Dr. Pengraff's office.

My mind is a blur of thoughts as I step onto the sidewalk, wondering whom I should tell first. *Will my mother deny it? Will she have some sort of excuse?*

I have no clue. All I know is that this changes everything. If I am pregnant with Jason's baby, then we can actually be together. But will he still want me? I rejected him. Made him feel as if his love wasn't enough.

God. I need to fix this. All of this.

And I will. As soon as I—

Screeching tires have me whirling around, just in time to see a blacked-out van stop right beside me. *What—?*

As the back door slides open, two muscular arms covered in ink reach out and grab me, the last thing I see being a dark set of eyes beneath a ski mask. Darkness takes my vision once more, and I'm left wondering if I'll ever get the chance to make things right. I want to. *God, how I want to.*

So as my consciousness fades, I throw out one last prayer to the powers that be. *Please, if you're out there, give me another chance.*

Jason

"Sir. She isn't in her vehicle."

Pressure builds behind my lids, and I swear I'm about to shoot laser beams with how furious I am. "What the fuck do you mean she isn't in her vehicle? Where is she?"

Armando's features take a bleak turn from concerned to scared. Armando is *never* scared. "Jason. I think she's been taken."

My heart stops and the world slows around me. I couldn't have heard right. Not possible. I have security around her 24/7. The idea that they took her is laughable, right?

"By the time her detail figured out she'd slipped out of the penthouse, it was already too late." He rubs at the back of his neck, his fingers squeezing at the guilt he undoubtedly feels.

"When they reached her vehicle, it had been parked for quite some time and there was no sign of her anywhere."

My eyes narrow, ready to rain down hell on him for letting this happen. "And where the fuck were you? You were the one in charge of her detail. *I trusted you.*"

"I know, sir. I'm sorry." He takes two dangerous steps forward before he's dropping a folder on my desk. "I was on the phone. Raul is missing and they think he's back in the states."

"*Fuuuuck.*" I'm ripping the envelope open and staring at photos of someone who looks like Raul boarding a commercial flight, the switchboard in the back showing that he is, in fact, back in the states. Yes, it says California, but who knows if that was just a connecting flight on his way to Florida. "When were these taken?"

"About forty-eight hours ago. But sir, there's more."

"Of course there fucking is." I throw my head back and growl.

"Based on the location of Ms. Kournikova's vehicle, we believe she was at Dr. Pengraff's office before she was taken."

For the second time in ten minutes, my heart stops and world turns. *Is she? Could she be?* It's been over a month, and yes, like some psycho, I'd been telling my men to keep an eye out for early pregnancy symptoms. I didn't buy the bullshit she said about not having ovulated or whatever.

Look at what happened to Catherine. She's in her forties, I double-gloved, and she *still* got pregnant. Clearly, I have super sperm. Those suckers probably waited around for her egg to drop, attacking it like little baby infusing vampires.

Oh god. If she is pregnant and something happens to that child because of Raul, so help me god, I will end him, once and for all.

"Find her. You need to do whatever it takes to get her back to me in one piece, or it's everyone's ass on the line. I don't give a shit. I'll paint this town red with the blood of everyone who let her down." Crumpling the photo of Raul in my hand, I glare at my old-time friend. "I don't care what it takes. You hear me? Bring her back to me."

"Got it." And with a nod, Armando moves to leave my office.

He might be my confidant and friend, but if he fails me one more time, he's as good as dead.

There's a knock at my door and I'm about to rip Armando's head off. "What?!"

"Jason?" Catherine's voice has my tone softening, but just a bit. The news I'm about to deliver can't be easy, even if she isn't close to her daughter.

"Catherine. Sit down." I point toward a chair in front of me.

"Is everything okay? I heard shouting." Her brows furrow and face pales.

There's no easy way of saying this, so I just spit it out. "Mila is missing."

"Missing? Are you sure she just hasn't gone off somewhere? You know how independent she is."

I'm rubbing a palm over my face, wishing it were that simple. That she'd just gotten tired of being trailed by my men. But the crumpled-up photo of my nemesis tells a different story.

"No. We think she's been taken."

"What?!" At this she startles, her previously pale face going even paler, if that's possible. "How? When? Who?"

"We aren't one-hundred percent sure, but my men are on it. We're doing whatever it takes to bring her back. Of that you have my word."

Catherine is up before I've even finished my sentence, rounding my desk and inserting her slender arms around my waist. "Jason, oh god. Thank you."

I give her a comforting pat on the back.

"You have nothing to thank me for." *I'm the reason she's missing in the first place.* Of that I have no doubt. I brought her into my world, one where this damned feud with a cartel has stolen her and our child's future.

No. Don't think like that. We *will* find her. And we *will* bring her back.

I'd been too lost in my thoughts to notice Catherine's hands slipping to my belt, her red-tipped fingers now trying to undo my zipper.

"Catherine, what the fuck?" I'm pushing her hands away forcefully, taking two steps back for good measure.

"Jason, I—I just wanted to thank you. Properly." She takes a step forward, but I hold up my palm. "You've been so good to me and my daughter. I wanted to show you how much that means to me."

"No, Catherine. Do not mistake my actions for something they're not." I round the corner of my desk, putting even more distance between us. "Mila is my world, and as soon as we get her back, I plan on letting her know this. I'm not letting her out of my sight for one goddamn minute, and that's something you better get used to. I'm sorry this is how you had to find out, but I can't live a lie this big anymore. I love your daughter, and I plan on building the rest of my life with her."

"But Jason. Our baby!" She's clutching her abdomen, big fat tears spilling down her face.

"I'll still be there for my child, but I can't continue to pretend that I'll lead a happy life by your side as anything other than a co-parent." Pinching the bridge of my nose, I let out a long breath. "I will always be that child's father, but living a farce with their mother will only do it more harm than good. I just can't do that."

"You can't possibly mean all of that."

"I do. Now, I understand if you don't want to live here anymore, but I promise I can set you up in whatever home of your choosing. For now, stay as long as you need. In fact, it's probably better. That way you can stay constantly informed with our search for Mila. *Shit*. I can't believe that's even something I have to say."

"Look, Jason." She drops her arms to her sides, a steely resolve coming over her features. "I see that you're upset right now. Probably not thinking clearly." Catherine walks toward the door but continues to speak. "Just know that I will be staying here, and we can revisit this once you've calmed down. Hopefully, you'll have come around once you've realized Mila is just off somewhere asserting her independence like she always does. That child isn't reliable, and that's something you best learn now before you drop me over her."

She's raising a brow as if I'm crazy, but the only crazy one here is her. She must be if she thinks I'll ever choose her over Mila. Hell, the only reason I slept with her in the first place was because she looked so much like her daughter.

But she doesn't give me the opportunity to respond because she's left my office as soon as the last words slip past her delusional mouth.

It's for the best. I'm in no state to talk down crazy. I'm barely hanging on by a thread and it's a miracle I could be as gentle with my news as I was.

Heading over to my phone, I know it's about to get a whole lot crazier. I'm getting ready to unleash WRATH's lethal sector on Raul and whatever minions he has left.

We annihilated his cartel's henchmen, killing off what we thought was every last one of them, save for him and his brother. It appears we must've missed a few.

Well, no more of that. Like men on death row, their fate is sealed and their blood marked as mine.

SINFUL CROWN

Chapter Twenty-Seven

MILA

here am I? My eyelids are heavy, each feeling as if they weigh a ton.

The last thing I remember was leaving the doctor's office. *Oh my god.* The van. The inked up arms.

Where the hell am I?

Looking around, I see that I'm in an all white room. No windows or doors. How did I get in here?

I need to get up. There had to be a way they got me inside. It wasn't magic, and as much as I'd like to believe in the possibility of teleportation, I don't think we've advanced that far in technology.

Getting up from the small cot I'm on, I realize I must have been sedated. Every movement I make is slow, as if I were moving through quicksand. God, I hope whatever it is doesn't hurt the baby. *The baby.*

My hands go to my abdomen, the thought of this little peanut being hurt propelling a determination in me I didn't know I had.

"Let me out!" I bang on the padded walls. Clearly they must have a way of hearing me, right? They couldn't have just left me here to rot, could they? *Shit.* Jason's words come back and haunt me.

You don't know the sick fucks we're up against.

Oh, yes. It sounds like they very well could leave me here to rot. But not without a fight.

Like a rabid animal, I claw at the walls, my words coming out more garbled than lucid. "Let. Me. Ouuuuuuut!"

"Calm yourself, child." One wall recedes before sliding to the side, the opening now revealing a massive wall of plexiglass and a darkness beyond.

But that voice. I'd know it anywhere.

"Father?"

"It's John, to you."

I'm blinking into the darkness, unable to understand what's going on. "*John?* What's going on? Why am I here?"

"And I thought you were the brightest of *El Jefe's* bastard children. Seems like you're just like the rest."

My throat has gone dry and the ringing in my ears has clearly messed with my head. Did he just say *El Jefe*, the notorious cartel leader, is my father?

"Ah. I see it's finally sinking in. About damn time." There's murmuring behind the glass, but I can't make out the other person.

None of this makes sense, but if he wants to play this game, I'll bite. Whatever to get answers from him. Maybe if I play him long enough, I'll find a way out. "Okay, I get you aren't my father. But what am I doing here? What do you want from me?"

There's a deep sigh. "This wasn't supposed to happen, but Raul, your uncle, went and offed *El Jefe*. It's now more important than ever that we find his will."

I'm trying to swallow through the sawdust in my mouth. "The will. Okay."

"Yes. The will. That's what we've been after this entire time. The whole reason Catherine seduced that manwhore Jason Crown."

My mouth hangs open. I can't help it. "Mother is in on this too?"

It's barely a whisper, but he hears it too, my words making him chortle. "She isn't your mother. She's your half-sister. The very first bastard child."

My mouth is hanging wide open. Just how many kids did this cartel leader have?

"Yes. My client was in line to take over his father's empire. He was promised to a rival leader's daughter, but of course, your father couldn't keep it in his pants. So Catherine was born."

My mouth is still hanging open. I could probably catch flies with this thing.

"By the time Austin rolled around, El Jefe's wife had developed a system of keeping the bastard children out of her hair. She didn't want any pesky children detracting from her own children's inheritance. Problem was, she was barren. Could never produce an heir."

"So if there's no heir, then who is in the will? The one everyone's trying to find."

"Austin Crown."

Holymotherfreakingshirtballs. "But why?"

"Despite his wife's covert tactics, El Jefe kept track of each and every one of his children. For some reason, he had his favorite, and it was Austin. Who knows? Maybe he reminded him of himself. There is a striking resemblance, after all."

"And mother—I mean Catherine. What did she want with the will?"

He chortles. "To alter it, of course. I was El Jefe's lawyer. And when his crew got decimated last year by the Cardenas cartel, I lost my biggest and only client. Them and the Crown brothers basically ruined me. So when Catherine proposed we find the will and collect on it, I jumped on board."

"Okay. All of that makes sense, but what does that have to do with Jason? Isn't Austin the one you're interested in?" My brows scrunch as my mind tries to piece together these facts like some sort of messed up jigsaw puzzle.

"Because Jason has the will. At least, that's what Raul told us. He'd been monitoring the Crown family for some time—ever since he became their silent partner."

My mouth has resumed its open fly trap position as I try to process everything I've just learned.

My mother isn't pregnant. She isn't really my mother. My

father isn't really my father. And I'm some sort of bastard cartel princess? Oh, and the man I'm in love with holds a will that basically gives all of a cartel leader's possessions to the Crown brother with the neck tattoos.

"While that's all fascinating, it still doesn't explain why I'm here. I'm not on the will and I didn't even know it existed, let alone have it."

"Of course you don't have it, stupid child." He makes a noise of disgust before there's a loud cracking sound. "But you're the backup plan... More like our main plan now. It seems Jason has taken a liking to you. Far more than we'd anticipated. And since Catherine hasn't been able to get into Jason's private quarters to retrieve it, using you as bait will have to do."

"Oh my god. You wouldn't."

"We would, and we have. Catherine asking you to visit, having you spend so much alone time with him, you think that was all accidental?" He snorts. "Please. As if we don't know of every time you two were together. I'd have to say, that blow job at the beach house was pretty entertaining to watch. Never thought I'd be into Daddy kink, but I have you two to thank for that."

I'm horrified, mortified, terrified... *all the ied's.*

"And now, thanks to Catherine's plan, we'll soon be in possession of the will."

"You two are monsters!" I'm lunging at the plexiglass, banging my fists against the wall even though it has little to no effect.

"We aren't the monsters. Your father was. You should have

seen some of the things he did." John lets out a deep sigh, as if bored. "But anyway, we should be done soon. Catherine had been waiting until we had you secured, making sure that we weren't followed."

"And now, what? You exchange me for the will?"

"Ha! You'd like that, wouldn't you? Oh, we'll be getting the will, but neither of you are coming out of this alive. You and lover boy are both going down with the ship."

"Ship? Are we on a boat?"

There's some more murmuring and then a series of clicks. "Yes. One of your father's mega yachts. This is where the drop will happen. Everything is in motion now."

Before I can ask any more questions, the white panel is sliding back into place, making the plexiglass and darkness beyond it disappear with it.

I'm fucked. If everything John is saying is true, then I have no hope of surviving this.

Throwing my head back, I scream with all that I have, praying against all odds that I'm given an answer. *Preferably one that'll set me free.*

Jason

"Sir, we have hit on a possible location. It's somewhere in the Appalachian Mountains." Armando is rushing into my office with what he deems as good news.

But it isn't good. *Not good enough.*

"I don't need approximations. I need the exact location."

And just when I'm about to hurl my computer across the room, Catherine saunters into the room, a smug expression on her face.

"I can help with that." She's raising a brow, her long fingers smoothing down her hair.

"What? What could you possibly—. Oh, you've got to be fucking kidding me." I'm glaring at her, begging against all odds that what I'm thinking isn't the case, but as she opens her mouth, she confirms the darkness I'd felt all along. She's evil. This woman is nothing but an abomination to this world.

"I know where and who she's with. And for the right price, I can give you that information."

Armando is lunging at her, but I stop him. She might deserve whatever he's about to dish out, but we need her. Alive and breathing so she can tell us what we need to hear. Mila's location.

"Name your price." I'm glaring at her over Armando's massive frame.

"The will. I need you to fork over *El Jefe*'s last will and testament."

I'm blinking at her, my face contorting as I try to understand what she's asking for.

"*The will.* What the fuck do you want with that?"

She rolls her eyes as if it should be obvious. "Only what's rightfully mine. Austin doesn't deserve any of that shit. I'm the firstborn. It should all be mine to do as I please with."

My mouth falls open and I feel Armando's body go lax, so

I finally release him, needing to regain my composure as I stumble back onto a chair.

"*El Jefe* was your father too?" I'm rubbing a palm over my face, wondering how in the hell this is all real.

"Yes. He was a manwhore. Couldn't keep it in his pants." Catherine says matter-of-factly as she looks behind the various paintings I have in the room. "Austin and me, we're just two of many bastard children he fathered. But *I* was the first, making me the rightful heir."

Wow. Not only is Austin fathered by the notorious cartel leader, but now he's also tied to my girl. I'm scrubbing a hand down my face, coming to terms with this new information. "So *El Jefe* was Mila's grandfather."

Catherine snorts. "No, silly. She's his bastard child, too. I'm just the half sister that got stuck with her." She moves on to my desk, opening drawers as if the document she's looking for would be laying out in the open. "I was broke and in my twenties when my father's attorney approached me, promising me a monthly allowance if I took her on as my own. Of course, I agreed. And now here we are."

I sit down on the chair across from her, needing a moment to process everything she's said. "Okay. Let's say I give you the will? What then? It's not like you could disappear, taking my child with you."

Catherine outright cackles. "Oh my god. You don't think I'd really get pregnant by you? At my age? Yeah, I'm not putting this glorious body through that. I've seen what it can do to women." She makes a face of disgust as she waves her hands at me. "Have you seen the size of a baby's head? No way in hell that's coming out of me."

Furious rage consumes me. So much so that I'm standing before I've had a chance to fully take in her words. In a matter of seconds, I have Catherine up against the wall, my fingers wrapping tightly against her throat.

She lied. This entire time, she's been lying, her stories having kept a tightly driven wedge between Mila and me.

"You fucking bitch." I'm hissing in her face when I feel a pair of hands on my shoulders.

"We need her alive, sir." Armando is bringing me back down from the mountain of fury I'd been on. One I'd gladly live and die on if it meant this woman's obliteration, making her incapable of hurting those I love.

Finally releasing my grip, I take a step back. "Where is she, Catherine? And I swear, if there's so much as a missing hair on her body, I will rain hurt upon you like you've never experienced before. I don't give a damn that you're a woman, or apparently Mila's sister."

Catherine clears her throat, her hand going up to the column of her neck, rubbing it tenderly. "I'm not telling you until I have the will."

"And I'm not giving you the will until you tell me and I confirm that she's there and safe."

Catherine raises a brow before pulling a cell from inside her bra. *Just how small do they make those things?*

"I figured you'd say as much." She taps on the screen, making the small electronic come to life before producing a video. "Here. You can see her in this room, a newspaper held up to the plexiglass in front of her."

My eyes narrow on the image, and sure enough, an enraged Mila is banging on the wall, a newspaper with today's date being pressed up against it. "How do I know she's still okay?"

Catherine rolls her eyes before pulling the phone away and tapping away at the screen. "Here. This is a live feed. She's sitting on the floor, crying like the little baby she is."

She's shoving the image in my face, one I'd rather not see again for the rest of my life. I'm coming, baby. *Daddy's coming for you.*

"Now. Where's the will?" Catherine is shoving the phone back into her bra, her eyes narrowed on mine.

"Armando. Detain her." My right-hand man does as I say, all while Catherine's face goes pale white.

"But—but we had a deal? You can't do this! She'll die if I don't call McComb back."

My body runs cold. Mila's father. No. Not Mila's father. *El Jefe's* attorney. That's where I'd heard his name before. *John McComb.*

All this time, he'd been playing the role of Mila's father.

Something Catherine said clicks into place.

'I was broke and in my twenties when my father's attorney approached me, promising me a monthly allowance if I took her on as my own.'

Oh, wow. This shit was orchestrated long ago, and all of it with no regard to the impact it had on my girl.

"Does he have her?"

"I'm not telling you anything more until you release me. Let me go! This instant!"

I let out a sardonic laugh. "Oh, fuck no, Catherine. I'm the one who's calling the shots now. It was your mistake using a cell phone to show me the live feed." I take a step closer, bringing my face as close as humanly possible without touching. "With my resources, I'll be able to pinpoint their location without you having to say a damn word."

"You asshole!" Catherine is wrestling against Armando's hold, but it's pointless. She isn't going anywhere. Not until I want her to.

"I've been called worse." Taking a step back, I round my desk and head to the door. "Now, Catherine. You're going to listen to what I have to say, and you're going to listen closely. Because one misstep by your part and I'll have no problem gutting you like the lying sack of shit that you are."

She nods, all while releasing an audible swallow into the otherwise silent room.

"Good. You're going to call John, tell him you have the will and that we're on our way. And remember... you say something more, hell, breathe a little funny, and you're as good as dead— unable to enjoy what measly existence you have left."

Catherine nods again, her already pale face going paler.

"Armando, please have her secured and facilitate the call. I don't trust myself to be present. I'm liable to come through the line and strangle that bastard myself."

Armando grunts. "Yes, sir. I'll have the men of WRATH set up the call, allowing us to trace their exact coordinates."

"I should have drugged you when I had the chance!" Catherine is screaming against Armando's hold while he ties her to my chair.

"*Should'a. Could'a. Would'a.* It's all too late. Frankly, I'm glad you hadn't thought this through. It gave me the opening to do what I'm doing now." I'm raising a brow and shaking my head. Knowing that she could have really fucked this up worse than she already had.

If she *had* drugged me and deliver the news while Armando was away and I was incapacitated, things probably would have turned out a little differently. Don't get it twisted, I still would have gotten my girl in the end. It probably just would have taken a little longer.

"Call me when it's over. I'll be in my room, preparing for the trip."

Armando nods, releasing another grunt in confirmation.

God. This day can't be over soon enough. I need to hold Mila in my arms and know that she's okay. Because lord help me, if she's not, I'm painting the town red with the blood of those who hurt her.

SINFUL CROWN

Chapter Twenty-Eight
MILA

I must've passed out from all of my screaming, crying, and pounding on the walls. Yes, I know it's highly unlikely that I'll be able to break free of this cell, but if I'm going to be trapped here, I might as well make whoever's listening on the other side as miserable as me.

Now that I'm awake again, I'm back at it. Refusing to give up on what little power I have left.

I'm banging away, hollering at the top of my lungs, when a loud voice comes over a speaker.

"Enough, you insolent child! I should just shoot you where you stand!" My body freezes at *my father's* words, being that he's not one to bluff. "I swear I should——."

John's words are cut off by the sound of a machine gun

raining through the speaker, the terrifying sound filling the tiny box I'm in for two whole seconds before the audio goes dead.

Oh my god! What's going on? Who else is out there?

Minutes that feel like hours go by when I hear a voice that has my knees buckling where I stand. *Jason. He's here.*

"Hang in there, baby. We're getting you out!" His soothing words come shooting through the speaker, and I swear, they're almost as good as his embrace.

A river of tears and pent-up hurt is ripping out of me now. My whole life, I thought the two people who brought me into it did not want me, and only part of that was true. They didn't want me, but they were not the ones responsible for my birth. No, those two threw me away like a piece of trash.

But here, on the other side of this wall, is this man who's willing to risk life and limb to save me—to give me everything I need and more.

I'll gladly endure whatever bullshit I lived ten times over if it meant that I could have this man hold me in his arms once more.

I'm irrevocably his, and I can't wait to spend the rest of my life by his side if he'll let me.

After what feels like an eternity, the same white wall slides back, revealing the plexiglass and darkness beyond it.

"Jason?"

"Yes, baby. I'm here. We're just trying to get this—." More bullets sound off and I hear Jason grunt out in pain. "Fucking hell. You just won't die, will you?"

"Jason!" I'm screeching, pounding on the glass and

refusing to believe that they've shot my man. That can't be. I can't have him so close, only for him to be ripped away at the last second. Life isn't that cruel, is it?

"Jason! Answer me!" I need to hear his voice—hear that he's okay—because I can't see for shit through this damn wall of glass.

There's a rustling on the other side before the speaker comes roaring back to life. "Miss Kournikova, it's Armando."

Oh god. "Where's Jason? Armando! Where is he?!" I'm sobbing hysterically, knowing there could only be one reason Jason isn't answering himself.

"He's hurt, miss. But I'm getting you out and then getting us onto the chopper."

"Save him! Leave me here if you have to but save him!" I'm crumpling to the ground, knowing that I'd willingly give my life for his if it meant he could go on living.

The panel in front of me is sliding open and revealing the carnage that lay just behind it. My father, or the man who'd been playing my father, is lying in a pool of his own blood, a thick angry red slash adorning his jugular.

"Miss, don't look." Armando is urging me forward as he picks Jason up from the ground, a torn piece of fabric tied tightly around his abdomen. "I need to get him topside while keeping pressure on his wound. Are you okay to walk?"

"God, yes. Please, can I help?"

"Just keep walking. You'll need to keep your hands on him once we get in the air."

I nod, walking ahead of them both, even though I have no

clue where I'm going. *Wow.* John wasn't kidding. This is one hell of a yacht.

I'm making it out onto the deck when I see the massive helicopter on its very own helipad. *This is insane. Who has a helipad on a boat?!* Apparently, my father, the notorious cartel leader.

Taking steps two at a time, I'm practically diving into the chopper, turning around as quickly as my feet have settled on its floor. "Quick, lay him down."

Armando does as I ask, positioning him in front of me so I'm able to press down on the wound as he goes to fly us out of here.

"It'll be a good hour before we're on solid ground, miss." His somber tone says it all. He isn't sure if he'll make it. *But he has. He has to.*

"Hang in there, Daddy. I need you. Your baby girl needs you." I'm whispering onto his chest as my hands press down, praying with all that I have that he gets through this, because if he doesn't, I don't think I'll survive it.

We're at the beach house in Florida. It's the first place they brought us to after we landed the chopper in Miami.

Thank god there was a more than capable medical team on the landing strip, or I don't think Jason would've made it to the house.

Like a pack of guardian angels, they operated in the back

of the transport vehicle, using steady hands and capable maneuvers that enabled them to keep my man on this side of the earthly plane.

It's been twenty-four hours since the shooting that threatened to take Jason away, but thankfully, he's stable now.

Stable enough for me to take a moment and use the bathroom. It's been one hell of a day and I could surely use a splash of water to the face, at the very least.

I've just turned the water on when the phone in my pocket vibrates. With weary fingers, I pull it out and answer, praying that it isn't any more bad news.

"Hello?"

"Hi, is this Mila Kournikova?" a cheery woman asks.

"Yes, this is her."

"Great. This is Sandy from Dr. Pengraff's office. Congratulations, Miss Kournikova." She pauses, but I have no words. Not until I hear the rest of what she has to say. "The results of your pregnancy test came back as positive and the doctor wants you to come back in for some blood work. Just to make sure everything is going smoothly."

I was right. I'm pregnant. Pregnant with Jason's baby.

"Miss Kournikova? Are you there?" The woman, Sandy, pulls me back to the present.

"Yes. I'm sorry. Yes, I'm here."

"Okay, did you still want to see Dr. Pengraff?"

I'm nodding for a good three seconds before I realize she can't see me. "Yes, please."

"Fantastic. We can fit you in next Thursday at three. Does

that work for you?" There's another pause and I realize that with everything that's happened, I don't know where I'll be tomorrow, let alone next week.

"Um, I'm going to have to call you back to confirm. I'm not really sure of my schedule right now, but hopefully I'll have a better picture of it soon."

"Of course. But call us back as soon as possible. We want to make sure everything is progressing as it should."

I swallow thickly, wondering if whatever those assholes shot me up with affected the little peanut. "Yes, definitely. I'll be calling back soon."

"Great. Speak to you then." The all too cheery woman ends the line, giving me a second to breathe, but it isn't even a minute later when there's a knock at the door.

"Mila?" A deep masculine voice has my shoulders tensing. It's Austin, *my brother.*

He and the rest of the Crown family flew in last night. All of them—including my best friend—were up in the air not even an hour after having received my call.

It wasn't easy letting them in on what had transpired, but with how close they all are, I knew they'd want to know. And I wasn't wrong.

Cracking the door open, a pair of vivid green eyes stare back at me and I now see that they're much like my own. How had I missed it before? He and I may have different mothers, but we share the same father and that shows in the jade of our eyes and the slope of our nose.

"Austin? Is everything okay?"

"Yes, I just wanted to check in on you. You've been in there with Jason for a while and I haven't had a chance to talk to you about things." His eyes are narrowed and I can see that something is weighing heavily on him.

"You know you can always talk to me, right? Even in front of Jason." I place my hand in his, needing to give us that connection.

"Yeah, I'm not sure I'm ready to be near him." He scoffs. "I love my brother. Hell, I even came out here knowing what I do. But that doesn't mean I'm not tearing him a new asshole as soon as he wakes up."

I'm blinking up at him, confused. "I'm sorry. Did I miss something?"

Austin lets out a slow breath before he's releasing my hand and leaning against the door frame. "Those fuckers knew. They knew this entire time who my father was and didn't say a goddamn word to me."

My mouth is hanging wide open. *Holy hell.* That's one big secret to keep. "All of your brothers knew?"

Austin slowly shakes his head, his nostrils flaring. "Only Jason and Hunter."

I'm nodding, wondering why in the world they would keep such a thing from Austin. "I'm sure there's a good reason. They love you too much for there not to be."

Austin chuckles sardonically. "Yeah, I don't think that's possible. We're brothers. Even though we aren't blood, and there shouldn't be any secrets between us. I don't care if the virgin Mary herself came down and asked for it herself."

I roll in my lips and bite down, unsure of what to say. "I get it. I really do. Trust me. I'd been lied to my entire life, thinking that the two people who birthed me didn't love me. Only for it to turn out that they didn't birth me at all, and that I was only some discarded dirty secret."

"*Christ*, Mila. I'm so sorry." Austin's hands fall to my shoulders and squeeze.

"It's okay, brother. I'm not telling you this so you'll feel bad for me. I'm telling you because I know what it feels like when you're lied to." He's nodding, but I need him to really understand what I'm saying. "Look. Catherine and John lied to me my whole life, but the reasons they did it were selfish. I just don't see that as being the case with Jason. He loves his family too much to do that to them—*to you*."

Austin's hands fall from my shoulder as he lets out a deep exhale. "Maybe you're right, but I'm not ready to let it go. Regardless of their intention, it doesn't change the fact that it was wrong." He takes a step back into the hallway before continuing. "Anyway, I wanted to let you know that even if I'm not around Jason as much moving forward, I'll always be here for you. I mean it, Mila."

My chest warms at his words. "I've always wanted a big brother, and I can't believe that I'm finally getting one."

Austin chuckles. "Yeah. You not only have me, but I believe you've earned yourself the full panel of Crown brothers. Unfortunately for you, we're protective as hell, so don't expect to get a shit ton of freedom."

I balk at my brother's warning. "I guess you've never had

a little sister, especially one who doesn't deal well with authority."

I'm walking past Austin and toward Jason's room when I hear Anaya's laughter. "Oh, I knew I liked her."

"Shut it woman." I turn back in time just to see Austin playfully slap his wife's ass, her brow raising in defiance.

"Why don't you make me?" Anaya's words are the last thing I hear before I'm ducking back into Jason's room.

And it looks like I'm just in time. The doctor must have slipped out while I was talking with Austin, finally giving me some alone time with my man.

Making my way to Jason's side of the bed, I crawl onto it and press myself to his side. "Come back to me, please. I need you." Taking his hand in mine, I bring his calloused palm to my abdomen and spill the news I'm dying to share. "We need you. You're going to be a daddy. A real one. And I know you'll be the best there is."

"Baby." Jason's groggy voice has my eyes meeting his and I see so much love in them it threatens to make my heart burst. "A baby?"

He's pressing his hand into me as tears spill down my face. "Yes, *your* baby."

"Thank god." A smile that stretches from ear to ear touches his face. "Now you can't leave me. You're stuck with me for life."

I throw my head back and laugh. I can't help it. "God. As if I'd ever willingly do that."

Jason raises a brow. "You already did."

He's right. I did. But you can bet your ass I never will again. "I'm yours, Jason Crown. And there isn't a soul on this earth that could pry me away."

"There better not be. Or I'll hunt them down and end them." He's narrowing his eyes on me as his big hands go to my hips, slowly maneuvering me on top of him.

I'm about to straddle him when the door opens, and Matt's booming voice kills the mood.

"Oh no. You can't go sticking your flinker in her. Not for another two weeks, at least. Doctor's orders."

"Flinker? What are you, five?" Jason retorts, the exchange making me giggle.

"I'm sorry, but he's right. It's just, your hands. On me. They made me forget what Dr. Zuniga had said." I'm looking up at him bashfully, knowing that had his brother not come in, I'd probably be riding him right now—the action threatening to open up his bullet wound for the sake of our mutual release. "As much as I want to, it's better that we behave… for now."

"For now." Jason repeats, his eyes roaming over me as he licks his lips. "Lord knows I won't be able to keep my hands off you as soon as you start showing. *My girl, pregnant with my baby.*" The last bit is whispered, but it doesn't miss Matt's ears.

"Holy shit. Another Crown baby! This is cause for celebration." He whirls around, sticking his head out into the hallway. "Everyone! Get in here! Jason and Mila have some news to share."

My mouth is hanging wide open as one after another, all of the Crown family members pour into the master bedroom. Even

324

Austin who looks like he'd rather be pissing fire than standing in this very room—*and I fully empathize.*

But despite all of that, he's still here. *They all are.*

So even though this isn't how I envisioned telling everyone, I wouldn't want it any other way.

This family loves one another fiercely and that's something I'd never dreamed would come true for me. Belonging to such a wonderful group of people, knowing that they all have my back, giving me unconditional love and support.

And as my best friend strolls in at the tail end and Jason squeezes my hand, I know that this is right where I'm supposed to be. Celebrating this auspicious moment with the ones I love.

With a nod from my soul mate, I look toward our family and friends. Letting them in on this wild ride that's our life. "It's true, everyone… We're having a baby!"

Epilogue

JACE

I've never seen anything more beautiful in my life.

Mila, five months pregnant and laying on the bow of the boat, soaking up the sun's rays and making that caramel skin of hers glisten. *It's mouthwatering perfection.*

We're on our honeymoon, and if I could get her pregnant all over again, I would. *Fuck how I want to.* Claiming her body over and over again until all she knows of is me.

"Why don't you take a picture? It'll last longer." Mila pulls down her glasses, peeking over the rim at me with those gorgeous eyes of hers.

"Don't tempt me, baby. I just might."

She laughs as she raises herself onto her forearms. "No. God, no. It already took you forever to come out here. And why'd it take you so long? I thought we agreed. No work on our honeymoon."

Rolling in my lips, I lower myself and crawl over her delectable body. "Wasn't work. It was Jack."

"Oh? And what did your brother want?" She's raising a brow at me and I know I can't deny her the truth.

"Nothing. He was just letting me know the update on Catherine and Raul's whereabouts."

My girl squeezes her eyes shut. And this is just the type of reaction I didn't want on our trip.

"Where are they?"

"I'll tell you under one condition." I'm salivating at the mere thought of it.

"What is it?" Mila's eyes narrow, but the biting of her lip lets me know she's got a good idea of what I'm about to ask for.

I trail a hand up her inner thigh, stopping at the sweetest juncture known to mankind, giving it a quick slap for good measure. "You let Daddy lick that tight little pussy."

Mila lets out a gasp which quickly turns into a moan as I rub the spot I'd just abused.

Ever since she hit that second trimester, I swear she's hornier than I am, practically jumping me at every turn. Not that I mind. I would live inside her if I could.

"*Yes*. I agree. Hell yes, I agree." She's tilting her hips up into my hand and I'm thankful for this distraction, because what I'm about to tell her isn't really comforting.

"They're up in the Appalachian Mountains. Doing a damn good job of keeping their exact location private. But the men of

WRATH are on it, and between them and my brothers hunting them down, I have no doubt it's only a matter of time before those pieces of shit are pulled out of hiding."

"Good." She rubs herself harder on my fingers. "That's good. They're great at what they do." Mila stops, letting out a soft mewl before she undulates her hips once more. "Does that mean Austin is on talking terms with Hunt—."

My girl lets out an absolutely sinful sound and I'm not sure how I feel about it. "Baby, I get you're concerned about my brothers, but let's not talk about them while you're on the verge of getting off."

"Hey, Austin is my brother, too." Mila pouts.

I raise a brow and shake my head. "Now that you're officially a Crown, they're all your brothers. But that doesn't change me not wanting you moaning and talking about them at the same time."

Mila cackles. "Oh god, I'm just glad you didn't turn out to be my brother. Could you imagine? I'd have to go all Hale by K. Webster on you."

"Hale who?" I haven't even finished asking my question before Mila is grabbing my head with both hands and shoving it onto her heat.

"Enough words. I need you, Daddy. Please. Lick it and make it feel better."

Instantly, I'm groaning into her slit, my cock growing painfully hard in my trunks.

All she has to do is say the magic word and I'm all in, loving this game we play. The one where I take care of her needs and desires, no matter how dark. And god, how I revel in it. Making her feel cherished and adored. Protected and desired. All the while giving her unconditional love because she's mine. Mine until the day I die.

"Screw it. You're taking too long." Mila pushes me away and back, giving herself enough room to straddle me in place. "I'm taking matters into my own hands."

I can't help but laugh. "Shall I also play possum?"

Mila stills at my words, her nose scrunching up in that adorable way. "What?"

"You know… pretend I'm asleep. You seem to have a thing for taking advantage of me whenever I'm passed out."

Instantly, Mila's face flashes pink. "I—I don't know what you're talking about."

Biting the corner of my lip, I fight back a smirk. "Baby. You woke me up with head, and let's not forget the incident on this very boat…You do know that it's set up with surveillance cameras, right? State rooms not excluded."

Mila's face goes from flushed to pale in a matter of seconds. "Oh god."

I chuckle, squeezing her waist and rutting against her from below. "No not '*Oh god.*' More like, '*Daddy. Oh fuck, Daddy.*'"

"Nooooo." Mila buries her face in her hands, but I secure her in place. She isn't going anywhere.

"Don't be embarrassed, baby." I dig the pads of my fingers deeper into her supple flesh, anchoring her to me. "It was the first step of many that brought us here and I wouldn't change a damn second of it."

Just as I finish speaking, Mila drops down, pressing her upper body to mine. "I'm mortified."

"Seriously. Don't be." I rub my palms down her curvaceous hips, enjoying the softness of her skin against the callous of my own. "In fact. Why don't we recreate it."

I grind into her drenched slit, my hands deftly untying the knots on either side of her bikini before feeling the thin material fall away. *Fuck, she's perfect.*

Mila moans as I grind her on my hard length, the thick rod needing inside her this very moment. "That's right. Ride that cock just like before. Take what's always been yours."

"Jason," Mila whimpers, my name sounding like the sweetest of words falling from her lips.

"What, baby? What does my girl need?"

"This." She reaches down and pulls me out before I can even moan her name. "I need it, Daddy. I need it inside me. Right. Now."

She's rubbing the tip against her swollen clit, a shudder wracking her body with every upward stroke, and there's no denying her. Not when she's hungry for this cock.

"You know what to do, sweetheart." Lifting Mila, I position her right over my aching crown. "Fuck Daddy good and hard."

And like the good girl she is, my baby slides down inch by inch, sucking up whatever's left of my soul and tying it to her.

"Mmmph. Yesssss." Mila hisses as she fully seats herself on me. "You." *She pivots her hips and I swear I see God.* "Feel." *One more grind and she's clawing at my chest.* "So." *Shit. Shit. Shit. She's squeezing the ever-living-fuck out of my cock.*

"Good"

"Mila, baby. You keep throttling me with that vice grip and I'll have no choice but to paint your walls."

"*Yes*. Make me dirty." She slowly grinds up before coming back down, the sensation making my body coil with the need for release.

And because I can't deny this woman a damn thing, I turn us before lowering her onto her back, never once losing our connection. With a hand behind her head and another at her hips, I thrust up, hard and fast—our groans of ecstasy floating loudly through the bay and making it clear to anyone passing by that I'm claiming what's mine, what will always be mine.

"Fuck, baby. Your cunt feels so good." Slowly pulling out, I linger on every tingle of my spine and squeeze of my balls. *It's heaven.* Mila's body is what dreams are made of, the true definition of pleasure and paradise.

More. I need more.

I pull down her top, lowering my head and taking a mouthful of her tit, suckling the hard nipple all while I slowly push in and out of bliss.

Christ. I love the way she moans with every intrusion. Wanting to reward my baby, I gently bite down on the pebbled tip before lathing the battered flesh and giving it another swirl.

"*God*." Mila's legs wrap around my waist, the flat of her feet pressing hard into my ass. "Faster, Daddy, please. I need it. I need to come."

With a loud pop, I release her juicy tit and move both hands to her ass, lifting her up so the tip of my cock hits that magic button inside her walls.

"Ohhhhh. Shit." Mila whines and I know I've reached it, the spot that's sure to leave my girl a sopping mess.

Over and over again, I slide in and out—making sure to fuck her hard and slow, pulling out the most sinful of sounds.

She's whimpering now and I know she's close, her walls fluttering around my fat girth, squeezing beads of cum out of my tortured cock.

"That's it, baby. Come for Daddy." I free one of my hands, using the pads of my fingers to slap the side of her bouncing tit. "Milk that fucking cock."

Like a firing shot, my words are the trigger to Mila's release, her loud moans bouncing off the bay like music to my ears. *Fuck who hears.* She's mine and I don't care who knows it.

Yes, I may have over a decade on her, and she may have started off as my future stepdaughter—but she's mine now, and I plan on enjoying every whimper and moan. Starting *right-fucking-now.*

As if reading my thoughts, Mila clings to my body, her arms hanging on for dear life as the purest of pleasures runs through us both. And like a domino effect, her channel shuddering around me sets off my own release. *Christ.* The world fades and my vision turns dark as I tunnel my focus on the sensation exploding through me and into her womb. Life. That's what this is.

Mila woke up a part of me that was dead, never to surface until it had met its match. And here she is, all perfect and mine. *My very own sinful Crown.*

Thank you for taking a chance on Sinful Crown. Please consider leaving a review if you enjoyed it. Reviews are like precious gold to authors and it would mean the world to me to hear what you thought of my book baby!

MEN OF WRATH

Acts of Atonement: *A Single Dad Age Gap Romance*

Acts of Salvation: *An Age Gap Romance*

Acts of Redemption: *A Second Chance Romance*

Acts of Grace: *A Brother's Best Friend Romance*

Acts of Mercy: *A Stepbrother Romance*

CROWN BROTHERS

Filthy Crown: *A Single Dad Age Gap Romance*

Trojan Crown: *A Single Dad Age Gap Romance*

Feral Crown: *An Age Gap Romance*

Be sure to join my newsletter so you're updated with upcoming releases freebies. There's nothing like a fresh book hitting your inbox!

Let's stay connected. I'd love to hear what you thought of the book, what's on your TBR list, or simply how your day is going.

www.EleanorAldrick.com

Instagram
@EleanorAldrick

Goodreads
www.Goodreads.com/EleanorAldrick

Twitter
www.Twitter.com/EleanorAldrick

Facebook
www.Facebook.com/EleanorAldrick

THANK YOU
Acknowledgements

Sinful Crown marks book eight in my author journey, and even though it's hard to choose a favorite, I think this one takes the cake. I absolutely adore Jason and Mila, and I know their love story wouldn't be what it is today without the help of some really amazing people.

First and foremost, a million and one thank you's to Lauren and Suny. You two are rockstars, always keeping it real with me and telling me when my writing is just a little too crazy or something's just not right. I love you two to pieces and I know for a fact that my writing is the best it can be because of you both.

I also want to thank Anna Fury (if you haven't read her

Alpha Compound series, you need to get on that) who beta read Sinful Crown. This was a major fangirl moment. Thank you, Anna. I appreciate your feedback and am so lucky to call you a friend.

A huge shoutout also goes to Mary, my proofreader. Thank you for the work that you do. You are amazing and I appreciate the detail and dedication you put into every project. You're a gem!

And if taco tingle is your new favorite term, then you can thank Caitlen from momming.whilereading. She introduced me to this gem and I don't plan on letting it go. Like ever. It's absolutely brilliant!

I'd also like to thank everyone in the Sinfully Seductive Squad. You ladies are amazing, pumping me up and making me just as excited when I've got no energy left. If you've written a book, then you'll probably know the phases of writing. Inevitably, there comes a point where you've read your work so many times it all starts to blur together, but you ladies have kept me going and put that spark back into my writing. It means the world to me every time you share an edit or simply let me know how much you're looking forward to the next book. I just hope you know how much I appreciate and love you.

And last, but certainly not least, I am thankful for you. Thank you for taking a chance on my book. With so many titles out in the wild, you chose mine. I can only hope that you enjoyed the ride and that it has opened the door to a book friendship that will continue into the end of time.

Seriously, from the bottom of my heart, thank you.

      myself end up with someone who hasn't one fiction book to his name? I don't know, but I'm glad I did. Thanks, babe. You're my number one MVP.

      I'd also like to thank everyone in the Sinfully Seductive Squad. You ladies are amazing, pumping me up and making me just as excited when I've got no energy left. If you've written a book, then you'll probably know the phases of writing. Inevitably, there comes a point where you've read your work so many times it all starts to blur together, but you ladies have kept me going and put that spark back into my writing. It means the world to me every time you share an edit or simply let me know how much you're looking forward to the next book. I just hope you know how much I appreciate and love you.

      And last, but certainly not least, I am thankful for you, the reader. Thank you for taking a chance on my book. With so many titles out in the wild, you chose mine. I can only hope that you enjoyed the ride and that it has opened the door to a book friendship that will continue into the end of time. Seriously, from the bottom of my heart, *thank you.*

Made in United States
North Haven, CT
07 August 2022

22414236R00191